PUZZLE *Detective*

CRIME MYSTERIES TO SOLVE
WITH **LOGIC & DEDUCTION**

BY **RICK CARLILE**

CARLILE
MEDIA
www.CARLILE.MEDIA

Introduction

YOU ARE THE DETECTIVE!

Thank you for choosing Puzzle Detective! This book will give you hours of sleuthing fun as you accompany Lieutenant Falco Costanzo of the Los Angeles Police Department on four of his toughest murder cases. Pit your wits against high-society murderers in fun, challenging, solve-it-yourself mysteries!

Puzzle Detective cases are <u>**real mysteries**</u>.

That means you have to be a <u>**real detective**</u>.

— **Read the stories**. Good investigators use all their senses and listen to their intuition. How do you feel about the places you go, the things you see, and the people you meet?

— **Examine evidence**. Your investigations will uncover all manner of clues. What do they tell you about the case and your suspects?

— **Interview suspects**. People can be complex and manipulative creatures. Who is telling the truth, and who is lying to you — and why?

— **Solve puzzles**. Many clues conceal vital information, hidden in challenging conundrums. Can you untangle the enigmas and tease out the truth?

— **Crack codes**. Some secrets are intended to be understood only by the initiated. Will you be able to decrypt them and bring the truth to light?

— **Use forensic analysis**. Science and technology arm the investigator with powerful analytical tools. What will they tell you about your case's crime scenes and murder weapons?

HOW TO SOLVE

Each Puzzle Detective case has several sections:

1 — CRIME SCENE

Discover the basics of the case, the environment, and the victim.

2 — SUSPECTS

Meet everyone on your list of persons of interest.

3 — INVESTIGATION

Go where the leads take you! This section deals with **elements** and **clues**.

ELEMENTS

As you investigate, interesting **elements of the case** reveal themselves. These could be anything significant, such as:

— **Crime scene observations**. Possible murder weapons, puzzling objects, forensic samples…

— **Means, motive, and opportunity**. Evidence that tells you who had the reason and ability to commit the crime. Alibis, witness statements, record checks…

— **Unknown factors**. If the time of the crime is not obvious, when might it have been? If we're not sure where the crime took place, where could it have happened?

CLUES

The **Investigation** section is made up of **numbered clues**. There are two types of clues:

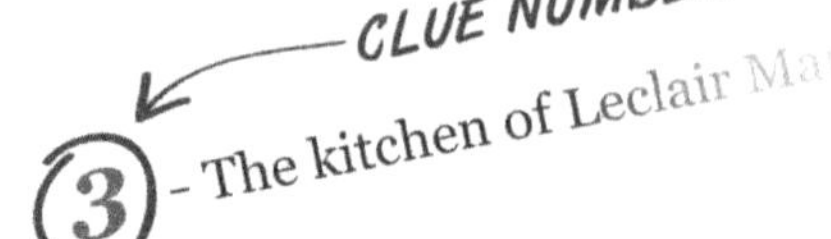

— **Crime clues**: some clues **connect elements to the crime**. For example, a clue might tell you that the murder weapon was the candlestick.

— **Suspect clues**: some clues **connect elements to suspects**. For example, a clue might tell you that Suspect X's fingerprints are on the candlestick.

4 — DETECTIVE'S NOTEBOOK

Your notebook has a list of all the **elements**, and all the **suspects**, in a grid.

Use the grid to solve the crime.

— When you find a **crime clue**, write the clue number next to the element. Highlight the element, or draw a line under it, so you know it's important.

— When you find a **suspect clue**, write the clue number in the grid where the element and the suspect intersect.

— **The guilty suspect is the one whose suspect clues are the same as the crime clues!**

In this example, the guilty suspect is **Suspect Z**, because we know that **elements B and E** are **linked to the crime**, and Suspect Z is **the only person who is linked to both elements B and E.**

Clues also connect Suspect X to element E, and Suspect Y to element B, but Suspect Z is the only one connected to both.

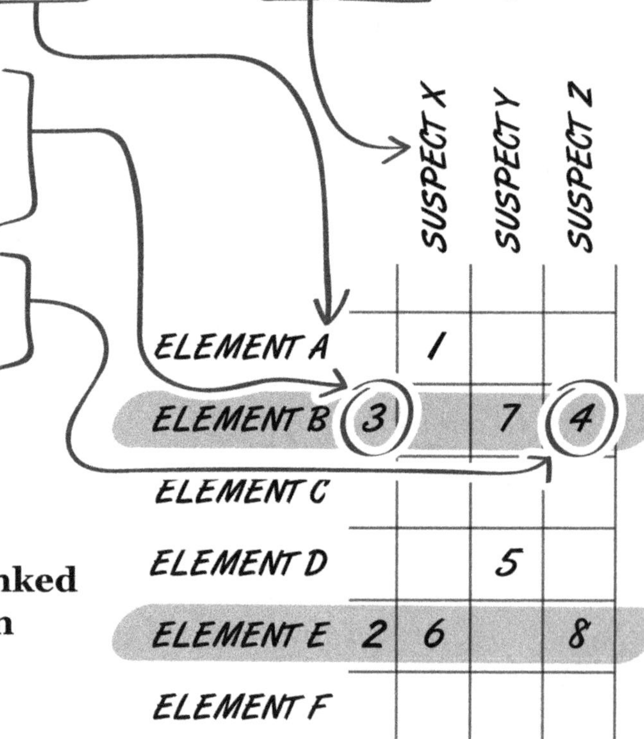

AN IMPORTANT MESSAGE FOR MURDLERS

You may be familiar with crime-themed logic puzzles like Murdle.
Those puzzles are designed so you can **infer negatives**.
For example, if Suspect X is connected to the candlestick,
Suspect Y **cannot** be connected to the candlestick.

But that isn't how investigations work in real life, so Puzzle Detective cases are different:
multiple suspects can be connected to the same element.

Anywhere from **NONE** to **ALL** of the suspects could be connected to any element.
So, when you connect something to one suspect, **don't cross out the other suspects**.

Puzzle Detective cases are **immersive mysteries**. Solving them requires not only **logic**
but also **insightful deduction** — just like in a classic detective story!

5 — SOLUTION

STILL WORKING ON THE CASE? HOLD IT!! THE "SPOILER ALERT" CRIME SCENE TAPE TELLS YOU TO GO NO FURTHER — UNLESS YOU WANT TO READ THE ANSWERS!

LERT SPOILER ALERT SPOILER ALERT SPOILER ALERT SPOILER ALERT SPOILER ALERT

Not sure exactly what a clue's telling you? No problem — this section **explains everything**, one clue at a time. At the end of the section is the name of the guilty suspect, and a copy of the Detective's Notebook grid with all the answers.

6 — CONCLUSION

LERT SPOILER ALERT SPOILER ALERT SPOILER ALERT SPOILER ALERT SPOILER ALERT

What would a mystery story be without a **detective dénouement**? This is the final section, where you lay out your case and **catch the guilty suspect!**

DIFFICULTY LEVELS & MISLEADING CLUES

Each Puzzle Detective case has a difficulty level: **Easy**, **Medium**, **Hard**, or **Fiendish**. As you progress, you will notice that more difficult cases have:

✓ More suspects,　✓ More elements,　✓ More clues,　✓ More in-depth investigations,

✓ More complex crimes, clues, puzzles, codes — and...

?? More **misleading clues**. These are either innocent (such as mistaken witnesses) or malicious (falsified records, for instance). Either way, there will be a suggestion in the clue that **something is amiss** — it's up to you to **take the hint** and **spot the red herring!**

9? When you think a clue may be misleading, **write it in your Detective's Notebook grid with a question mark**. Then, when you are ready to solve the crime, you can decide whether you want to **trust the clue — or ignore it**.

Happy detecting!

TABLE OF CONTENTS

Hollywood Ending

CASE #: 001

DIFFICULTY: EASY

DETECTIVE: LT. FALCO COSTANZO

UNIT: LOS ANGELES POLICE DEPARTMENT, ROBBERY-HOMICIDE DIVISION

CRIME SCENE

The early morning fog had only recently lifted when I arrived at Leclair Manor, a grand estate in the hills above the sprawling City of Angels. The call had come in early... Too early. Wiping the sleep from my eyes, I pulled my vintage convertible round to the front of the main house. I parked up behind a Rolls Royce and an Aston Martin — both European imports, just like my own classic automobile. These people had good taste! Looking around, I found a good-size rock and wedged it behind one of my auto's tires. These classic cars are like racehorses — temperamental — and my parking brake had been disagreeing with me recently.

The mansion stood silently, as if holding its breath, waiting for me to make the first move. The great old pile looked like it had been built for some 1880s Gilded Age tycoon, a Rockefeller or a Vanderbilt, but that was just an architectural fakeout — it was from the 1940s, built with movie money.

Ezra Leclair, a prominent Hollywood tycoon from a long line of prominent Hollywood tycoons, had been found dead in his study. It looked like foul play.

Walking through the front door, I was greeted by a high-ceilinged foyer adorned with what looked like priceless art. But what do I know? *Dogs Playing Poker* is more my speed.

The house was eerily quiet, apart from the whispered conversations of the staff, who were gathered in a tight group, chattering nervously.

The butler, Mr. Clarence, politely directed me to the back door, where I was informed that the recycling had already been picked up by the regular guy. After I showed my badge to clear up the confusion, Mr. Clarence accompanied me to the study.

Ezra Leclair's body lay sprawled across a Persian rug. Papers were scattered chaotically around his mahogany desk and the floor; a single glass, half-full of a rich, burgundy liquid, sat precariously close to the edge. The deceased showed no external signs of struggle, but had suffered a crushing head wound. Nearby, a shattered crystal vase decorated the polished hardwood floor with sparkling, scarlet-tinted fragments. It looked like the murder weapon. Lead crystal is *heavy*, and a vase made of the stuff would be no joke as a bludgeon.

After roaming the mansion, I determined that there were only two ways the murderer could have escaped the crime scene: down a back alley between the main house and the outbuildings, or through the garden gate. Then, Mr. Clarence told me about a third way: a tunnel built for some nefarious purpose now lost to history. It led from a hidden door in the study, through the basement, and out behind the house.

SUSPECTS

I turned my attention to the list of suspects, each of whom had a possible motive for wanting Ezra out of the picture.

- First, there was **Annie Galloway**, Ezra's on-again, off-again starlet lover, whose relationship had deteriorated into a series of explosive arguments.

- Then came **Elias Russell**, his hard-charging young business partner.

- Finally, **Gertrude Reed**, Ezra's reclusive younger sister, who had always lived in the shadow of her more successful sibling.

INVESTIGATION

1 — As I sifted through the remnants of Ezra Leclair's study, I discovered a series of unsigned, anonymous letters hidden behind a desk drawer. One in particular stood out. It was crumpled and folded, as though it had been read and reread, and its contents almost dripped with desperation and anxiety. Phrases like *I can no longer stand the pressure*, and *Your demands are driving me to the edge* indicated a person deeply tormented by Ezra's influence and expectations. My experience told me that someone this fearful of Leclair might well stop at nothing to protect themselves. It looked like they were on the edge.

2 — The very first evening of the investigation, I was woken in the wee small hours by the phone ringing. Disentangling myself from the bedsheets, I snatched up the receiver.

"What kinda time you call this?" I yelled.

"Uh…" It was Officer Kennedy. I'd left him to keep watch on the crime scene after hours. "It's about half past three, Chief."

I looked at my watch. It showed a little before midnight. "Aw, gee, would ya look at that. My watch stopped. Thanks!" I hung up the phone, wound my watch and set it to the correct time, and settled back down to sleep.

A couple minutes later, the phone rang again.

"You gotta listen, Chief — it's the sister, Miss Gertrude. I caught her sneaking into the security room at the mansion. She was trying to delete video of her hanging around the back alley around the time of the murder. Says she was hiding behind the house having a cigarette — nobody knows she still smokes. She swears she just thought we'd get the wrong idea when we found out. Whaddaya want me to do?"

I didn't know what to think. Was she just a nervous lady telling the truth about having a hard time kicking a tobacco habit, or did she have more to hide?

3 — The kitchen of Leclair Manor was as grand as the rest of the house, with stainless steel appliances and countertops gleaming under harsh fluorescent lights. The smell of freshly baked bread wafted through the air. Maria, the housekeeper, had asked to meet secretly with me to tell me something relevant to the case.

"Lieutenant Costanzo, there's something I should tell you about the night Mr. Ezra was killed. As I was leaving to go home, I saw Miss Annie coming out of that nasty basement tunnel. She didn't notice me, but I saw her. She looked frightened. I didn't think much of it at first, but then…"

4 — The garage smelled of motor oil and old tires, a comforting scent. I knew that Joe, Leclair's mechanic, was something of a confidante to all the mansion's inmates. I asked him if he'd seen anyone acting strangely recently. "Funny you should ask," he replied. "Just the other day, Annie brought her car in. She wasn't her usual self — looked like she'd seen a ghost or something." He paused, searching for the right words. "She mentioned Ezra, how things had been *getting out of hand*. Said she felt like she was constantly living on the edge because of him. Something about how he was always holding things over her, making her scared of what he could do."

5 — Returning to the scene of the crime, I found myself once again in Ezra Leclair's study. The room was as chaotic as I had left it. It was here that I hoped to find more concrete evidence, something that could illuminate not just *how*, but *why*.

I set to work meticulously going through each document, each piece of correspondence. Ezra's financial records, personal letters, and meeting schedules painted a picture of a man at the apex of his career, but it was his email records that caught my attention. Sitting at Ezra's computer, I pulled up the emails and began to read.

One email in particular caught my eye — clearly the product of great frustration. Another email, sent just a few days before Ezra's death, was even more pointed.

```
TO: ezra-leclair@crystalclearpicturesinc.com
FROM: all_lies_ruses@burner-email.org
SUBJECT: Re: Continued Delays
```

Ezra, this can't go on. You refuse to see
reason and keep blocking my initiatives.
If we don't expand aggressive investment
in new markets, we'll fall behind. Your
short-sightedness is jeopardizing everything we've built.

```
TO: ezra-leclair@crystalclearpicturesinc.com
FROM: all_lies_ruses@burner-email.org
SUBJECT: Re: Re: Continued Delays
```

Ezra, I've had enough of your roadblocks.
If you don't step aside and let me take
the lead on this venture, there will be
consequences. I won't let your inability
to adapt ruin my career. This is your last
warning.

Who sent the emails? The sender had used a *burner* (disposable) email address to hide their identity, but maybe I could figure out who it was... What might the email address *all_lies_ruses* mean? A *ruse* is a trick, or subterfuge... Was the clue in the meaning, or was I looking at it the wrong way around?

6 — Exploring the dusty, unlit basement tunnel, I discovered another letter, much the same as the ones I'd found hidden in the study, but looking more recent. Lying on the floor, it had little dust cover; it hadn't been there long. The killer must have taken it from Leclair, hoping to hide their motive, and dropped it in the tunnel in their haste to escape.

7 — Dr. Kinsley at the forensic lab tells me he has discovered a latent handprint at the exit of the basement tunnel, using a ninhydrin solution to reveal the amino acids deposited by the skin's ridges. He believes that the print is recent, as it is very clear — the ninhydrin test produces less well-defined results with older prints.

In the following image, the enhanced handprint photo is at the top, and the three suspects' fingerprint record cards are below. Whose handprint is it?

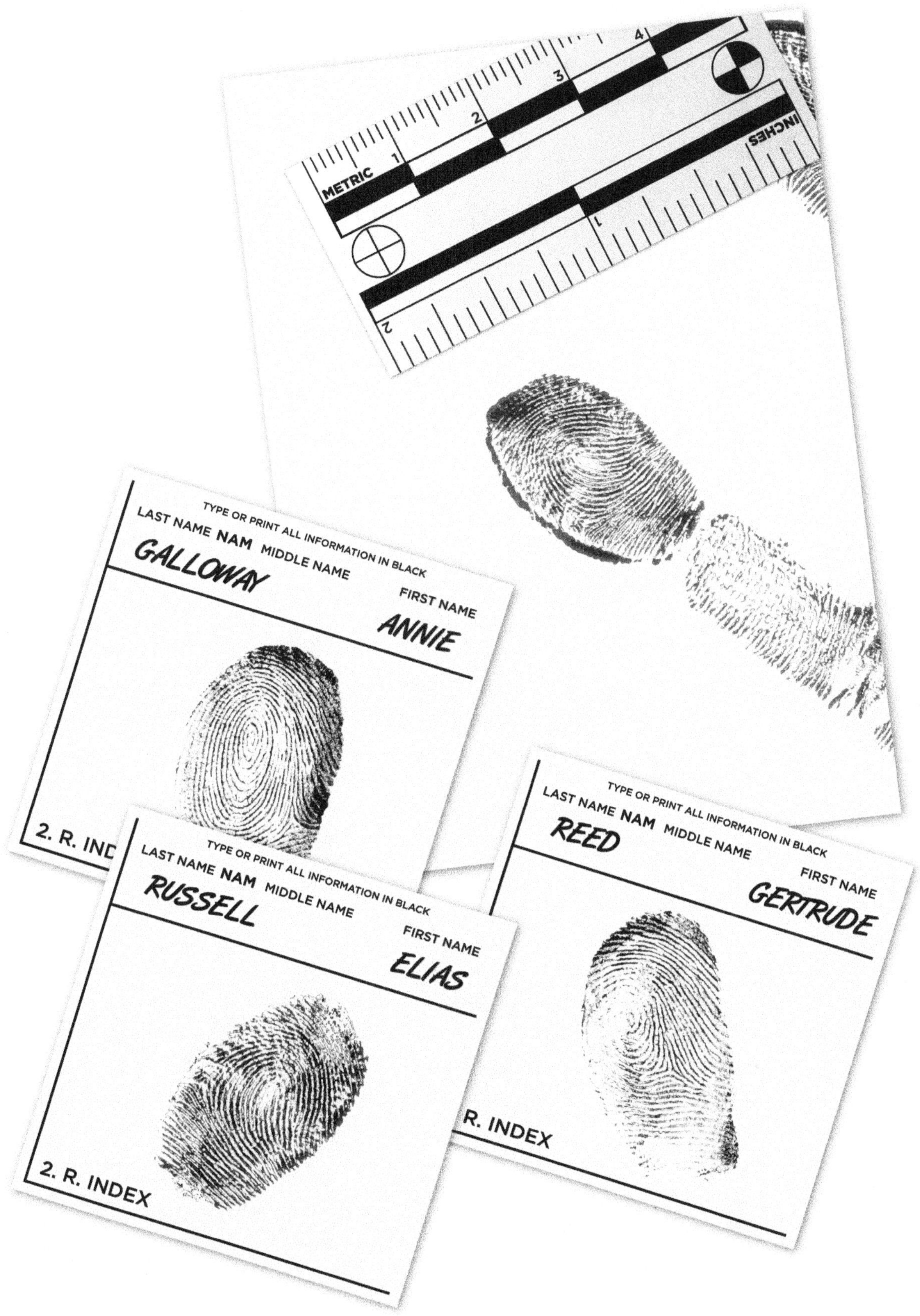

8 — After a hearty meal of spaghetti and meatballs in the mansion's kitchen, kindly prepared by Maria the housekeeper, Mr. Clarence confided in me that Ezra's sister Gertrude had always resented Ezra for "hogging the limelight." Ezra had always been the outgoing, extrovert type — a natural showman... But Gertrude always resented it, and thought she deserved an equal say in how the family business was run.

Pouring another glass of wine, Clarence whispered, "Some people even say that Ezra 'doctored' his father's will to give himself a majority of shares in the company. But of course, the poor old dear can't prove anything..." He leaned even closer. "Just between you and me, even if he did, I wouldn't blame him. Miss Gertrude doesn't really have the right character for business. A lovely lady, but not the hard-nosed, enterprising type."

Who is the guilty suspect?

———————————————

	Annie Galloway	Elias Russell	Gertrude Reed
Envy			
Ambition			
Fear			
Garden Gate			
Back Alley			
Basement Tunnel			

Turn the page to see the solution!

SOLUTION

- *1, 6* From the letters discovered behind the desk drawer and later found in the basement tunnel, we determine that the murderer's motive was fear, and that the tunnel was their escape route. Leclair must have been threatening some course of action — perhaps blackmail — against the person who killed him. The murderer must have taken the letters to hide their motive, dropping one in the tunnel and unaware that more remained hidden in the study. Therefore, the suspect whose motive was fear and who can be placed at the basement tunnel, is the guilty suspect.

- *2* Gertrude Reed behaved very suspiciously, but the evidence she was trying to hide (being in the back alley) does not appear to be related to the crime.

- *3* Maria revealed that Annie had been seen leaving the basement tunnel.

- *4* Joe the mechanic let us know that Annie was frightened of something Leclair might do to her.

- *5* Looking at the *From* email address, *all_lies_ruses@burner-email.org*, the first thing that occurred to me was the strange grammar in the phrase "all lies ruses." Why not say "all lies *and* ruses," if the meaning was of primary importance? The only reason one would do so deliberately is that one *had to* — and why would one have to? Perhaps because it was not the meaning, but the *letters* that were important — maybe the address was an anagram… Do any of the suspects' names use the same letters as *all lies ruses*? *Annie Galloway*? Nope, one letter too many… *Gertrude Reed*? Correct number of letters, but no; the letters don't match… *Elias Russell*? Yes, that's it! It was Russell who sent the emails — his thwarted ambition caused him to threaten the victim out of frustration.
  However, this ambition is quite different from the fear we know to be the killer's motive. There is no reason he would have taken and tried to hide the letter; we must look elsewhere to explain that behavior.

- *6* See #1.

- *7* The fingerprint found in the basement tunnel matches Elias Russell.

- *8* We learned from Mr. Clarence that Gertrude Reed was envious of the victim.

The guilty suspect is therefore

Annie Galloway.

	Annie Galloway	Elias Russell	Gertrude Reed
Envy			8
Ambition		5	
Fear (1)	4		
Garden Gate			
Back Alley			2
Basement Tunnel (6)	3	7	

CONCLUSION

I stood in the grand library of Leclair Manor, facing the suspects, who were seated in a row of overstuffed wingback armchairs. The household staff watched in hushed silence, the weight of the moment pressing down like the thick fog outside. Officer Kennedy and several other cops stood around the room, looking quietly menacing in their dark uniforms.

"You're probably all wondering why I've gathered you here today," I intoned dramatically.

This was met with a general *tsk*-ing and rolling of eyeballs. "Goodness me, *do* please enlighten us, Lieutenant," drawled Elias Russell, with more sarcasm than was really polite.

"You betcha, Mr. Russell," I replied. "You're an ambitious guy, aren't you? There's nothing wrong with that, is there?" He shrugged noncommittally. "But Ezra was standing in your way. Not letting you flourish and bloom, right?"

Russell blushed a little, perhaps at being described in such florid terms. "I won't deny it."

"And you used the basement tunnel; your fingerprints put you right there at the scene of the murderer's escape."

"Well, actually…" he started to speak, but I cut him off.

"And Miss Gertrude!" I swung round to face her; she had begun to visibly perspire. "The little sister. You know, you did yourself no favors at all when you tried to monkey with the surveillance video, did you?"

She began to mumble flustered excuses, but I didn't let her get any further. I turned to Annie Galloway.

"Annie," I began, calm yet resolute, "it's over. We know you killed Ezra Leclair."

Annie's eyes widened, her breathing quickening. "I — I don't know what you're talking about," she stammered, but her voice lacked conviction.

I spoke quietly. "Ezra couldn't accept that the relationship was over, could he?"

She drew in a shaky breath, the fight slowly leaving her. "Lieutenant Costanzo, you have to understand. He wouldn't let me go. It was as if everything I was — or could ever be — was tied to him, and he wouldn't let me break free."

"If he was violent, a jury would understand."

Annie seemed surprised. "Oh, no, it was nothing like that. It was my career, everything I'd worked for, all the dreams I had... Movies, Hollywood... he said he'd take it all away." She swallowed dramatically. "He could do that, you know." Tears began to well in her eyes. "He was a powerful man. It would have been so easy for him. Just a few words to the right people, and I'd be blacklisted. I knew he was serious."

Gertrude finally found her voice. "You mean... you murdered my brother over... over a *job?*"

Annie was affronted. "Oh, no, Gertrude — you have to believe me. Not a *job*. No, a whole *career*."

"That'll do," I said, and gestured to the uniformed cops. "Guys, take her away." I turned my back and walked out of the library, as Officer Kennedy and the rest of the polyester-clad posse descended on Annie Galloway. I left Leclair Manor shaking my head.

Hollywood, huh? I thought. *There's no business like show business. Boy, there sure ain't.*

The Silent Siren

CASE #: 002

DIFFICULTY: MEDIUM

DETECTIVE: LT. FALCO COSTANZO

UNIT: LOS ANGELES POLICE DEPARTMENT, ROBBERY-HOMICIDE DIVISION

CRIME SCENE

The marina lay baking in the sun's hazy glow, lending the scene a smoggy auburn tint that made it look like a vintage photograph. My coat flapped lazily in the late morning breeze as I observed the scene, and the water slapped against the dry, salty wood of the dockside. From off in the distance came the *clink-clink* of metal hardware tapping boats' masts as they bobbed in the swell. What a relaxing place. I wondered how much you had to make to keep a boat here. But then, I don't know much about boats except that the pointy part is usually the front.

I didn't have to be an expert to know that the *Siren's Call* was a real beauty. A sleek, white-painted sixty-footer, with varnished teak decks and shining brass brightwork. I sure didn't need to worry what she cost, not on a cop's salary — forget it! She was the perfect vessel for a man of the world who spent his valuable time and considerable fortune enjoying the finer things in life — a man like Martin Phillips.

Phillips was known to his friends as *Club* on account of the huge number of societies to which he belonged and funded: literary clubs, fine dining clubs, wine clubs, sports clubs, you name it.

Club Phillips was a charismatic figure in his early fifties, with graying hair and a weathered charm, who navigated through high society with savoir faire and aplomb. His reputation preceded him — a connoisseur of the avant-garde with an unerring eye for people and places of interest, a collector of experiences worth more than any treasure.

No one knew for sure where he had made his money, but he moved in the kind of circles where it's impolite to ask too many questions. The kind of circles where you never know exactly who you're talking to, where European counts and *contessas* mix seamlessly with billionaire arms dealers and fugitive fraudsters. Whatever the truth, Club must've had plenty of spare time on his hands in order to fit in his many *bon vivant* activities.

Well, he wasn't going to have to worry about spare time anymore. On account of how he'd been found slumped over the helm — that's what I would call the steering wheel — of his yacht. Dead as a doornail.

Salvatore Russo, the marina's night watchman, had been making his dawn patrol and noticed the distinctive silhouette of the boat-owner draped across the large hardwood wheel, lit by the first rays of the morning sun. Assuming that Phillips was probably just a hung-over casualty of the night before, Sal called out jokingly at first... but on boarding the yacht, he was shocked by the gruesome truth.

"It's how he would've wanted to go," Sal said all of a sudden, jolting me out of my reverie. "You know, in the captain's chair."

I turned my attention to the scene of the crime. The cockpit and the whole deck area were a mess; it looked like a struggle had taken place. I noticed that what looked like a boat racing trophy lay on the deck where it appeared to have been discarded. As far as forensics went, I figured there wouldn't be much to go on; the *Siren's Call* cockpit was open to the weather, and it had rained overnight. But if there was something to find, I would find it. You bet I would.

SUSPECTS

Before long, I had my cast of suspects. They were what you might call a motley crew.

- **Vaughn Gibbons** was first on my list. A culinary genius and minor celebrity, his most ambitious venture — a new high-end restaurant — was teetering on the edge of bankruptcy. It was no secret that the tweed-clad Gibbons blamed Phillips, his friend-slash-rival, on account of a scathing review Phillips had "jokingly" placed in a prestigious Los Angeles society magazine. It seemed that not everyone got the practical joke's humor, and customers were staying away in large numbers.

- **Sherry Earle** had been Phillips' close confidante and, some said, lover. A charming but rather directionless intellectual, the two had spent long days together but, friends said, had recently drifted apart. Some particularly gossipy folks suggested that Earle had discovered Phillips seeking romantic refuge in the arms of another.

- **Jazmine Boykin**, a renowned stage actor and performing arts theater impresario, was Phillips' creative partner in a long-running theatrical venture. Despite every appearance of success, behind the scenes the shows that Phillips bankrolled were losing money like a sailor on shore leave, and the rumor was that he was about to withdraw his funds.

- **Raven Fowler** was a name known to everyone in the LA arts scene (or so she told me). The culture vulture behind numerous jazz and literary happenings in the city, she and Phillips were said to have shared a strange kind of mutual fascination; not quite romantic... but not quite platonic, either.

INVESTIGATION

1 — Phillips' right hand was formed into a fist, as if ready to defend himself against the person who struck him down. But as I slowly pried open the clenched fingers, a gleam of light off metal showed me it was no mere defensive reaction. A fancy-looking silver key was pressed tightly into the man's hand. I held it up in the sunlight to get a better look. Etched into the finely-carved key head was the legend *Athenaeum Private Library — Founding Member*. It could be no accident; Phillips must have pulled the key from a pocket or somewhere around the boat's cockpit, and gripped it tightly in his hand in his last moments — his final act, a crucial clue to his murderer's identity.

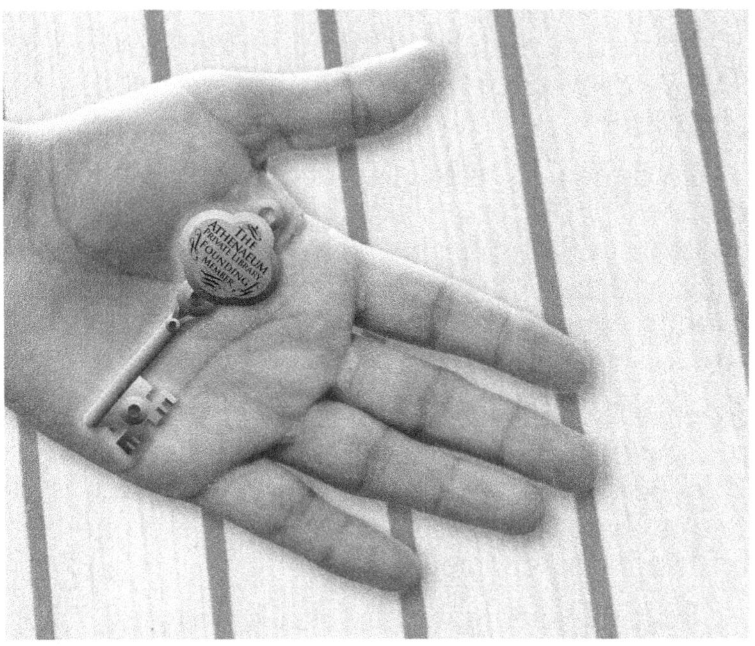

2 — While examining the luxurious cabin inside the *Siren's Call*, I noticed something strange about the wood paneling beside the captain's desk. With a bit of tinkering, the panel swung open to reveal a hidden safe. Deep scratches and dents around the faceplate showed that someone had been trying to force it open, though it seemed without success — it was locked tight. As I leaned closer, I saw a small tuft of fabric caught in the secret panel's door jamb. It was a distinctive pattern of Harris tweed, just like the heavy jackets famed chef Vaughn Gibbons insisted on wearing even in the heat of the kitchen.

3 — I stared with consternation at the forensic report. I kept rereading the section about the likely murder weapon:

The victim exhibits pronounced ligature marks encircling the neck region. The pattern is consistent with compression from a fibrous material. The markings display a distinct linear configuration with slight diagonal striations, indicative of a rope with a specific weave pattern. [...] Microscopic analysis of the neck area reveals embedded fibers, determined to be consistent with hemp, aligning with typical though old-fashioned nautical equipment.

Bizarre, I thought. I'd had the guys go over the boat tip to tail (sorry, *prow* to *stern*) and they'd found none of the rigging or mooring ropes missing, out of place, or bearing any forensic clues. The whole boat was kept immaculately tidy, with a place for everything and everything in its place — *shipshape*, as they say. So where could the murder weapon have come from?

4 — The crime scene tech guys were real excited to let me know they found a strange powder on the victim's face — they figured it was a theatrical pancake makeup product called *Encore Epoxy*. As the name suggested, the makeup was supposed to stay put even under the hot lights and sweat that theater actors have to tolerate for hours on end.

Under the pretext of learning more about the wonderful world of stagecraft, I was able to snoop around Jazmine Boykin's dressing room at the performing arts theater as she regaled me with unrepeatable and slanderous stories about various celebrities I'd never heard of. And there it was, on the crowded makeup table: a big tub of *Encore Epoxy*. The stuff looked like drywall mud. But Boykin claimed she hadn't been near the *Siren's Call* in weeks...

I confronted her about it, asking why her makeup should have been found on the victim's face.

"Dahling," she laughed, "in the theater game we're all kissing cousins, dontcha know? It'd be strange if some of us didn't rub off on one another, now wouldn't it?"

5 — In his forensic report, Dr. Kinsley notes that the victim bears numerous marks and scars. Some, long-healed, appear to be the result of a surgical process on his left shoulder-blade area.

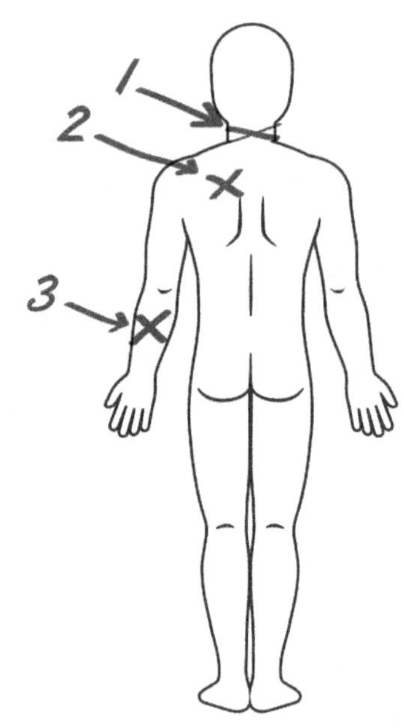

More interesting are those on Phillips' left forearm, labeled *3* in the *Marks & Wounds* section of the report. Dr. Kinsley believes they are postmortem contusion injuries, inflicted by a blunt object.

Intrigued by this, the doctor investigated further and discovered numerous blisters partially hidden by the contusions. In Kinsley's opinion, these blisters are consistent with a recent tattoo-removal process. The only practical conclusion, he suggests, is that the murderer tried to conceal the blisters.

6 — I wondered what I was doing as I found myself at the *Golden Hour Lounge*, a faded haunt near the docks where the air was thick with the scent of old cigarettes and desperation. *Meeting Benny "The Whisper" Walker* was the answer, though it wasn't a very good one. Benny had the honor of being about the least reliable confidential informant on our books.

Benny leaned conspiratorially over his drink. "You ain't gonna believe this, Lieutenant, but I saw Vaughn Gibbons messin' with ropes just last week. Real old-lookin' ones, too."

I sighed. "Go on."

Benny squinted, as if pulling the memory from the haze of his fuddled mind. "Yeah, in the back alley by that artsy restaurant joint, the *Velvet…* erm, *Curtain, Velvet Rope…* anyway, you know the place. He had this coil of it, just like the kinda rope a sailor might use for, uh, tying down the, uh, sails."

"Did he tell you what it was for?" I asked wryly, sipping my coffee.

"Nah, he didn't see me," Benny replied, winking, as if that lent his tale more credibility.

"Interesting you remember it so clearly," I countered mildly, setting my cup down. "Seeing as the *Velvet Rope*'s been closed for renovations the past three months."

7 — Searching the tool locker of the *Siren's Call* yielded an interesting find: an old, wood-handled claw hammer. Someone had painted the handle orange, presumably so it could easily be found even in an emergency. Boating is all about being prepared for the worst. And speaking of *the worst*, standing out clearly on the hammer's handle were dark spots of what I'd bet was dried blood.

*****

A few days later, I received an evidence box from Dr. Kinsley at the forensic lab. Inside was the hammer, a note from the Doc, and a bunch of printouts covered in spidery charts. I scanned the note, eager to find out what he'd discovered about the bloodstain…

Lieutenant,

On the next page are the DNA test results from that orange claw hammer you found.

There is residue of TWO individuals' DNA on the handle. I think one is the hammer's owner, Martin Phillips. You can figure out the other one!

Look at the attached DNA test printouts. The first printout is the crime scene sample from the hammer. Each "spike" on the chart is known as a "marker." Each marker has a "tab" underneath, showing the marker's numeric value.

The chart is divided into five sections, or "loci" (the plural of "locus," meaning "place" in Latin). These are the places on the chromosome from which we extract data. Each locus has a name, such as "D13S317."

Each locus on the hammer's chart has four markers: two results from one person, and two from the other person.

Why two from each person? Because we all inherit a marker from each parent: one from the father, and one from the mother.

Note that, where two markers have the same value, the spikes "stack" on top of the other, making one BIG spike. For a "stacked" result, there is only a single numeric tab.

The second printout is Phillips' DNA test result. After that are the test results from the suspects.

To discover the other person's identity, remove Phillips' data from the crime scene sample. Look at the suspects' test results. Who matches the remaining data in the crime scene sample?

By the way, the spikes on the crime scene sample aren't very high, compared to the suspect samples. That's because it's not a great quality sample — I think someone tried to destroy the DNA with bleach...

Good luck!

Dr. Kinsley

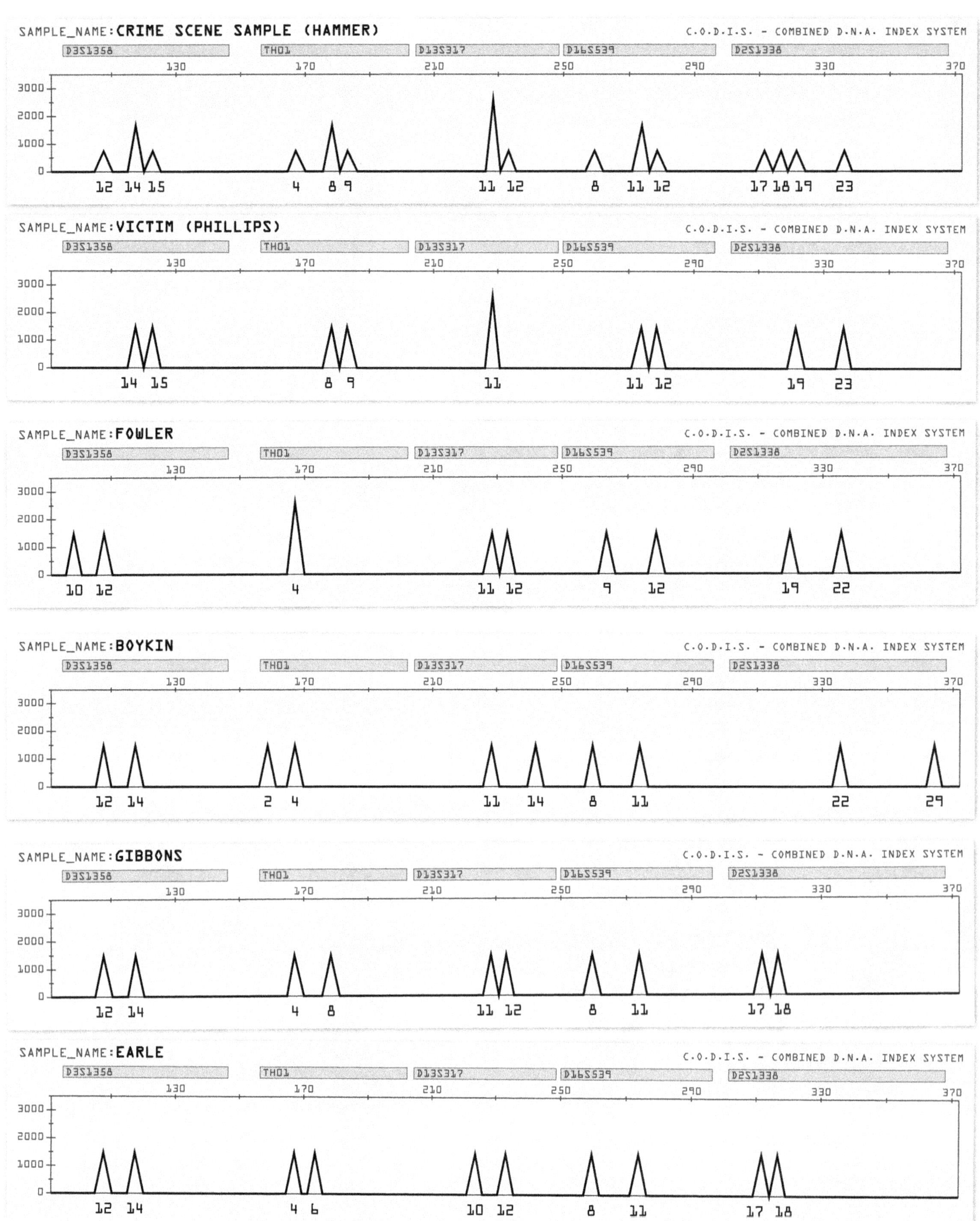

8 — I asked Sal Russo, the marina watchman, about Phillips' nautical adventures. I figured Russo was the kind of guy that someone like Phillips might feel he could speak freely with.

"Sure," Sal replied. "We used to talk about all sorts." He chuckled. "His regular friends weren't exactly sailors." I laughed; I'd met them, and they sure weren't. "Well, he didn't sail that much the last few years. But about four, five years back he took a big trip all the way down to the Galapagos islands, to take in all the wildlife. And speaking of wildlife, he took those two women with him... Miss Sherry, and that other one, named after a bird... what was her name?"

"Raven," I said. "Raven Fowler."

"Right, that's it. Imagine, those two ladies on the same boat. I'm amazed he hadn't thrown himself overboard by the time they got to Avalon Bay."

"Hard to get along with?" I asked.

Sal shrugged. "Naw, just what you'd call 'high maintenance,' I guess. And they both hated each other. Tried to hide it, but you could tell. Guess nobody taught 'em to share. Course, they did have one thing in common."

"Oh yeah? What was that?"

"Club showed me this tattoo on his left arm he'd got down there in the Galapagos, from a guy in San Cristobal. It was this bird, looked kinda like a big seagull with these huge, flappy, bright blue feet. About the most awkward-lookin' thing I ever saw. He said it was a blue-footed booby, kind of a local symbol of the Galapagos. Apparently, they dance for each other, the males and females, like folks tryin' to dance tango wearing diving fins. Said he got the tattoo as a memento of their trip. Asked the ladies to join him, but they didn't fancy showin' off a blue-footed booby on their arms at their high-society cocktail parties... can't say I blame them. Club managed to convince them to get the tattoos in the end, but smaller, in what he called 'a more inconspicuous location.'"

9 — For a cop, having an actor as a suspect is like a vacation — you can just sit back, take it easy, and let them talk about themselves. Jazmine Boykin went one step further: she handed me a huge leather-bound scrapbook stuffed with newspaper clippings from her performances. "Here you go, Dogberry dahling, it's all in here — the good, the bad and the spiteful backstabbing." She'd taken to calling me *Dogberry* on account of that was the name of a cop in some Shakespeare play. I wasn't sure it was a compliment. Either way, I couldn't help thinking of Huckleberry Hound.

I spent a sleepy evening skimming through the newspaper clippings. She had an impressive portfolio of work, all right. Then it hit me, and I jolted upright — there it was! A color photo from a Sunday arts magazine, a review of Boykin's all-female production of *Death of a Salesman* from a year or so ago... Boykin kneeling on the front stoop stairs of a wooden house, looking like she was fixing a loose board, her arm raised — holding a very distinctive orange claw hammer... I squinted, looking closer. I'd swear that was the hammer I found in the *Siren's Call*'s tool locker.

10 — I pulled up to the door of Raven Fowler's sun-drenched loft in the arts district. She greeted me with a warm smile and a slight raise of her eyebrows. The apartment was an elegant mess, with canvases stacked against the walls. The air was heavy with the scent of oils and turpentine.

"Lieutenant Costanzo, what a surprise! To what do I owe the pleasure?"

"Good afternoon, Ms. Fowler. I hope I'm not interrupting. I just had a couple of questions about your recent activities."

"Of course," she said, motioning me to a seat. "How can I help? You must excuse me if I seem tired, I've been *so* busy recently, *sooo* many irons in the fire."

"I've been checking with local ship chandlers," I began, sensing that it might be best to avoid getting drawn into the quicksand of small talk. "Seems you made an unusual purchase of some very specific nautical rope. Old-fashioned, natural hemp. I'm curious what you wanted it for."

Raven chuckled, leaning back thoughtfully. "Ah, yes, that rope. It's part of a piece I'm working on for the upcoming jazz festival. I'm calling it *Tangled Waves* — it represents the flow and complexity of jazz."

"I see," I said, nodding as if I saw. "This kind of rope, it's not what most sailors these days use though, right? It's a very special kind."

"That's right. How very observant of you, observant and knowledgeable. It's *so* refreshing to see one's tax dollars hard at work."

"Hemp. Hemp rope," I persevered.

She sighed. "I needed that exact type of rope because, well... I got the inspiration right on Club Phillips' yacht. "She paused for effect, her eyes meeting mine. "I was on the *Siren's Call* a while back, lounging on the deck, watching the rigging move and swing in the breeze. It struck me as elegant, a musical dance — rhythmic, but free-form, improvised, never the same twice... *Jazz*."

"Nice."

"I wanted to incorporate that same movement into my art piece, so the choice of rope was crucial to convey that rhythm. You know how Club liked to have everything on his yacht perfectly appropriate for its age; he'd never have used anything as crass as —" she shuddered "— *nylon* rope."

11 — Interviewing Sherry Earle at her cute little home in the hills, I was intrigued to notice the handmade plant hangers decorating her porch. "I made them myself," she said proudly. "Club gave me the rope, didn't have any use for it. He told me that you have to replace the ropes on a sailboat every few years — the salt isn't good for them."

12 — The police radio in my car squawked into life. I wrinkled my nose at the burst of static. The reception was terrible. "You better speak up," I yelled into the mouthpiece.

"It's officer Kennedy. I'm calling about the bartender."

"Bart who? Speak up!"

"No, the bartender from the jazz place, the *Riff Raff Club*."

"What?"

"The *Riff Raff Club. Riff Raff*!"

"You got a dog in there?"

"Listen, Lieutenant, that's Raven Fowler's place. The bartender called us. He said that Phillips was there with Fowler the day he was killed. Apparently, he spent the whole afternoon there."

13 — It turns out that the Athenaeum Library Club is a strange and extremely exclusive organization. The club Secretary met me in an intimidatingly vast, echoing entrance hall, full of marble and gilt ornaments. "My dear Lieutenant," she intoned, "you can't simply expect us to give our membership list to any Tom, Dick, or Harry who asks." She glanced with disdain at the grubby sheets of paper in my hand. "Even with a subpoena."

With a wave of her hand, she directed me to a marble plaque on the wall. "Our founding members list is not only public, it is quite literally written in stone — but in code! I'm sure it will not dwarf a policeman of your evident," she looked over her glasses and down her nose at me and sniffed, "...*intellect*."

I examined the plaque, mystified. Sensing my confusion, she added, "All right, one clue: Mr. Phillips was always our most *prominent* founder."

Who else is on the list?

Who is the guilty suspect?

____

	Vaughn Gibbons	Sherry Earle	Jazmine Boykin	Raven Fowler
Athenaeum Library				
Jazz Bar				
Theater				
Restaurant				
Clothing Fibers				
Makeup				
Tattoos				
Surgical Incisions				
Hammer				
Rope				
Trophy				

Turn the page to see the solution!

SOLUTION

- *1* The silver key clenched tightly in Phillips' hand told me that the Athenaeum Private Library had to be closely related to the murder.

- *2* The tweed clothing fibers found on Phillips' safe at the crime scene indicate Vaughn Gibbons had been there, and may have been interested in something he believed was in the safe.

- *3* The forensic report told us that the murder weapon was a hemp rope.

- *4* Jazmine Boykin admits to (possibly) being the source of the theatrical makeup found on the victim.

- *5* The forensic report also told us that someone deliberately injured the victim's forearm postmortem. The only plausible reason to do this would be an attempt to conceal the fact that the victim had recently undergone a tattoo removal procedure. Therefore, the murderer is likely to be a person with a connection to the removed tattoo, who would be implicated by the fact that Phillips evidently wished to no longer be reminded of the connection.

- *6* Benny Walker's testimony was not very believable, considering the fact that the club at which he claims to have seen Gibbons was closed. Either a legitimate case of mistaken location or, more likely, simply an attempt to extract yet more money from the Department.

- *7* There are two basic ways to solve the DNA puzzle and discover whose bloodstains are on the hammer.

The first, observational method, is to take a ruler and examine the spikes, seeing which suspect's spikes add to the victim's to create the sample graph (bearing in mind that the bleach-contaminated crime scene sample's spikes are smaller than those of the other, higher-quality samples).

The second, mathematical method is as follows. First, we follow Dr. Kinsley's advice and remove Phillips' results from the crime scene sample chart.

Phillips has the following result markers:

Locus D3S1358: 14 and 15.
Locus TH01: 8 and 9.
Locus D13S317: 11 and 11 *
Locus D16S539: 11 and 12.
Locus D2S1338: 19 and 23.
* We know there are two *11* markers in locus D13S317, because it's a *stacked* spike, with only one numeric tab in the locus — Dr. Kinsley told us to expect this.

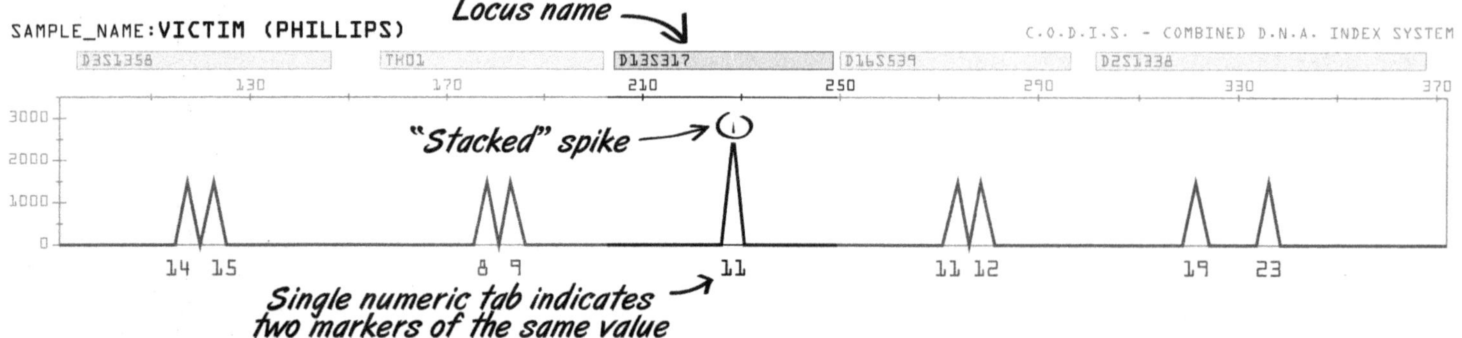

Going back to the crime scene sample chart, the key to solving this puzzle is to realize that the medium-height stacked spikes can represent two result markers, and the taller stacked spikes represent *three* markers.

This is the only logical conclusion, considering that we know Phillips has two *11* markers in locus D13S317. If we removed *all* the *11* markers from this locus in the crime scene sample, the only remaining marker in the locus would be a single *12* — and this is not possible, as Dr. Kinsley told us that *everybody* has two markers in each locus (the *12* spike is too short to represent more than one marker). Therefore, we remove Phillips' two *11* markers and retain one.

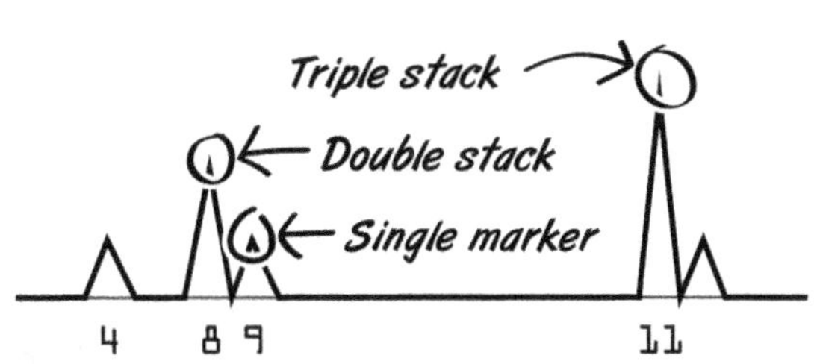

Eliminating these markers means the crime scene sample chart looks like this:

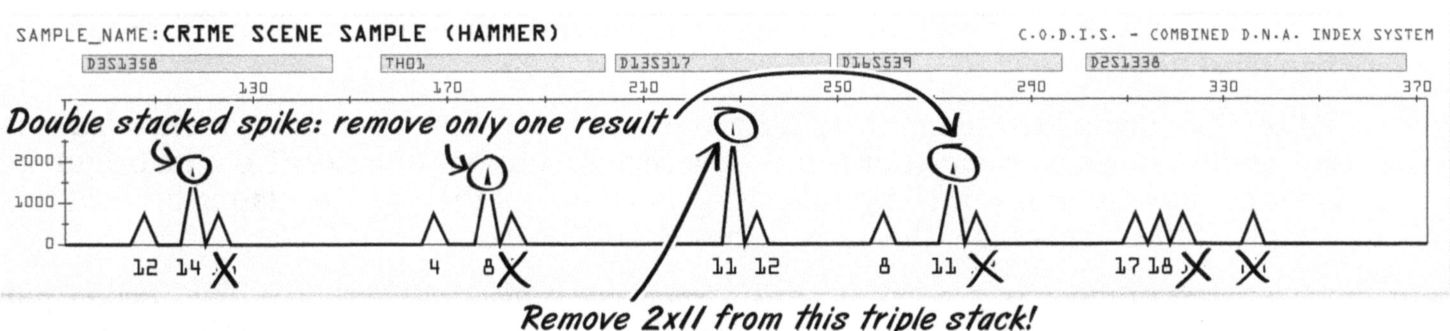

This means the other bloodstain must belong to a suspect with a DNA chart with the markers in the thick line below:

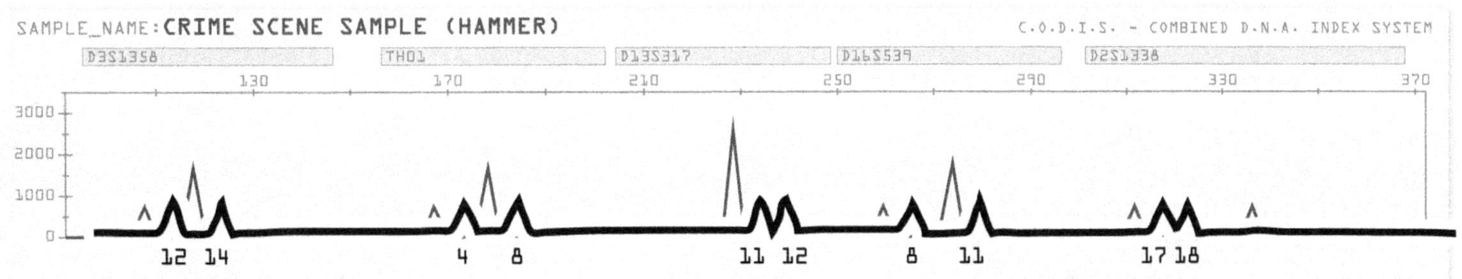

So, we're looking for someone with the markers:

Locus D3S1358: 12 and 14.
Locus TH01: 4 and 8.
Locus D13S317: 11 and 12
Locus D16S539: 8 and 11.
Locus D2S1338: 17 and 18.

Therefore, Vaughn Gibbons' DNA is on the hammer! Considering the clothing fibers as well as his blood on the hammer, it looks like Gibbons intended to steal something from Phillips' safe and injured himself trying to force his way into it. I bet if I took another look in that tool locker I'd find a chisel, or some similar tool, showing marks of recent use.

- *8* The conversation with Sal Russo told us that both Sherry Earle and Raven Fowler were linked to the tattoo. Either could have wanted to conceal the fact that Phillips removed the tattoo, indicating that he fell out with one or both of them.

- *9* Jazmine Boykin's connection to the hammer is noteworthy. However, the time elapsed since the theater production — around a year — indicates the connection may not mean much. Sometimes a coincidence is just a coincidence... Not often, but sometimes.

- *10* Raven Fowler had the opportunity to take rope from her personal stash and use it to murder him.

- *11* Sherry Earle's handmade hemp rope plant hangers connect her to the rope. Evidently, she has a good supply of it, courtesy of Phillips. Like Fowler, she could easily have brought it with her to the crime scene and taken it away once the deed was done, aligning with the fact that no rope on the boat was missing or out of place.

- *12* That Raven Fowler was at the *Riff Raff* jazz bar with the victim on the day of the murder is certainly interesting, but without any further connection to the crime, we have to regard it as mere happenstance.

- *13* In the Athenaeum Private Library puzzle, the list of founding members was encoded using a *Caesar cipher*, in which each letter is moved a certain number of letters from its origin. The code is said to have been invented by Julius Caesar (the quotation on the plaque hints at this). For example, if the number is 1, then *A* becomes *B*, and so on.

In this case, the number is 7 — so, for example, *A* becomes *H*. There is a clue in the quote (*Across seven seas...*). There are also seven names in the list. The club Secretary gave us an oblique clue ("dwarf your intellect," she said, referencing the Seven Dwarfs from Snow White).

Her more obvious clue, that Martin Phillips is the most prominent founder, i.e. first in the list, lets us work backwards from *THYAPU WOPSSPWZ* and discover that *M* is seven letters back from *T*, *A* is seven back from *H*, *R* is seven back from *Y*, and so on.

Moving each letter back seven letters gives us the decoded list:

MARTIN PHILLIPS
AUGUSTUS FAIRFAX
PENELOPE DUPREE
SHERRY EARLE
THADDEUS REMINGTON
JAZMINE BOYKIN
VAUGHN GIBBONS

We discover that all of the suspects are listed as founding Athenaeum Private Library members except Raven Fowler.

Even if we don't realize it's a Caesar cipher, we can still figure out the puzzle — but it takes longer. For example, we know that one of the members must be *Martin Phillips*: a first name of six letters, and a last name of eight letters. There's only one such entry in the list, the first one. The fact that the first entry also has a double *S* in the same position that *Phillips* has a double *L* tells us we're on the right track. There *is* a name in the list with a first name of eight letters and a last name of six, *WLULSVWL KBWYLL*, which could conceivably be *Phillips Martin*, but the lack of a double-letter in the first word (corresponding to the double *L* of *Phillips*) makes it unlikely.

So, this gets us started — knowing these letters means we can fill out the list like this:

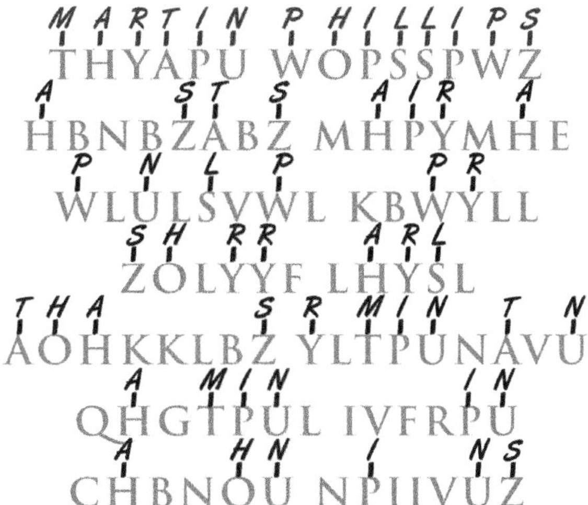

Now, we can go back to our list of suspects and see if anyone fits... One name stands out: *ZOLYYF LHYSL* is looking a lot like *Sherry Earle*. We're missing only two letters, one of which occurs three times — and if *L* is code for *E*, everything fits. Now we know the letters *E* and *Y*.

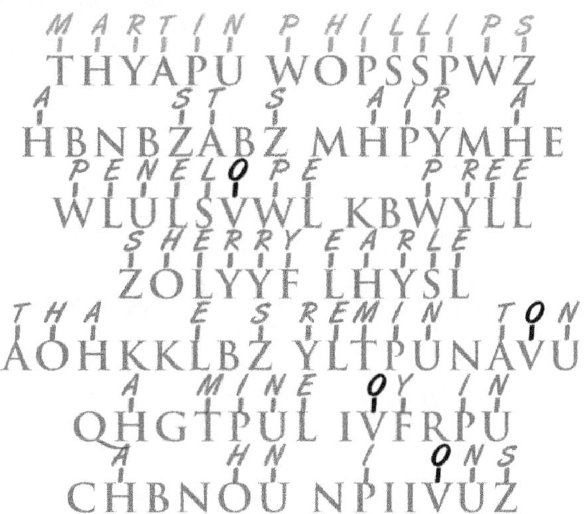

Looking at the remaining unknown letters, we can hazard a guess that *V* is code for *O*: what else could fill the blank in the name *PENEL_PE*?

Now, we can fill in the blank for the surname *REMIN_TON*. *N* has to be code for *G*.

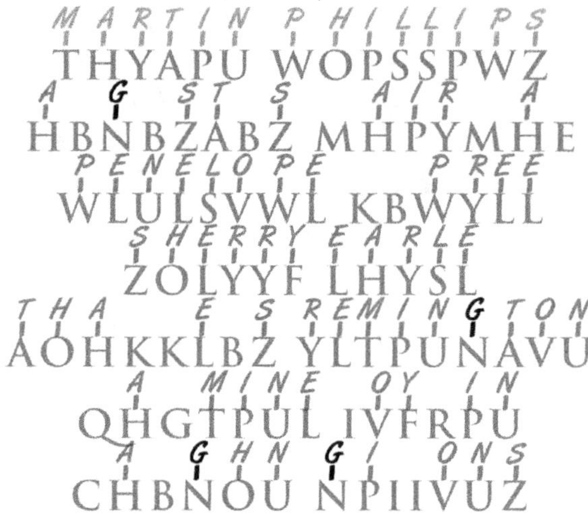

The last two names in the list are now mostly complete. Looking at the list of suspects, we cannot escape the conclusion that they are *Jazmine Boykin* and *Vaughn Gibbons*. Now, we have our answer. None of our suspects are named *Augustus*, *Penelope*, or *Remington*, so these names can be ignored.

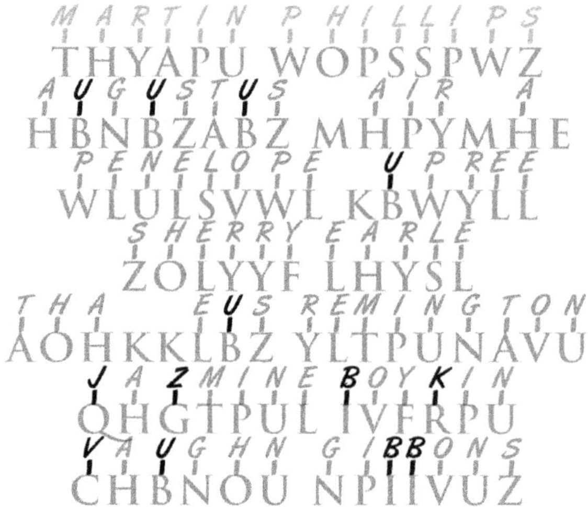

Although, of course, the blanks in the first name *THA___EUS* mean that *K* must be code for *D*; no other letter would fit. For the sake of completeness, *Augustus'* surname remains elusive, but considering that the only letters we have not yet uncovered are *C*, *F*, *W*, and *X*, we can test them against *_AIR_A_* to achieve a successful conclusion.

The guilty suspect is therefore

Sherry Earle.

	Vaughn Gibbons	Sherry Earle	Jazmine Boykin	Raven Fowler
Athenaeum Library (1)	13	13	13	
Jazz Bar				12
Theater				
Restaurant				
Clothing Fibers	2			
Makeup			4	
Tattoos (5)		8		8
Surgical Incisions				
Hammer	7		9	
Rope (3)	6?	11		10
Trophy				

CONCLUSION

We stood on the boat dock, the early evening sun casting two long shadows over the water. Sherry Earle's face was composed, betraying none of the inner tumult that I knew lurked beneath her calm exterior.

"It was the key," I said. "That was your mistake. It was his dying act, grabbing it. It meant his murderer had to be one of the Athenaeum's co-founders. If you'd taken it out of his hand, I might not have figured it all out."

She shook her head. "I thought I saw him take something from the cockpit's cabinet. But it was all so quick, so... so violent. I had to get out. By the time I calmed down enough to think about it, it was too late to go back."

"You must've hated him. To do that to him, I mean."

Her lips pressed to a thin, bitter line. "I wanted him to remember us forever. Evidently, he felt differently."

"I understand," I replied comfortingly. "Nobody likes to be rejected."

Sherry's façade crumbled, and tears glimmered in her eyes. "It's not just that. It was intolerable. When I saw he'd removed that tattoo, it was like he'd erased everything that had meaning to me. Erasing memories. Memories we could never get back... I believe that the purpose, the *meaning* of life, is to make great memories. Making a beautiful story. Like a director making a great movie, one wonderful scene after another. Do you believe that too?"

I didn't answer. It seemed as plausible a theory as any, I guess.

Rogues' Gallery

CASE #: 003

DIFFICULTY: HARD

DETECTIVE: LT. FALCO COSTANZO

UNIT: LOS ANGELES POLICE DEPARTMENT, ROBBERY-HOMICIDE DIVISION

CRIME SCENE

The evening draped the city in a velvet shawl of shadows. Traffic lights blinked all the way down La Cienega Boulevard, illuminating the cars that crept through the LA twilight. The white stucco edifice of the Arnette Gallery loomed up above me, its monumental smoked glass doors a haughty symbol warning the casual passer-by to keep on passing by: *Members only — and, buddy, you ain't in the club.*

Officer Kennedy must've seen me hesitate, because he heaved one of the huge doors open and beckoned me inside. "Hey, Lieutenant," he said, "good of you to show up. Follow me."

Inside, the usual hum of cultured conversation had been replaced by the low chatter and murmured questions of bystanders and police. Officer Kennedy's shoes clicked on the polished marble floor as we walked across the atrium. Everywhere, exhibits overwhelmed the senses — bold strokes of color danced across the white expanse of its white walls, and massive, sharp-angled steel sculptures caught the light, sending it off at crazy angles.

"They found her in the storage area, Lieutenant, it's kind of an art warehouse," Kennedy informed me as we maneuvered through the labyrinth of carefully arranged exhibitions. The gallery's grand central hall gave way to narrower passages lined with less gigantic works.

As we reached the back of the gallery, we passed through a pair of thick soundproof doors and turned down a corridor that led us away from the public eye and into the practical day-to-day running of the establishment. Here, the aesthetic shifted abruptly. The sleek perfection of the gallery front morphed into utilitarian simplicity — walls of exposed concrete and brick, plastic-covered floors, and harsh overhead lighting.

Kennedy pushed open a heavy door to reveal the warehouse, a vast, windowless space lined with towering shelves that stretched toward the ceiling, each one weighed down with carefully wrapped artwork and labeled crates. The refreshing smell of the pinewood crates filled the air.

Rosetta Arnette lay sprawled across an extra-large packing case. It was big enough to hold a refrigerator. A slim, blonde figure dressed in a severely cut black pantsuit, I recognized her from the newspapers' society pages. An overturned wineglass on the case stained the wood a deep red. I noticed a wine bottle standing on the floor nearby, about three-quarters empty. *Could be poison*, I thought.

I ran my fingers through my hair. "OK, Officer, whadda we got?"

Kennedy licked a finger and flicked through his notebook. "Rosetta Arnette, aged fifty-four, divorced. Husband's out of the picture, on the east coast. One child, daughter, estranged — at college in Europe."

"Any other men in her life?"

"It seems not."

"Okay, keep checking until you're sure. Carry on."

"Yessir. Occupation, gallery owner. Harvard-educated. Lives alone — one of those stilt houses out in the hills."

"Who found her?"

"The night security guard came on duty about an hour ago and started his rounds." Kennedy looked over his shoulder. "Hey, Stan, come over here, would ya?"

I'd noticed the old fellow in the brown guard's uniform. He was one of those guys who look like they've seen a lot in life, and it's taken all the color right out of them. Like an old, faded photograph.

"Tell the Lieutenant what happened, Stan," Kennedy encouraged.

"Well, it's like this, see. I'm on duty at 6 PM, so I get here a little early to get set up. Maybe a quarter to six."

I broke in. "You replace the day guard?"

"Sure, usually. But today's Sunday, so the gallery was closed. There's just a night shift Sundays."

"All right, carry on."

"So the first thing I always do is check the perimeter from the outside. That way I know nobody's getting in. Then I go through the building, first the public spaces, make sure no one's hiding in the bathrooms, that sorta thing, then finally the private areas."

"That's when you found her."

"Right. Just came through the door and there she was, just like you see her now. Gave me the shock of my life, you betcha."

My brow furrowed. "You saw her as soon as you opened the door?"

"Oh yeah, right away. Just like I said."

"But this was Sunday. The place was closed — the lights should've been switched off all day. And this place hasn't any windows — which means if you saw her as soon as you came in the room, the lights must've been on."

"I guess you're right. I didn't think about it."

I turned to Kennedy. "Officer — we got time of death?"

"Sorry Lieutenant, the ME's running late."

"Never mind."

"Hey," Stan spoke up. "In case it helps — there was a false alarm report at midday. This place has got an alarm that rings at central office. When it goes off, we send out a car to check it out. They give those guys special keys, access all areas — they sweep the whole place. I saw it in the log. Everything was OK at noon."

SUSPECTS

Before long, I had examined the crime scene, learned all I could about the victim, and compiled my list of suspects. It turns out that the art world is not always the refined, pleasant place one would like it to be, and the list of individuals with shady backgrounds or reason to wish harm to Rosetta Arnette was as long as my arm — but five prime candidates stood out.

- **Jeffrey Gardner**: an art dealer in his early forties. Born and raised in Chicago, he carved his niche in the art world by identifying and promoting emerging artists. His charisma and eye for talent brought him widespread acclaim, eventually leading him to Los Angeles, where he established a chic gallery on Melrose Avenue.

  Jeffrey and Rosetta Arnette's paths often crossed in social circles, and they collaborated on exhibitions. Their relationship took a bitter turn when Rosetta secured an exclusive contract with a high-profile artist who Jeffrey had been courting for years. The deal was a significant blow to his gallery's prestige and financial prospects. Jeffrey had on more than one occasion threatened to expose Rosetta's — in his words — "unethical dealings."

- **Denise Kinney**: an art critic and columnist for a popular lifestyle magazine, known for her incisive critiques and unyielding opinions. With a degree in Art History from UC Berkeley, Denise climbed the ranks from a small-time blogger to a respected voice in the art community. Her sharp-tongued reviews were known to make or break artists and exhibitions.

  Denise had a complex relationship with Rosetta Arnette. Over the years, Rosetta's gallery had been a frequent subject of Denise's columns, with reviews oscillating between glowing praise and harsh criticism. Rumor has it that Denise recently discovered some troubling information regarding alleged forgeries being passed through Rosetta's gallery.

- **Kenneth Haddad**: a middle-aged, reclusive artist; a staple of the Los Angeles art scene. Known for his moody, magic realist paintings, Kenneth once enjoyed the adulation of critics and collectors alike. However, recent years have seen his influence wane, with younger, more avant-garde artists overshadowing his work.

  Rosetta Arnette had been Kenneth's patron for many years, hosting numerous exhibitions dedicated to his art at her prestigious gallery.

  In recent years, however, tensions flared between the two. Rosetta had become increasingly candid about diversifying her gallery's offerings, expressing a desire to reduce the focus on traditional art in favor of artists with a fresher style. Rosetta's decision not to feature Haddad in an upcoming high-profile exhibition was not well received by the artist, whose most recent public outburst against his treatment even made it to the Entertainment & Arts section of the Los Angeles Chronicle under the headline *I've Haddad Enough!*

- **Alexander McCullough**: an affluent art collector, known for amassing an eclectic and prestigious collection that spanned continents and eras. Funded by family money, his acquisition strategy was marked by a keen eye for value and a strategic approach to building a collection balancing historical significance with cutting-edge contemporary works. Alexander considered Rosetta Arnette a trusted advisor and valued collaborator, purchasing numerous high-profile pieces through her gallery.

  However, Alexander's relationship with Rosetta recently took a troubling turn. It was discovered that a rare piece he acquired through her gallery was (I quote from the auctioneer's report) *not as exclusive as initially presented.* That's to say — a forgery.

- **Rochelle Phelps**: an art broker with a flashy lifestyle and a reputation for her discerning eye and resourceful networking skills, known for maneuvering within the more shadowy elements of the art market. Based out of an elegant Malibu beach house but often found globetrotting art fairs and auctions, Rochelle has made a name for herself brokering hyped-up deals for pieces that often fetch exorbitant prices.

  While Rochelle's expertise allowed her to supply Rosetta with rare and sought-after pieces, her methods have sometimes been controversial and, some said, bordering on the unethical.

INVESTIGATION

1 — The crime scene was bustling with activity. Photographers, uniformed officers, and forensic experts all moved like pieces on a chessboard, each intent on their own assignments. But I was only interested in the ominous pinewood packing case on which Rosetta's body had lain until recently.

I lifted the lid cautiously and shined a pencil flashlight into the dark interior. Inside was a dim form wrapped in layers of thick plastic, held in place by expanded polystyrene forms which looked cut specially for the piece's odd shape. Some kind of modern art sculpture, I figured. Packing and handling art is serious business — you can't just wrap a Van Gogh in cardboard and send it through the mail. You need specialist shippers.

Then the beam of my flashlight caught it — stuffed down between the side of the sculpture and the wall of the packing case, barely visible. I reached in and fished it out triumphantly — a blue cardboard document folder. Aside from the color, it was a lot like the ones we use for case files at headquarters.

Inside the folder were only a few sheets of paper. Photocopies, they looked like, or printouts — scanned documents or receipts of some kind. Lists of numbers, and strange, angular symbols. They didn't mean anything to me — yet.

But this sure did: on the first page of numbers was a big, round wine stain, an impression of the base of a wineglass in reddish-purple liquid. I knew, from long experience of spilling wine, the fact that it hadn't turned darker yet meant it was fresh — a few hours old, at most.

"Hey, Kennedy, get over here with an evidence bag — take this to forensics, I wanna know if the wine stain matches the wine in the bottle — fast!"

Something told me that it would.

Whatever the purpose of the mysterious folder, the fact that Rosetta had tried to hide it with her last breath indicated that the folder and its contents had to be relevant and important to the case.

2 — Back at headquarters, I spent hours poring over the documents from the blue folder I'd found in the packing crate. Among the photocopies were a bank receipt and what looked like a carbon copy of a withdrawal form. They appeared to reveal a substantial transaction from Rosetta's account just the week before her untimely demise. The form's *Method of Disbursement* field read *Cash*.

I dialed Arthur Reilly, Rosetta's bank manager, and leaned back in my chair. After a few rings, he picked up. I introduced myself.

"Lieutenant Costanzo, what can I do for you?"

"I'm interested in a large withdrawal made from Ms. Arnette's account." I gave him the details from the form. "What can you tell me about it?"

Reilly paused, the sound of fingers tapping at a computer keyboard coming down the line. "Yes, I see it here — a significant sum withdrawn around midday. The teller involved is on shift today. Let me call her over for you."

Within moments, the teller was on the phone, her voice radiating professionalism. "This is Julie speaking. How can I assist you?"

"Julie, this is Lieutenant Costanzo with the LAPD. I need you to walk me through a transaction with Ms. Arnette from Thursday. You remember it?"

"Oh, yes, absolutely. It was rather unusual. Ms. Arnette seemed quite agitated when she requested to withdraw the funds. Not that we don't get a few nervous customers, but..." Julie trailed off as if considering how much to say.

"Nervous, how? Did she seem like she was in a hurry?"

"Well, she kept glancing around the bank, checking over her shoulder. I found it odd, especially when she simply stuffed all that cash into her handbag. Considering the amount, I was worried for her safety."

"Uh-huh. And then what did she do?"

"Well, there was this other person waiting for her. A short, blonde lady. In her mid-thirties, maybe. I saw Ms. Arnette open her handbag so the other lady could see inside, and then they walked out together. I figured she was there for additional security, so I stopped worrying about the money... Lieutenant, is this something to do with her... well, her murder?"

It was a good question. I thought about it. Everything happens for a reason, and these documents being in the blue folder was no exception. "Yeah," I said. "But exactly *what*, I don't know... We're gonna have to wait and see."

3 — Later that day, I was nursing a cup of coffee that had grown cold an hour before. I was sifting through constellations of reports when the phone on my desk rang, breaking the silence. It was Arthur Reilly, Ms. Arnette's personal banker.

"Lieutenant Costanzo?" he asked.

"Yes, speaking," I said, stifling a yawn. "Hello again, Mr. Reilly. How can I help you?"

"I believe I have some information that might be pertinent to your investigation into Rosetta Arnette's..." He paused, searching for the right word. "...unfortunate passing."

"Go on," I urged.

Reilly took a breath before plunging in. "On Sunday, a couple of minutes after 4 PM, Ms. Arnette contacted me requesting an immediate loan. I..." he hesitated, "I could sense some urgency in her tone."

"Hold on a minute," I replied. "You said 'Sunday.' You mean to say your bank clients can just call you at home on the weekend? It takes me two weeks to get an appointment with my bank manager."

"Well, Lieutenant, here at the Venetian Bank we pride ourselves on our accessibility. It's a little different in the world of, uh... *private wealth management.*"

"Gee, it sure is," I replied, running my hand through my hair. "You mentioned a loan. What kind of amount are we talking about here?"

"Significant. Let's say it was large enough to involve considerable risk assessments, even for someone of her financial standing."

I leaned back in my chair, thinking. "And did she mention the purpose of this loan?"

"Ms. Arnette was rather discreet, as was typical of her business dealings," Reilly admitted. "It was a quick call."

"And did the loan request have any connection to the large cash withdrawal we discussed earlier?"

"No, not as far as the bank is concerned. Two separate incidents."

"I see. You seem very confident about the time of the phone call, Mr. Reilly."

"I should be. Every call that comes in on my business line is timestamped and recorded. Bank rules. In this business we live in a world of *know your customer* regulations — *KYC*, it's called — and if you knew *our* customers, you'd know why the regulations are so strict."

"A bunch of wise guys, huh?"

"Lieutenant, you have no idea."

4 — There was the tinkle of a bell as I opened the door of Gardner's gallery and stepped out of the hustle and bustle of Melrose Avenue into an oasis of calm.

Soothing ambient music filled the air as the door closed behind me, and I found myself in a bohemian enclave of earth-toned decor, the scent of incense, and fluffy green shag carpet that would've been right at home in the Playboy Mansion, circa 1971. To say it was a contrast to the Arnette Gallery's stark marble caverns would be the understatement of the year.

I was going to take a leisurely look around, but as I was deciding which direction to walk around the gallery, a dapper but flustered-looking man with an erratic mop of dark hair detached himself from a group of people talking quietly nearby and, to my surprise, began trying to shoo me back out the door.

"Look, I'm really not interested, okay?" he said with a world-weary sigh. "I've told you before, I can't give valuable wall-space to every self-proclaimed genius who walks in off the street!"

I tried to set him straight, but he just barreled right on. "Why don't you try the Outsider Art Collective in Venice Beach? They're *much* more likely to have space for someone of your —" he paused and sniffed before finishing "— *ilk.*"

I didn't say anything this time, because by now I had my badge wallet in my hand, discretely held open at waist level. I looked him in the eye, then looked downwards, and his gaze naturally followed mine. It was like someone had thrown a toaster in his bath. "Oh!" he exclaimed loudly, and I thought his socks were liable to pop off with surprise.

Heads turned towards us, and he began to apologize profusely, fluttering his hands around like a southern belle with the vapors.

"You *are* Jeffrey Gardner, right?"

"Indeed, of course. My most sincere and abundant apologies, Lieutenant, you must understand, we get a never-ending stream of bedlamites and eccentrics approaching us, wanting us to display their hobo daubings, so when you came in I naturally assumed... well, yes, quite naturally, I'm sure," he burbled in embarrassment.

"No problem, sir," I tried to calm him down. "Is there somewhere we can talk?"

"Yes, yes, certainly. Please, come with me." Gardner took me by the arm and led me to what was evidently his private office. The green shag carpet was even deeper and more luxuriant in here. Perhaps it needed mowing.

"Coffee?" Gardner offered as we entered his private enclave. I nodded gratefully, and he busied himself at a bar tucked in between shelves of art books and vinyl records.

"I guess you know why I'm here, Mr. Gardner."

He affected a casual air that didn't quite come off as nonchalant. "Ah, the incident with poor Rosetta, I suppose?"

"That's right. I'm making the rounds, talking to her associates." I paused, measuring his reaction. "Trying to get a feel for the undercurrents of the art world, you might say."

Gardner studied me for a moment, tapping a finger idly on his desk. "Rosetta was... a formidable presence, no question. We moved in overlapping circles. Certainly, we had our, um, differences, over matters of business."

"Oh, believe me Mr. Gardner, I understand. Art can be a cut-throat world. It's a high-stakes business, after all."

He gave a soft chuckle. "Indeed. The art world is filled with beauty and passion, Lieutenant, but that passion can also be fierce."

I leaned forward slightly. "Any particular tensions you might've noticed recently? Within those overlapping circles you mentioned, I mean."

Gardner waved a hand dismissively. "Oh, the usual disagreements over contracts, gallery spaces, deciding upon whom the fickle and fleeting spotlight of fame should next alight. We gallery owners are not without a modicum of power, you know."

I nodded encouragement, keeping quiet so he'd continue.

"Of course, I wasn't always a moneygrubbing businessman. As a younger fellow, I had high hopes that my own artistic muse might carry me to the pinnacles of fame and fortune. Observe —" he waved his arm theatrically at a wall covered in framed pictures. I'd noticed them earlier. They were striking, and attractive — stark white forms on backgrounds of a beautiful deep blue that made me think of cloudless skies.

"They look like old-fashioned blueprints," I said, rather more bluntly than I'd intended.

To my surprise, he was pleased by my reaction. "Indeed! You're quite right, Lieutenant, in a sense that's exactly what they are. *Cyanotypes*, a kind of photographic printing. My medium of choice. Exactly the same process by which early blueprints were reproduced, and — obviously — the origin of their name."

"I see. They're tremendous. But I guess success was... elusive?"

Gardner shook his mop-like head. "Sadly, so. The mind, no matter how elevated its mentation, is slave to the whims of the base body to which it is tethered — as Ariel is the prisoner of Prospero. One has to eat, after all, and beautiful thoughts do not fill the beggar's bowl. I tried to peddle my poor little works; I thought I'd found a mentor in a famous collector, Alexander McCullough, but the sunlight of his gaze was fleeting and he soon turned elsewhere, leaving me out in the cold. So I opened my first gallery and became a hunter after the almighty buck. A fleet-footed quarry, but one which is much more easily speared from this side of the canvas, I can assure you."

*****

Back at headquarters, I sat back in my chair with my feet up on my desk, thinking deeply. I think best with my eyes closed. Sometimes I think so deeply that I enter a strange, trance-like state, and also snore.

Suddenly, I was wide awake. That was it! That's what had been bugging me. The word Gardner had used to describe his blueprint art — *cyanotype*. Somewhere in the back of my mind, a little voice was screaming that word at me.

I looked it up. It turned out that, like regular photography, the process was as much chemistry as art. When preparing the reactive paper, two chemicals — potassium ferrocyanide and ferric ammonium citrate — are combined to create a solution that is then used to coat the paper. Then, when ultraviolet light is applied, ferric ferrocyanide is created — also known as *Prussian blue*. Just like a developing photograph, the areas where the chemical is concentrated slowly turn a dark blue, whereas the areas where it is absent retain the color of the paper.

Apparently, Prussian blue is one of the oldest synthetic dyes, and quite safe, but by applying an alkaline solution one can isolate hydrogen cyanide gas from it. And from there, it's child's play to treat the hydrogen cyanide with an aqueous solution of potassium hydroxide, evaporate the solution, and be left with powdered potassium cyanide — one of the most lethal poisons known to humankind.

I sat back and rubbed my eyes. Cyanide, eh? Well, whaddaya know!

5 — The sun had dipped below the horizon, casting long shadows across the city streets as I made my way to the Medical Examiner's office. I rapped on the frosted glass door and let myself in.

The ME was hunched over a stack of charts, his glasses perched precariously on the end of his nose.

"Evening, Larry," I said, pulling up a chair. "I'm hoping you've got some good news for me."

"Good news is my business," he replied, flipping a page with a flourish. "You're after a time of death for Rosetta Arnette. Well, she died prior to 5 PM."

"Okay," I said, pen poised over my notepad. "What are we basing this on?"

Larry adjusted his glasses. "Primarily *livor mortis* — postmortem lividity. The pooling of blood that settles in the lower parts of the body, after the heart has stopped pumping it around. It typically takes a couple of hours after death before it becomes visibly apparent, so, given the time of examination, we can confidently say she was dead before 5 PM Sunday."

6 — Nature can reclaim just about anything, if you leave it long enough. Kenneth Haddad's sprawling Laurel Canyon property must've exuded glamor a long time ago, but now its overgrown condition betrayed the artist's dwindling fortune. The paint peeled away from the walls, and unruly vines crept every which way.

I knocked on the front door, half expecting it to fall off its hinges. Haddad opened it cautiously, revealing dark, fatigued panda-bear eyes, wild, uncombed hair and a thick beard. I saw he was wearing a threadbare bathrobe, and hoped there was some clothing underneath. The home's interior bore signs of former opulence: gilded frames and plush, faded furniture.

"Kenneth Haddad?" I asked, managing a smile and showing my identification.

"In the flesh," he replied drily. "Excuse my appearance. Rare to have anyone come by these days." He turned and started to wander back inside, beckoning me with an air of resigned courtesy, so I followed him. "Without an appointment, that is," I heard him mutter angrily.

His art was everywhere, not only framed on the walls, but stacked in unframed piles on the floor. Most of the paintings' subjects were everyday stuff: suburban houses, night-time scenes with yellow-lit windows that made you want to peek in and see what people were up to inside. I liked it instinctively. I'm no critic like Denise Kinney, but to me it seemed clean-lined and kind of honest, but with this kind of — oh, I don't know — *mythical* quality that let you know the artist was capable of looking at the world in a benevolent, understanding way. Looking at the unkempt, irritated guy in front of me, I reflected that the art and the artist do not always mirror one another.

"What brings you here, Detective?" Haddad asked, hitching his bathrobe tighter.

I got down to business. "I'm investigating Rosetta Arnette's murder."

Haddad raised an eyebrow, feigning surprise, but there was a flicker of interest in his eyes. "Indeed. And why come to me?"

"Well, I gotta look at all the angles. Your name came up, given some recent, uh, artistic differences."

Haddad snorted softly, turning away. "Artistic differences. That's a delicate way to put it, Detective. Rosetta had her ideas about progress, and I had mine. But disagreement doesn't make me a killer." He paused. "Though, she was a real witch, of course. An absolute bloodsucker."

I said nothing, hoping he'd elaborate, but something told me he wasn't going to be easily drawn any further on the subject.

Haddad considered me with a worn expression. "Are you keen on art, Detective?"

"It's *Lieutenant*, actually. And, well, gee... I guess I don't know much about it. But I know what I like."

"Splendid! You know your own mind. The mark of an honest man. Here —" he motioned towards a stack of canvases "— take a look. I've got plenty you won't find in galleries these days. You might see something you like. I'll make you a good deal. You'd be getting a steal."

It was too good an opportunity to miss. I began thumbing through one canvas after another. They were all variations on the same theme, the suburban landscape. "Fantastic work. You've got a real eye," I remarked.

He shrugged with modest acknowledgment. "They used to call the style *critical modernism*. Never really liked the label, myself."

I moved on to a second stack of dusty canvases. I was starting to notice similarities between his paintings, now: every tract house was the same, or at least very similar... subtle differences only. The characters — men, women, children, even the dogs — all looked nearly identical; cookie-cutter people. Even the plants around the houses were the same; I noticed that every painting contained the same strange, blue-flowered bush, usually in a garden but sometimes growing wild on a hill, its vibrantly-colored stems incongruous among the surrounding earth tones, like indigo arrows of color. I pointed it out to Haddad.

"Well noticed," he said. "That's *wolfsbane*. As the name suggests — the bane of wolves — it was used historically as a way of keeping vicious predators at bay. *Aconitum variegatum* — also known as monkshood, on account of the flowers' shape. I think the symbolism is obvious. Protection from monsters, real and imagined. The homeowner's craving for security. Safety in a vicious world. An illusion — unattainable."

I pulled a canvas from the stack. Looking down from a point high in the air, it showed a flock of black birds flying over the familiar landscape of tract houses. Down below a human figure was running. It wasn't clear if he was a jogger, or if he was fleeing from the birds, like in that Hitchcock movie. It seemed to be a recurring theme across numerous paintings.

"How much you want for this one?" I asked. Haddad named a figure that set me back on my heels.

"Wow, OK." I raised my hand in mock supplication. "I'll have to think about it. Run it past my wife. She'll want something that goes with the furniture in the den, I guess."

Haddad said nothing. I was grateful for that.

7 — I drove out to see McCullough at his family estate in the hills outside of Los Angeles. The winding driveway led me to a stone mansion that looked like a European castle, but on a smaller scale, like it had been designed based on something the architect once saw on a tin of German sugar cookies.

I stepped out of my car, and the crunch of gravel underfoot seemed uncannily loud. The only other sound around was a lawnmower droning away somewhere in the distance.

As I approached the entrance, the heavy wood and glass doors swung open, revealing Alexander McCullough himself. He exuded charm, effortlessly poised, attired in a tailored suit that seemed sculpted to his form. The guy probably practiced his poses in front of the bedroom mirror.

"Lieutenant Costanzo, welcome to my humble abode," he greeted me with a serene smile.

"Huh — humble ain't really the word I'd choose," I replied, glancing at the towering ceilings and polished wood. "Thanks for agreeing to meet with me."

"Of course. Please, this way," he replied, gesturing toward a sun-drenched room lined with bookshelves and display cases. "What can I do for you, Lieutenant?"

"Could you tell me where you were Sunday afternoon? Say, noon until five?"

He rubbed his chin thoughtfully. "Well, actually, most of the day I was recording an episode of *Timeless Treasures*. We wrapped up around four. They asked me to come in to the studios to appraise an interesting piece a viewer had brought in for evaluation — jade carvings."

"Jade carvings, huh? Where'd they come from?"

"Kyushu."

"Gesundheit."

"No, Lieutenant, Kyushu is in Japan. The most southerly of the four main islands."

"Wow — an ancient Japanese artifact," I mused. "I didn't know you were an expert."

"Oh, well, that's decades of travel and study for you," he replied, green eyes alight with satisfaction. "As a matter of fact, I based the thesis of my visual anthropology degree at Stanford on the Ainu people of Hokkaido. Remarkable artists. I spent a month with them."

I nodded as if I knew what he was talking about. "*Timeless Treasures* — that's a great TV show. My wife watches it all the time. She keeps bugging me to take her collection of vintage *Looney Tunes* figurines in for appraisal."

It was McCullough's turn to nod in bemusement. "I, uh... I see."

"So, anyway, after *Timeless Treasures*, where did you head off to?"

"I returned home. Spent the rest of the day working on a piece I've been writing — an essay on traditional artistic ethics. Alas, no one was around to observe me, but I assure you, Lieutenant, you have my word on it."

8 — I was stuck in stop-go traffic on the 405, and my classic automobile's temperature gauge was starting to climb into the red, when officer Kennedy's voice blared out of the police radio speaker at me. I asked him what he wanted.

"Lieutenant, it's about Gardner."

"What gardener?" I said, distracted.

"You know, Lieutenant, the fine arts dealer."

"The fine art stealer?" I was quite confused now. "The gardener's stealing the art?"

"No, Lieutenant, *dealer*. Mr. Gardner. He's a fine arts —" pause "— *dealer*."

"Oh, him. What about him?" I thought I could see some steam escaping through the panel gaps around the auto's hood.

"Turns out he's got an alibi up until four o'clock. At a new gallery opening — the whole event was recorded, it's up on the Internet. There's no breaking it."

"Understood. What about after four?" There was a definite smell of hot engine coolant coming from the air vents in the dash now.

"Nothing concrete, Lieutenant."

I pressed the push-to-talk button on the radio mic, but before I could reply there was a loud bang from in front of me and the car's hood unlatched and sprang up amid a plume of steam.

"Lieutenant, are you OK?" Kennedy's worried voice came over the speaker. "What was that?"

I just sat back in the driver's seat and concentrated on breathing deeply as the honking of angry drivers started up all around. "Nothing, Kennedy, nothing important. Just send a tow truck, would you?"

9 — The bank teller had mentioned "a short, blonde lady." One person on my list matched the description perfectly: the sharp-tongued art critic Denise Kinney.

The bungalow court where Kinney resided was a quaint relic of a bygone era, a cluster of charming but weathered adobe homes that hummed with history. The vintage neon sign at the entrance flickered like a fading star.

I parked my car and ambled up the path to Kinney's bungalow. Considering her status as a minor but respected celebrity in the art world, the place was more run-down than I'd expected. I figured a successful critic like her would more likely opt for something a little more upscale, a slick apartment with an ocean view, perhaps.

Moments after I knocked, the door swung open to reveal Denise. She was impeccably dressed, her presence immediately radiating the fierce confidence she brought to her often-scathing critiques of the art world.

"Lieutenant Costanzo," she greeted me. "This is a surprise. What brings you to my home?"

"Well, it turns out, mostly nostalgia," I said, gesturing at the bungalow. "These places have so much history. Hollywood royalty used to call places like this home."

A flicker of pride crossed her face. "Indeed. That's why I love it here. It's like living in a chapter from LA's golden age."

I rapped my knuckles on the adobe wall and hazarded a guess. "What do you call this style, Spanish Colonial?"

"Not bad, Lieutenant, you're close: Mission Revival."

We exchanged a few more pleasantries about the bungalow and its storied past, but I could tell she was growing restless. I switched gears. "Now, Denise, the real reason I'm here. I have to ask about your visit to the bank with Rosetta Arnette."

She didn't skip a beat or bother trying to pretend it wasn't her. Maybe she was the honest type, or maybe she knew there'd be no coming back from a lie like that, if she was proved wrong. "Sure. What about it?"

"Well, why did you go along with her?"

She smiled suddenly. "Oh, that's easy — security. Rosetta was making a large withdrawal and needed someone she could trust."

I looked at her diminutive stature and tried to figure out how to put the next question politely. "You, uh, have martial arts training, maybe?"

"Oh no, silly! I have a gun. It's all legal, concealed carry permit and everything." Her hand dove into her jeans pocket and I thought for a second she was going to pull out a weapon, but her hand returned with a brown leather wallet. She extracted a plastic card and handed it to me.

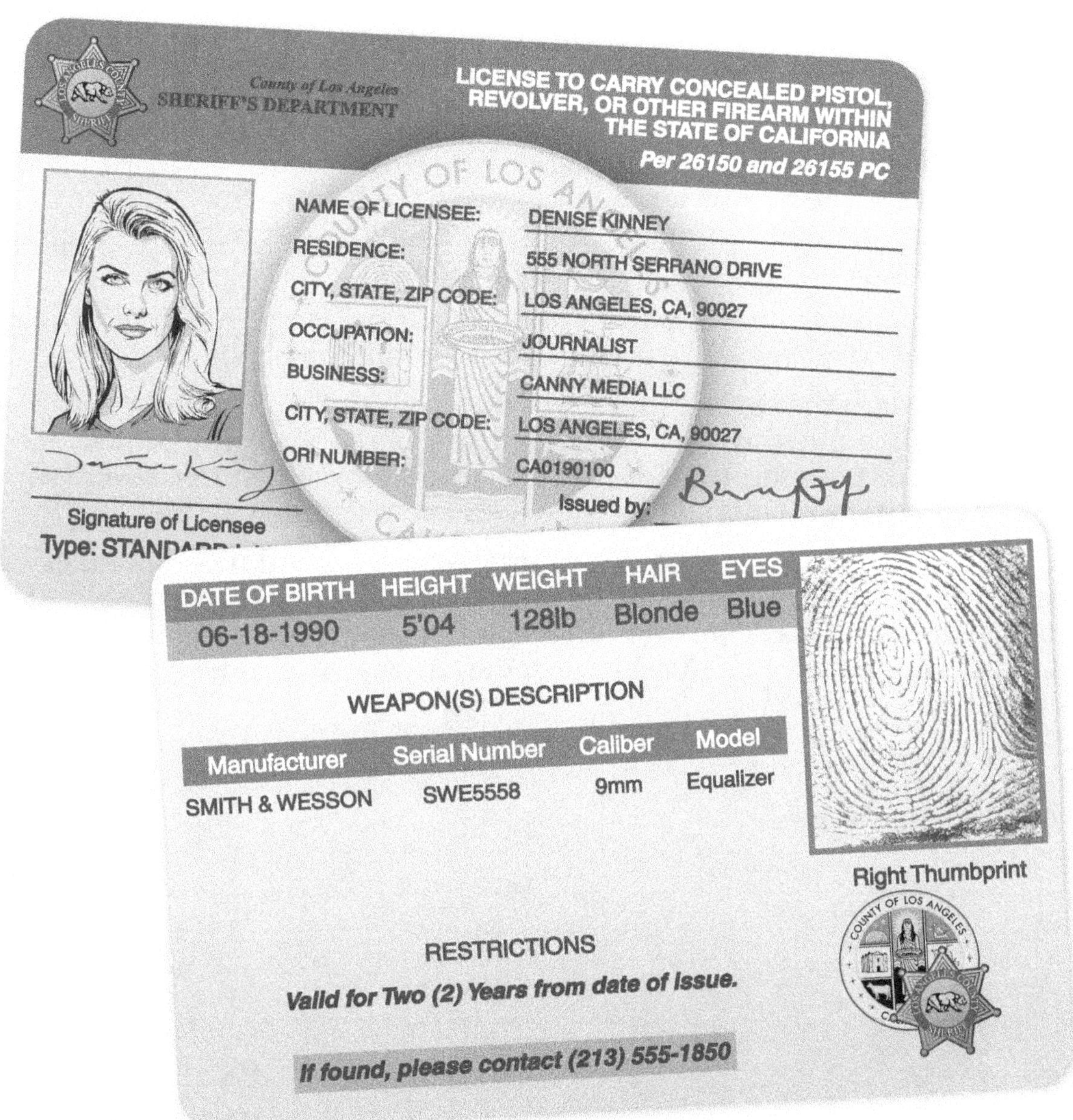

"Nine millimeter... I'm no firearms expert," I apologized, "but don't most ladies with a, uh, smaller frame, prefer a lighter caliber, like .380?"

Denise shrugged. "Maybe. But this is California — ten rounds maximum legal magazine capacity. If that's all you can carry, why not pack the most punch you can?"

I didn't really have an answer to that one, so I shrugged and moved on. "So, what did you and Rosetta do after you left the bank?"

"I dropped her at her gallery," Denise replied smoothly. "Made sure she got through the door safely, then drove off. After that, it was her business."

"Uh-huh. Speaking of her business, what did she need the money for?"

Denise shrugged and raised her eyes, as if remembering. "She *told* me it was to pay for an artwork from some artist who wouldn't deal with banks, only in cash. Sure, there's a lot of kooky guys out there. But I don't know if I really believed her... you know, the art business can be kind of *shady*."

10 — The label on the large, plain, manila envelope said only *Lieutenant Costanzo — Urgent*. No sender's name, no return address. Someone had dropped it into the Department's mailbox after hours.

Rosetta Arnette's murder had hit the headlines, and the trickle of tips and leads coming in to the Department had become a flood. Most of them were dead ends, but I wondered if this one would be different.

The fact that it was anonymous was a good omen. Most of our lousy tips come from people trying to score a buck or make a name for themselves, so the fact the tipster chose to stay out of the limelight suggested they genuinely thought they had something significant. Rightly or wrongly. Either way, I was willing to take a chance on it.

I picked the envelope up, tested its weight, and felt out the corners. I ripped open the seal and slipped out a single sheet of paper. Torn out of a spiral-bound notebook.

The pre-printed fields at the top told me it was the kind of stationery used by a medical professional to take notes when meeting with patients. I wondered who would have access to such a document. The note-taker themselves, of course. An employee of their clinic. Maybe a family member. No one who'd want their name to come out in connection with the case, that was certain.

I figured the doc didn't find the patient very interesting; several bored doodles were sketched unprofessionally around the page. And the writing seemed even harder to read than the indecipherable scrawl that serves as a private language between doctors and pharmacists. Then I laughed to myself. The old *da Vinci* trick! I wondered what it all meant, and why it had been placed in my hands...

135 - October 17 / *Rosetta Arnette*

PATIENT / **SESSION**

Patient expresses concern regarding escalating alcohol consumption.

Patient attributes this to elevated stress induced by two individuals, A & D.

These individuals both exert significant influence over her actions, yet in conflicting and opposing manners. Rational self-awareness? Or avoidant rationalization?

11 — I was back at my desk when Detective Manion of the Major Crimes Division knocked on my office door. He was a former Marine; a big guy with blond hair and the air of a football linebacker twenty years and forty pounds past his prime but still gung-ho enough to make real trouble if he wanted to.

"Lieutenant Costanzo, I got something you might want to have a think about," he said.

"Hey, Brian!" I was happy to see him; he was one of the old-school good guys. "Come in and take a load off."

He did so, and my guest chair creaked alarmingly as the load in question was transferred to it.

"What can I do for you?" I asked.

"Maybe I can do something for you. Or maybe it's nothing. Either way, it's one of our confidential informants. The CI works as a bodyguard and part-time enforcer for the LA Mafia. Low rent type, pretty far down the food chain, but sometimes he sees things. He says he was working security for a meeting at a downtown restaurant one lunchtime. Claims to have seen an unfamiliar guy meeting with his boss. When he asked his buddy who the guy was, he was told *Some dude named McCullough — and none of your damn business*. The name rang a bell — you mentioned you'd been talking to this Alexander McCullough, the collector. Figured it might be your guy."

"You never know," I replied. "What about the description of this lunch guest?"

Manion shrugged. "I looked up your art collector online. No reason it couldn't have been him."

My McCullough was a pretty average-looking guy. No offense to him; I mean average height, weight, like that. And LA is a big city. Maybe it meant something, maybe not. "Thanks Brian," I said diplomatically. "I'll bear it in mind."

12 — I was just leaving headquarters to get lunch at a nearby food truck when Officer Kennedy ran down the steps and grabbed my arm.

"Lieutenant, the guys at Technical Investigation wanted me to let you know they got some text messages from Ms. Arnette's phone you might be interested in. Messages to McCullough."

"OK, fire away — what do they say?"

"Sure, let me see," Kennedy rustled a sheaf of papers, finally finding the right one. "Here we go. She writes to him: *I've been to the bank — withdrawal complete. Now it's your turn*. Then he writes, *Prove it!* ...and she replies, *No problem*. That's the last message."

"When was this?"

"Uh... Friday. Friday afternoon."

"I see. Hey, you wanna grab some lunch? My treat."

Kennedy looked worried, for some reason. "Where did you have in mind, Lieutenant?"

"Well, I was gonna get a couple sloppy joes at the *Belly Buster* truck round the corner."

I thought I saw Kennedy turn slightly pale. "Yeah, no, thanks all the same, Lieutenant. I've seen you eat... I mean, uh, I'm not that hungry. No offense."

"Hey, none taken," I replied, picking at a mustard stain on my tie.

13 — Navigating through the tangled mess of Laurel Canyon roads, I arrived once more at Haddad's ramshackle residence. I rapped the tarnished brass knocker a couple times, and the artist appeared, looking if anything scruffier than last time.

"Oh, Lieutenant Costanzo," he intoned wearily, "back for more of my sparkling company, I see."

"Mr. Haddad," I began, cutting straight to the heart of it, "I need to know where you were between midday and 5 PM on Sunday."

"Of course you do," he replied, scratching his beard. "Uh, I was teaching art classes online, through a video app. Noon until, well, I guess around five o'clock."

I raised an eyebrow. *Teaching?* The idea of this irascible scarecrow influencing impressionable minds made my jaw drop.

Kenneth nodded, misunderstanding my evident disbelief. "I know, right? I'm becoming a real tech nerd. It's part of a community outreach program for a local university. They rope me in every now and then — you know, to inspire new artists and fund my modest existence."

"You got proof of this?"

"Well, the sessions are recorded. I can show you the schedule and log you into the university's system if you want."

I waved him off. "You know what? Let's save it for the techies back at the office. I'll have my people verify it. Are you sure the lecture finished at around 5 PM?"

The artist looked a little embarrassed. "Well... dealing with those snot-nosed students means I usually have to take the edge off... I guess I got outside a few glasses of scotch. Maybe more than a few. I *think* it was around five — but the video will tell you for sure."

*****

Later, back at headquarters, a digital file arrived in my email. I enlisted Officer Kennedy's help to open the video, and we started to watch.

Haddad appeared on-screen, his unkempt hair and scruffy robe unchanged. There was a large glass of brown liquid and ice on the table next to him. He took a drink from it from time to time, as he delved into the nuances of creative expression with a theatrical fervor. Meanwhile, apparently unknown to Haddad, the students were carrying on their own narrative in the chat window. Each comment was scrutinizing Haddad's wild appearance or describing his home as something out of a post-apocalyptic B-movie. I noticed Kennedy was having a hard time containing his amusement. I wanted to get through the class quickly, so I hit the *skip* button. In fast-forward mode, Haddad's lecturing became even more frantic, and his drinking arm twitched the glass to and from his mouth erratically.

The timestamp in the top right corner of the video was ticking away... But something was wrong. "Hey, Kennedy, what's going on with this timestamp?" I blurted out. "It's not showing us the time!"

"Oh, right, I forgot to mention," he replied. "The tech guys told me about that. It's some weird format they call *daily epoch time*. Basically, it shows the number of seconds elapsed since the start of the day. So, at one minute after midnight, the daily epoch timestamp would be *60*. Because sixty seconds have elapsed. Make sense?"

"I guess..." In the video, Haddad had finished yelling at the students, picked up his notes, and had just left the screen. "Hey, pause it here — this is the end of the class. Back it up to the last time we can see Haddad... That's it. Pause it. What's the timestamp say?" We looked at the screen.

"OK, " I said. "Haddad claims he was in the class until 5 PM. Is he telling the truth?"

"Hmm…" Kennedy pulled out his phone.

"Hey!" I admonished. "Don't use a calculator, that's cheating!"

Kennedy gave me a sour look and picked up a pad and pencil. He began scribbling away. "OK, so there's sixty seconds in every minute… That's three thousand six hundred seconds in every hour… Multiply by twenty-four… That's eighty-six thousand, four hundred every day…"

Could I figure it out before he did?

14 — Boy, these rich folks have an easy life. Or at least, they like to make us working stiffs think they do. Maybe they've got tons of problems and stress, and they just hide it well. We Italians have a word for "making it look easy" — *sprezzatura*. That's why I don't dress fancy. Makes you look like you're trying too hard. Better it should look like effortless elegance instead, I thought, flicking some remnants of lunch off my jacket.

I was leafing through a copy of *Architecture & Interiors* magazine from a couple years back. It was a pretty highbrow rag. Not my regular kind of reading material, but they had a piece on Rochelle Phelps' house in Malibu. The article was the typical frothy puff piece that made you wonder how much people paid to appear in the magazine, and whether they got their money's worth — but the photos of the house were spectacular.

ARCHITECTURE & INTERIORS
page *48*

AT HOME WITH
Rochelle Phelps

words by **Anna Dyne** &
Annie Sthetic
photos by **Holden Gower**

After navigating the dynamic and often unpredictable art world, broker Rochelle Phelps emphasizes the importance of balancing career and personal passions.

"This is where I find inspiration, connect with loved ones, and truly embrace life," she explains while standing in the sunlit atrium of her Los Angeles home.

The meticulous renovation of her mid-century modern dwelling reflected a shift in aesthetic preferences. When Rochelle acquired the property in 2021, she envisioned a transformation that would seamlessly blend modern sophistication with artistic flair.

After several months into the redesign, she had a revelation. "I realized the original character held exceptional charm that could be harmonized with my vision," she notes.

Rochelle, whose journey began in global art trading and who is now chair of the prestigious annual Venetian Bank Arts Festival, found that the home's inherent design qualities resonated with her professional ethos.

"I'm moving away from traditional galleries and towards spaces that offer warmth and intimacy. The coziness of these rooms speaks volumes," she remarks, transitioning from the airy atrium into the intimate library.

Exotic shrubbery frames the residence's entrance

Suddenly, I pulled my feet off the desk and sat up straight. I could hardly believe my eyes — there it was again! Outside Phelps' front door... those same strange, blue-flowered bushes, like in Haddad's paintings. What had he called them?

15 — Denise had told me she was home all day Sunday, but of course I wasn't going to take her word for it. Harry Tremont, the bungalow court's super, was the guy I needed to talk to.

I knocked on the door of a bungalow that looked just like all the others, and within a minute was answered by a middle-aged, nervous-looking man who was wiping his hands on an oily rag. Or rather, he was wiping his oily hands on what had previously been a clean rag. I introduced myself and explained my business.

Harry sighed. "Ah, Sunday — the electrical upgrade. New breaker boxes for the whole court." He beckoned me inside, where a hodgepodge of photos, bills, and scrawled notes were pinned up on a cork board — the closest thing Harry had to an office.

"Sunday was hectic," Harry continued, sinking into a worn armchair. "Edison Electrical Services sent their team around noon. I had to keep tabs on the whole operation, keep them on schedule. Lucky us, getting it done on a Sunday. The only time everyone would be home to let the contractors in, though... Weekend overtime, you know." He rubbed his thumb and forefinger together in the universal sign for *money.*

"I get it," I replied. "Cost you an arm and a leg, I bet."

"You know it. I can tell you this, Lieutenant — Denise was definitely home. Had to be, or the work wouldn't have gotten done. I knocked on her door to let the guys in. Even chatted with her a bit while the crews were working. Same goes for the rest of the neighbors. I must've ping-ponged across this court a dozen times to make sure Edison's team did their job."

"You're absolutely certain about the time?"

Harry nodded vigorously. "Certain. I was there until just before four o'clock and the contractors left. Guess they figured they couldn't run out the clock any longer. I remember the time 'cause I had to sign their timesheet. Then, I let Denise know she could lock up, or get going, if she wanted."

16 — I pushed through the intimidating doors of the Arnette Gallery once again, a letter-sized manila envelope stuffed with papers under my arm. I'd called ahead, and Arnette's assistant — ex-assistant, I corrected myself — a young woman named Lydia, greeted me with a nod.

"Lieutenant Costanzo, come in. How can I assist you today?" she asked. She seemed very professional.

"Afternoon, Lydia. I've got something here that might interest you," I replied. "We found a USB thumb drive among Ms. Arnette's personal effects, and it's loaded with photos of paintings." I waved the envelope at her. "I have the printouts here. Mind taking a look?"

"By all means." I handed her the envelope, and she spread the color prints around the reception desk.

"Ah, yes. This is unmistakably Kenneth Haddad's work," Lydia said. "He's quite the character — a critical modernist, one of the originals."

"I see; Kenneth Haddad..." I paused. "Odd that with all their public disputes, she'd keep a drive full of his paintings in her pocket."

Lydia hesitated, then leaned closer. "Well, between you and me, Ms. Arnette was planning something a bit sneaky. She thought Haddad's style had been out of favor long enough that she could orchestrate a revival of his work. You know how these things work, in cycles, like in fashion."

"What's sneaky about that?"

"Well," Lydia continued in hushed tones, "Not to speak ill of the dead, but she wanted to use Haddad's exclusion as a tactic — make him think he was finished, out of luck forever. That way, he would agree to a heftier gallery commission on his sales when she pretended to finally relent, against her better judgment — he'd agree to anything if he thought it was his only way back onto the scene. And she'd make a killing."

"Well, that's an interesting strategy," I said mildly, raising an eyebrow. "But doesn't it seem, uh, kind of risky? The guy's got quite a reputation for being volatile."

"You may be right. I hate to say it, and God forgive me, she was a good boss to me... but maybe she got what she deserved."

17 — "Lieutenant, you might want to see this." Kennedy slapped a newspaper cutting down on my desk.

LOS ANGELES CHRONICLE

You've Been Haddad

By
Maude Clonet
Arts Beat
Correspondent

Notoriously outspoken former celebrity artist Kenneth Haddad hit the jackpot this week as the image rights to his back catalog sold for a sum in the high six-figures.

The buyer, operating via "Stone Script LLC," a company whose ownership remains anonymous, has not yet been identified.

Speculation is rife among the cognoscenti as to what this shadowy buyer would want with the intellectual property. Haddad hasn't had a gallery exhibition in years and is generally considered an out-of-touch has-been. His style has fallen out of favor in recent years, reportedly leaving him close to destitution.

Haddad in happier times.

Chronicle art critic Denise Kinney noted, "I can't imagine what they were thinking. Who on Earth would want to pay so much for a catalog of so little value? I mean, this is the twenty-first century! No wonder they want to remain anonymous. Frankly, the only possibility that occurs to me is that this is some kind of money laundering activity. Or cover-up for a blackmail payment, maybe. Though don't print that, of course. You're not recording this, are you?"

Get Off My Lawn

Known as a recluse, Haddad himself was unavailable for comment yesterday, instead choosing to remain largely silent about his unexpected windfall. "I don't know who the buyer is, and I don't care!" he yelled at this correspondent from behind the door of his sprawling Laurel Canyon home.

"Go away before I call the cops," the artist wittily quipped.

My first reaction was to echo the disbelief in the article. Why would someone pay top dollar for a has-been artist's back catalog? And why hide their identity? There had to be more to the story.

"You know," I told Kennedy, "There isn't really any such thing as an *anonymous* LLC — that's *Limited Liability Company*, in case you didn't know." Kennedy's eye-roll suggested he was well aware. "You can set up layer after layer of shell companies, but if they're incorporated in most states, the ownership structure is a matter of public record. Every Secretary of State's website has a business search engine. And in the few states public disclosure isn't required, we can easily subpoena the information. Even non-law-enforcement folks can look into other records like property purchase deeds to figure things out. Sooner or later someone looking hard enough is gonna find what they're looking for."

Kennedy didn't say anything.

"I bet you're wondering why I'm telling you this, right?"

"Nope," Kennedy sighed. "I'll start looking."

*****

The sun was low in the orange sky when Kennedy returned to my desk. "Well, Lieutenant, it took a while. Like you said, one shell company inside another. Different states. But here you go, I think I found the signature you're looking for." He handed me a printout of what looked like a badly scanned, badly photocopied government form.

<u>**REQUIRED**</u> **SIGNATURE:**

Rosetta Arnette

Signature of a member or an authorized representative of a member.

(In accordance with section 608.408(3), Florida Statutes, the execution of this document constitutes an affirmation under the penalties of perjury that the facts stated herein are true. I am aware that any false information submitted in a document to the Department of State constitutes a third degree felony as provided for in §817.155, F.S.)

SECRETARY OF STATE
TALLAHASSEE, FLORIDA
12 MAY – AM 8:40
FILED

18 — I was pacing up and down in my office, mulling a few things over, when the phone rang. I picked up the receiver. It took me a few seconds to place the raspy voice on the other end — then I realized it was Kenneth Haddad on the line.

I sat down at my desk and grabbed a notepad and pencil. "What can I do for you, Mr. Haddad?"

"Well, it's about poor Rosetta," he began, his tone uncharacteristically oozing concern. "I didn't think it was important when we talked before, but I just remembered that a couple weeks ago, late at night, she called me. Must've had few glasses of wine, from the sound of it."

Huh. Rosetta hadn't struck me as the type to make casual late-night calls. Particularly not to someone she was supposed to be feuding with. "What did she want?"

"She was... distraught," Haddad continued, pausing dramatically. "She said that everyone knew I was a recluse, which was a little insulting — but I was intrigued, so I didn't hang up right away. She wanted to know how I dealt with it."

"What do you mean?" I was puzzled.

"Well, apparently, her dealings with that art critic, Kinney, were really getting under her skin. Claimed Kinney was hassling her something awful. Really intimidating her. Made her frightened of going to work, even leaving the house. "

"Why? What do you mean, *dealings*?" I felt like I was missing something.

"She wouldn't spill too much. Kept mentioning she just didn't want to face the world anymore. Said Kinney was a real devil when the mask slipped off. But when I prodded for more, Rosetta just clammed up."

"I thought they were friends, Rosetta and Denise — weren't they?"

"Who knows, Lieutenant? Who knows what people are like behind closed doors? Sometimes they hide their true colors, don't they? But you only have to read Denise's newspaper column to see she's a nasty, venomous little... I mean, *not a very nice person.*"

I frowned to myself. Rosetta didn't strike me as the kind of person to let herself be taken advantage of; she was a scrappy fighter, not a recluse like Haddad. How did this new piece fit into the puzzle?

19 — I sat at my desk and examined the document in front of me, the green-shaded desk lamp flooding the desktop with yellow light. The lab had finished their analysis of the wine stains on the papers and let me have them back. As I'd suspected, the stain matched the bottle at the crime scene.

Now I had to figure out what the documents were, and what Rosetta Arnette had been doing with them — why she'd had them in the warehouse, why she was examining them while drinking her wine, and why she'd stuffed them down the side of the packing case — in what might well have been her last act before dying...

The first page was self-evidently the most important, because it was the one with the coded messages.

The original document was clearly a list of transactions, probably from a bank or other financial institution. There was a watermark on the paper of what I figured was a winged horse, or Pegasus, though its head and forequarters were covered so I couldn't be sure. Probably the institution's logo. The document had a list of money transfers and *To* and *From* fields, but the names of the sender and the recipient had been covered by pieces of paper before the document was scanned or photocopied. At least that told me the sender and recipient were the same for all the transactions.

Each of the pieces of paper was covered in strange symbols. The same type of symbols were on another piece of paper that looked like it could be a covering note, at the top of the document.

TRANSACTION LIST

FROM:

TO:

ACCT: 000641 3624

DATE RANGE: YTD

DATE	$AMT	STATUS
01-15	35,362.74	ACCC - SUCCESS
02-15	38,854.52	ACCC - SUCCESS
03-15	42,265.97	ACCC - SUCCESS
04-15	45,745.46	ACCC - SUCCESS
05-15	51,982.26	ACCC - SUCCESS

It was vital that I figure out what these coded messages were — this was a pivotal piece of evidence. It had to be a cipher of some kind, where each symbol is a substitution for a letter. I wondered if there was any logic behind which symbol was assigned to each letter. Maybe, maybe not. Either way, the most common letter in the English language is *E*, so there was a good chance that finding the most-repeated symbol in the cryptic messages would let me know which symbol represented that letter. I started counting…

A while later, I had my answer: not counting the dashes, of the eighty-nine symbols in the document, the most common symbol was the square — there were fourteen of them.

Now, in English vocabulary the *second* most common letter is *A*, but in everyday English text it actually tends to be *T* (on account of how the vocabulary is full of thousands of weird and wonderful words, but in conversation we use only a handful of common ones). I looked at my notes again…

Or was there a smarter way to approach this?

20 — There were a couple of crime scene photos from Rosetta Arnette's office that still bugged me. A stack of paintings and a scrap of paper… I kept coming back to them. What did they mean — if anything?

21 — I leaned back in my chair, contemplating the computer screen in front of me. The title *Canvas of Culture: Interrogating Semiotic Constructs in Ainu Traditions* stared back at me accusingly. Beneath the title was, *Master of Arts Thesis, Alexander McCullough, Visual Anthropology, Stanford University.*

McCullough's talk of visiting Japan had piqued my interest, so I'd dug up the thesis he'd mentioned from the university's online library. They had every student's published work, no matter how old, obscure, or tedious.

What now interested me even more was a long passage in the text. The academic work was supposed to deal with traditional arts, but included a long and quite irrelevant section concentrating on how the Ainu hunters create and use poisons. There was a passage quoting from a nineteenth-century British explorer:

"Pipichari has given me a small quantity of the poisonous [aconitine] paste, and has also taken me to see the plant from the root of which it is made, the *Aconitum Japonicum*, a monkshood, whose tall spikes of blue flowers are brightening the brushwood in all directions.

The root is pounded into a pulp, mixed with a reddish earth like an iron ore pulverized, and again with animal fat, before being placed in the arrow. [...] They claim that a single wound kills a bear in ten minutes. [They] say that if a man is accidentally wounded by a poisoned arrow the only cure is immediate excision of the part."

— from "Unbeaten Tracks in Japan," by Isabella Bird, pub. John Murray, London, 1880.

22 — I rubbed my temples, feeling fatigue setting in. But the day wasn't done yet. It was time to delve into Denise Kinney's personal universe — her newspaper column. The Los Angeles Chronicle's website had an archive going back years.

Immediately, I realized I'd bitten off more than I could chew. Every article was chock-full of terms like *non-linear dialectics* and *deconstructing meta-narratives.* Yecch.

Just as off-putting was her attitude. *Vicious, snide,* and *catty* were all words that came to mind. I guess fancy folks like that kind of thing, makes them feel sophisticated — but it just made me want to tell her, *Go write about something you actually enjoy!* Still, she must've been doing something right; clearly her opinions were well respected in the LA art world. For what that's worth.

Then I spotted a link to her biography. Relieved, I clicked through, hoping for something more digestible. The bio was an interesting mix of personal insights and professional milestones. But there was one particular segment that made me stop and lean forward: *My father's exemplary career as an industrial metallurgist greatly influenced my critical outlook. His innovative work with hexacyanoferrate complexes in steel treatment opened my mind to the intricate beauty of both art and science.*

Hexacyanoferrate complexes. There was that little old syllable again, hidden away in the middle of the first word. I looked up the scientific phrase, adding the name *Kinney*, clicked the first link that displayed, and read:

tive. This redox couple is reversible and entails no making or breaking of Fe–C bonds.

Development [Edit]

Hexacyanoferrate complexes are chemically stable compounds that contain cyanide ions bonded to iron.[11] Dr. Kinney was instrumental in developing the use of potassium cyanide, reacting with iron salts under specific conditions, to synthesize a unique hexacyanoferrate solution that yields a reflective surface ideal for optical and sensory technologies.[citation needed] This solution is then utilized to form layers on steel surfaces, or introduced into baths for electrochemical treatment.[12]

See also [Edit]

- Potassium ferricyanide
- Ferrocyanide

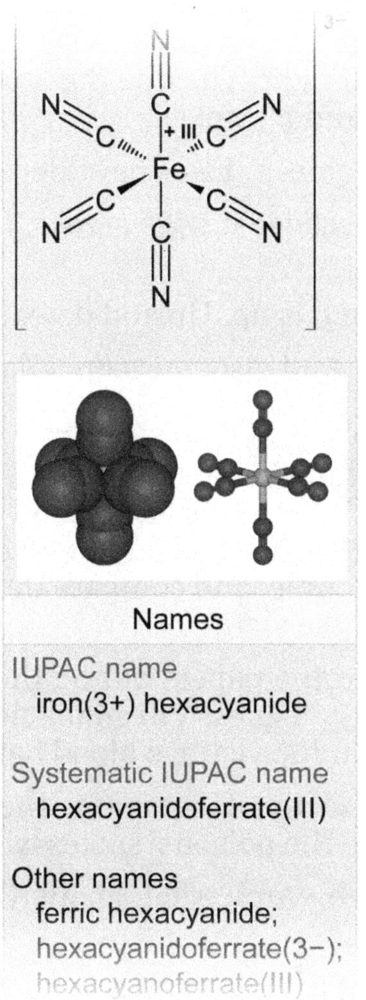

Names

IUPAC name
iron(3+) hexacyanide

Systematic IUPAC name
hexacyanidoferrate(III)

Other names
ferric hexacyanide;
hexacyanidoferrate(3−);
hexacyanoferrate(III)

23 — Dr. Kinsley called me to come visit him at the forensic laboratory. As soon as I arrived, he waved a sheaf of papers under my nose. The papers were covered in charts and graphs.

"Some interesting news, Lieutenant! We have discovered traces of a most unusual substance in the victim's bloodstream. Without a doubt, the murder weapon was poison. Moreover, while the same poison was present in the wineglass found at the scene, the wine bottle from which the liquid came was free of the substance. Just normal, though rather expensive, wine. Interesting, would you not agree?"

"You bet, Doc." It's best to keep your replies short with Doc Kinsley; he has a tendency to *go on*.

"As you know, we use Fourier-transform infrared spectroscopy to analyze substances that may be involved in a crime. The process works by sending light through a sample of the substance across a wide spectrum of wavelengths, and seeing how much light is absorbed by the substance at each wavelength. Every chemical has a kind of absorption fingerprint, which lets us know if a given compound is present in our sample substance. This so-called fingerprint is made up of *absorption peaks*, or spikes on the graph. Every chemical has a different set of absorption peaks."

"Sounds simple enough," I mumbled, offering the Doc no excuse to embark on further lecturing.

"Indeed. In this case, where poison is suspected, we analyzed the victim's blood. Now, this gives us a pretty complex graph, what with all the different substances present in the blood sample — proteins, lipids, carbohydrates, and other metabolites. Then, we looked at several of the possible poisons that could have killed the victim, based on the observed symptoms. Finally, we identified the key frequency range, shown on the graphs' x axis."

"Uh, wait a sec..."

The forensic scientist looked at me over his glasses. "The x axis is the line on the graph that goes left to right. The line that goes up and down is called the y axis. Remember the mnemonic, 'x is across, and y's up.'"

"X is a cross?" I was bewildered.

"Yes, because it goes across, from left to right. And the letter X is literally *a cross*. Two lines, crossing."

"And so y is up. Up and down."

"Right. And also, *wise up*. Like, get smart, don't be a bonehead."

"All right, take it easy, Doc," I said, a little affronted.

"So, I think you'll find it quite interesting — only one of the poisons has all its spikes present in the victim's blood. Bear in mind that the lower concentration of the poison in the victim's blood means the spikes won't be quite as prominent as they are in the pure samples. Look at the spikes for each sample, and compare the spikes to the victim's blood. Can you tell which poison was used to murder the victim?"

I spread the papers out on the desk, with the *Victim's Blood* graph at the top. "Hmm," I said, insightfully. "I guess I'm gonna need a ruler for this one. Maybe a pencil, too... Hey, Doc, do *all* the spikes from the victim's blood have to be in the poison's sample?"

"Not exactly, Lieutenant, the poison is just *one of* the compounds in the victim's blood. Examining the poisons' spikes will tell you which spikes are relevant."

"Uh-huh. And what about these 'valleys' in the victim's blood sample — do they mean anything?"

"Well, if there's a valley — or 'trough,' we call them — in the victim's blood, that means you can eliminate any poison that has a spike in that position."

"Gotcha, Doc." I set to work.

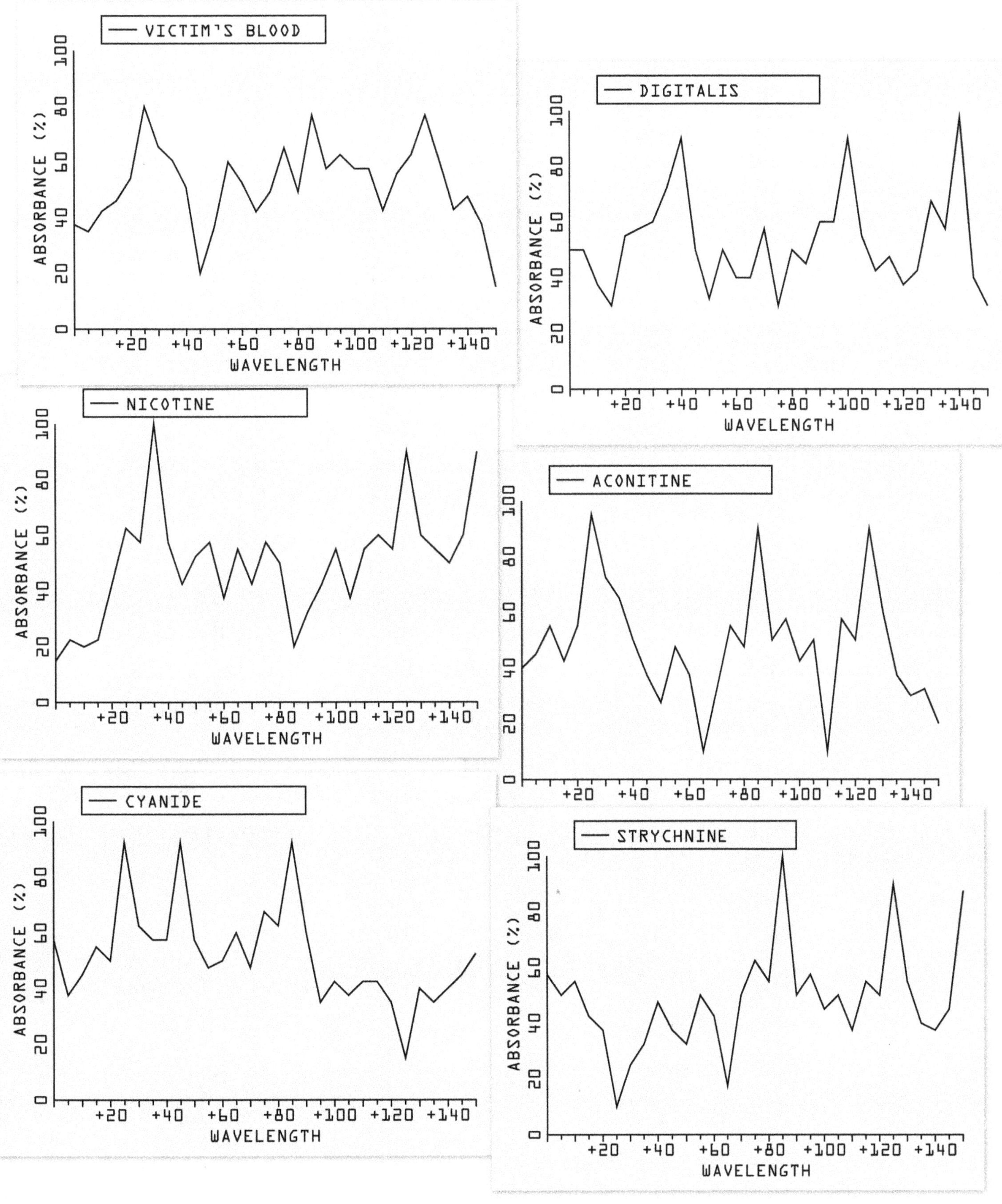

VICTIM'S BLOOD
ABSORBANCE (%)
WAVELENGTH
DIGITALIS
NICOTINE
ACONITINE
CYANIDE
STRYCHNINE

24 — I could use a cup of joe, so when Rochelle Phelps suggested meeting at the *Artisan Expression* coffee house, I readily agreed. The place was fragrant with the aroma of roasted beans and humming with the quiet rhythm of cool jazz.

Rochelle was seated at a corner table, her outfit a perfect blend of understated chic, sipping a frothy cappuccino from an oversized china cup. I ordered at the counter and went over. She glanced up as I approached, offering a composed smile and a wave.

"Lieutenant Costanzo," she greeted me, motioning to the chair across from her. "I appreciate you meeting me here. Busy day, dontcha know?" She had a jaunty, mid-Atlantic accent of the kind you don't often hear anymore, except in old movies.

"The pleasure's all mine, ma'am," I replied, settling into the seat. I explained why I needed to talk to her, and we discussed Rosetta Arnette for a minute. Then, the barista set a steaming cup the size of a soup bowl in front of me. I took a sip, letting the rich, warm flavors wash over me. Then I took out my notebook and pencil and got down to business. "Ms. Phelps, I need you to tell me where you were on Sunday. Noon until 5 PM... and if anyone can vouch for your whereabouts."

Rochelle inclined her head, her sleek hair catching the light. "Well, Lieutenant," she began with a little sigh of relief, "that shouldn't be a problem. It's all a little embarrassing, though..."

I shrugged. "If it gets you off a murder charge, how bad can it be?"

She laughed. "Why, Lieutenant, you're so right. You see, all day Sunday I was obliged to attend traffic school. On account of a little run-in I had with the highway patrol in my Maserati. I said to the judge, surely *reckless driving* means *driving without getting into a wreck*, but he didn't have a sense of humor and made me spend all day in a stuffy classroom listening to a funny little man going on about defensive driving. I've got a certificate to prove it."

It seemed pretty airtight. The companies who run these court-ordered courses have to be able to prove the attendees were actually sitting in the classroom for the required attendance time.

"All day? That's terrible. They didn't give you time for lunch?"

Her face clouded over. "Oh, yes, I'd forgotten about that. We were free for an hour, from noon. Hardly time for a breath of fresh air, let alone a nourishing meal."

Just then I got the coffee shop's joke name — *Art-is-an Expression*. Very droll. Rochelle frowned, puzzled by my unexpected smile. "Why, Lieutenant, did I say something amusing?"

"Oh, no, ma'am. It's just sometimes things take a little time to, you know, percolate through my mind. My apologies."

Who is the guilty suspect?

———————————————

	Jeffrey Gardner	Denise Kinney	Kenneth Haddad	Alexander McCullough	Rochelle Phelps
Aconitine					
Cyanide					
Nicotine					
Digitalis					
Strychnine					
Midday to 1 PM					
1 PM to 2 PM					
2 PM to 3 PM					
3 PM to 4 PM					
4 PM to 5 PM					
Hidden Documents					
Memory Stick					
Mafia Contacts					
Secretive Purchase					
Drinking					
Bank Withdrawal					
Intimidation					

Turn the page to see the solution!

SOLUTION

- *1* The wine stain on the documents in the blue folder was recent, indicating that Arnette placed the folder inside the packing case on which her body was found shortly before her death. Evidently these documents are closely related to the murder.

  The fact that she placed the documents inside the packing case suggests that she was hiding them — either so they would not be found by someone on the scene, or (realizing she had been poisoned) so they would be discovered by investigators.

- *2* The bank withdrawal must be relevant to the murder, because we already established that the contents of blue folder found hidden by the victim at the murder scene are central to the crime, and the withdrawal slip was discovered in the folder.

- *3* The conversation with Rosetta Arnette's banker, Arthur Reilly, shows that she was alive at 4 PM on the day of her murder.

- *4* Gardner's interest in cyanotypes shows he's familiar with the poison cyanide.

- *5* The Medical Examiner is confident that Rosetta was dead by 5 PM. We already know from the conversation with Arthur Reilly that she was alive at 4 PM, so the murder must have occurred during this period.

- *6* Haddad's habit of including the blue-flowered bush wolfsbane (*Aconitum variegatum*) in his paintings indicates a familiarity with the poison it contains — as its botanical Latin name suggests, aconitine.

- *7* McCullough has no alibi between 4 and 5 PM.

- *8* Gardner's gallery opening engagement gives him a solid alibi until 4 PM, but he has none between 4 and 5 PM.

- *9* Kinney freely admits to being involved in the large bank withdrawal.

- *10* The doctor's notepad text was written backwards, right to left — mirror writing — just like Leonardo da Vinci used to do. Maybe as a way to prevent people understanding his notes, or maybe because it's a way for left-handed people to avoid smudging the ink (when writing left to right, a left-handed person's hand passes over what they've just written).

  Some people can read mirror writing just fine, but I found it easier, as the name suggests, to reflect it in a mirror and read it that way. The doc's lousy handwriting made it tricky even then, but I got it in the end. The notes read:

Patient: Rosetta Arnette

Session: 135 - October 17

Patient expresses concern regarding escalating alcohol consumption.

Patient attributes this to elevated stress induced by two individuals, A & B.

These individuals both exert significant influence over her actions, yet in conflicting and opposing manners.

Rational self-awareness? Or avoidant rationalization?

The doctor tried to keep the identities of individuals *A* & *B* confidential in his notes, but his bored doodles reveal their names:

CHEF — FREE — GARDEN — NERD

and

ROW — SHELL — PHI — HELPS

The last two doodles took me a moment to figure out — I'm not exactly an expert on the Greek alphabet — but the message was clear: the stress-inducing influence of Jeffrey Gardner and Rochelle Phelps was causing Arnette to drink more than she was happy with.

- *11* Detective Manion's clue suggesting McCullough might have ties to the LA Mafia was well-intentioned but too weak to trust. Probably misidentification.

- *12* The text message on Rosetta's phone, sent to McCullough, indicates that he was involved in the bank withdrawal — though he was not the intended recipient of the money, otherwise he wouldn't have asked her to *prove it*. When she writes *Now it's your turn*, it suggests McCullough is also supposed to provide money.

- *13* "Got it!" I said. "OK..." I looked at my calculations. "The timestamp on the video reads *57720*. That means fifty-seven thousand, seven hundred and twenty seconds have elapsed since the start of the day. There are three thousand, six hundred seconds in each hour, so all we need to do to get the real time is to see which hour the timestamp number falls into... Like this —" I showed Kennedy the calculations on my notepad.

```
1 AM = 3,600 x 1 = 3,600 seconds
2 AM = 3,600 x 2 = 7,200
3 AM = 3,600 x 3 = 10,800
4 AM = 3,600 x 4 = 14,400
5 AM = 3,600 x 5 = 18,000
6 AM = 3,600 x 6 = 21,600
7 AM = 3,600 x 7 = 25,200
8 AM = 3,600 x 8 = 28,800
9 AM = 3,600 x 9 = 32,400
10 AM = 3,600 x 10 = 36,000
11 AM = 3,600 x 11 = 39,600
12 AM = 3,600 x 12 = 43,200
1 PM = 3,600 x 13 = 46,800
2 PM = 3,600 x 14 = 50,400
3 PM = 3,600 x 15 = 54,000
4 PM = 3,600 x 16 = 57,600
5 PM = 3,600 x 17 = 61,200
```

"Sure," said Kennedy, "but you could've saved half those calculations right away by remembering that 10 AM has to be 36,000 seconds, because it's ten hours of 3,600 seconds each. No offence, of course, Lieutenant."

"Uh, well, it's better to be certain. Being methodical never hurt anyone, *Officer*."

"And from there it's pretty easy to double that 36,000 and get 72,000. That would be the timestamp after an additional ten hours, i.e., 8 PM. That number's much too high, so we can look at the halfway point. Half of 36,000 is 18,000 — an easy calculation. So, adding five hours, or 18,000 seconds, to our initial ten hours — making 3 PM — gives us a total of 54,000 seconds. Now, that's pretty close to our target number. What happens if we add another hour, or 3,600 seconds? We get 57,600 — 4 PM. Just 120 away from our target, and a hundred and twenty seconds is two minutes, of course. Haddad left the class at 4:02 PM, almost a full hour before he claimed."

"Yes, Kennedy, that's the answer at which I *also* arrived."

"Sure, *eventually*. A binary or dichotomic search is usually much more efficient than the linear approach."

I gave him what they call an *old-fashioned look*. "The point is that Haddad's whereabouts are accounted for by his online class until just past 4 PM, but after that — who knows?"

- *14* The photo of Phelps' front door in *Architecture & Interiors* magazine shows the blue-flowered shrub, *Aconitum variegatum*, that can be used to produce the poison aconitine.

- *15* Kinney's super gives her a good alibi until 4 PM on Sunday. But from then on, she's got nothing.

- *16* The photos of Haddad's paintings connect him to the memory stick on which they were found.

- *17* The newspaper cutting and Kennedy's administrative research links Haddad to Arnette's secretive purchase (his image rights).

- *18* Haddad's phone call claiming that Arnette was being driven to reclusive behavior by Kinney's intimidation has every hallmark of a maliciously misleading clue. It doesn't fit with what we know about Arnette, and Haddad's obvious animosity towards Kinney indicates he may just be trying to land her in hot water. He probably read what she said about him in the recent newspaper article.

- *19* The notes on the photocopied/scanned document are written in a *pigpen cipher*, in which each letter of the alphabet is replaced by a symbol based on a grid, like this:

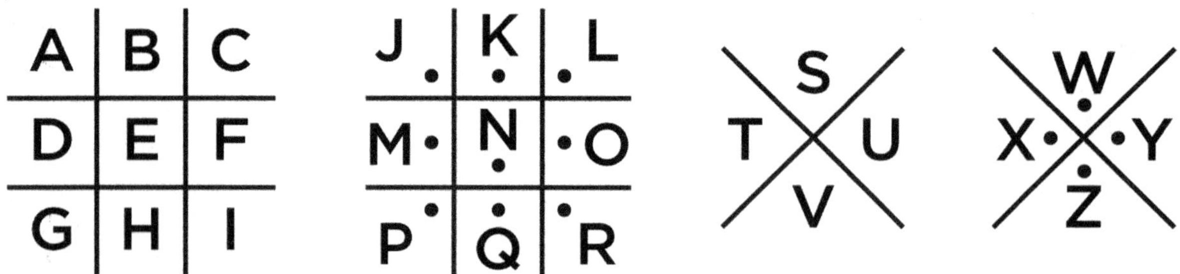

Each letter's position on the grid gives it a unique symbol made up of the lines and dots around it. For example, the letter *A* has lines below and to the right, and no dot. No other letter has this exact combination. *J* is similar, having the same lines below and to the right, but it has a dot.

That means we can use these lines and dots to create an alphabet cipher, like this:

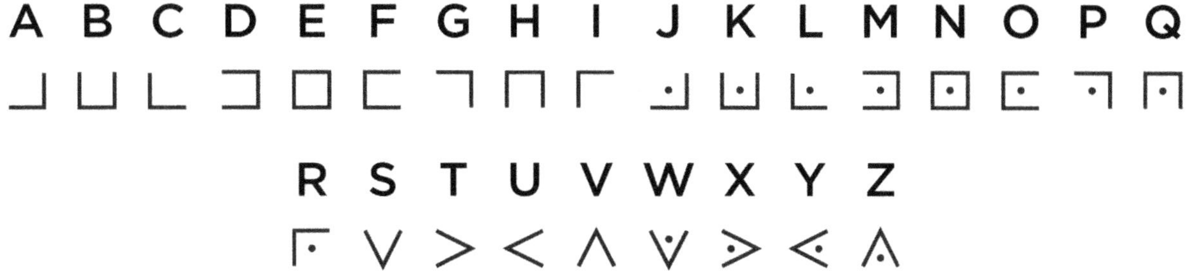

I could've kept on working the letter frequency technique I used to figure out that the letter *E* was probably represented by the square symbol, but the "smarter method" I mentioned was to realize that the *From* and *To* fields in the document had to be names. We'd already figured out that the square symbol was likely the letter *E*, so the *From* field looked like:

E**E* (*9 letters*)
********** (*10 letters*)

and the *To* field looked like:

****E**E (*8 letters*)
E* (*6 letters*)

It wasn't much of a stretch to see which names of people we already knew involved in the case fitted those numbers of letters and pattern of *Es* — Alexander McCullough and Rochelle Phelps.

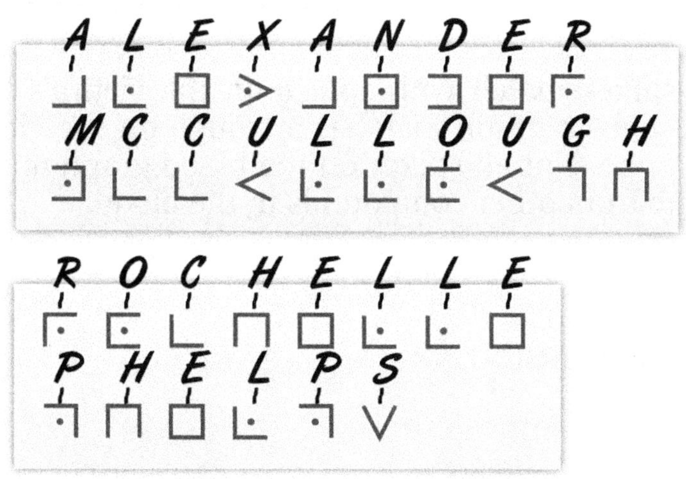

Also, a surprising number of our suspects had double letters in their names. Looking for repeated symbols in the coded message was also a smart move. For example, the repeated symbols corresponding with the double *C* and the double *L* of *McCullough* — and, even better, the latter symbol's repetition in the correct place for the double *L* of *Rochelle* — told us we were on the right track.

So, once we had the *From* and *To* fields figured out, using those known letters to work out the rest of the message was reasonably straightforward.

Oh yeah, and the watermark on the stationery? It wasn't a winged horse. The tail and feet were all wrong. It was a winged *lion* — the historical symbol of the Venetian Republic and, I later realized, the logo of the exclusive Venetian Bank. We already knew not only that Arnette banked there but also — from the magazine article — that Phelps was in charge of the arts festival the bank sponsored, indicating that she too might well be a client. If I'd figured that out a bit sooner I would've looked for Phelps' name right away in either the *From* or the *To* field.

So, decoding the cipher, we get:

Covering note:

TO - DENISE KINNEY

HERE IS THE TRANSACTION LIST

FROM - JEFFREY GARDNER

Bank document:

From:

ALEXANDER MCCULLOUGH

To:

ROCHELLE PHELPS

Evidently, Gardner sent a list of transactions (money transfers from McCullough to Phelps) to Kinney. All four of these suspects are connected to the documents.

- **20** The scrap of paper on the pile of paintings in Arnette's office was a currency band, used by banks to organize their paper money. There's a good chance that the discarded band came from the large bank withdrawal, but the fact that it happens to be lying on what appears to be one of Haddad's paintings is not inherently meaningful.

- **21** McCullough's travels in Japan familiarized him with the use of aconitine.

- **22** Kinney's father's work on hexacyanoferrate complexes indicates a probable familiarity with the poison cyanide.

- **23** The spectroscopy analysis identifies the fatal poison placed in the victim's wineglass.

The *Victim's Blood* graph has spikes on the *Wavelength* axis at 25, 55, 75, 85, and 125. It has troughs (inverse spikes) at 5, 45, and 150.

The correct poison graph must have all its spikes match with spikes on the victim's blood graph. As Dr. Kinsley told us, if a spike on a poison graph matches a trough on the victim's blood graph, the poison cannot be the correct one. Not all spikes on the blood graph must be present on the poison graph — they could come from other compounds in the blood.

The poison graphs have the following spikes:

Nicotine: 35 (no match), 125 (match), 150 (trough)
Digitalis: 40 (no match), 100 (no match), 140 (no match)
Cyanide: 25 (match), 45 (trough), 85 (match)
Aconitine: 25 (match), 85 (match), 125 (match)
Strychnine: 85 (match), 125 (match), 150 (trough)

Aconitine is the correct poison.

- **24** Phelps' court-mandated traffic school gives her an alibi all day — except for the lunch hour, between midday and 1 PM.

The guilty suspect is therefore

Alexander McCullough.

	Jeffrey Gardner	Denise Kinney	Kenneth Haddad	Alexander McCullough	Rochelle Phelps
Aconitine (23)			6	21	14
Cyanide	4	22			
Nicotine					
Digitalis					
Strychnine					
Midday to 1 PM					24
1 PM to 2 PM					
2 PM to 3 PM					
3 PM to 4 PM					
4 PM to 5 PM (3, 5)	8	15	13	7	
Hidden Documents (1)	19	19		19	19
Memory Stick			16		
Mafia Contacts				11?	
Secretive Purchase			17		
Drinking	10				10
Bank Withdrawal (2)		9	20?	12	
Intimidation		18?			

CONCLUSION

Alexander McCullough looked wistfully at the walls of his study, covered in beautiful art and exotic artifacts from his decades of globetrotting. I could tell what he was thinking: *There won't be much of this, where I'm going.*

"You're right, of course, Lieutenant. I poisoned poor Rosetta. It was the only thing I could do. You see, we were being blackmailed."

"Blackmailed about what?" I kept my voice calm. Unemotional, but understanding.

He paused before deciding. "I suppose it doesn't matter if I tell you, now. My wealth —" he gestured expansively around the opulent room "— is not what it appears. Not anymore. I was nearly bankrupt; all the family money, accumulated and guarded over generations, *gone*. I couldn't let it get out that I was broke. My reputation would be in tatters. So I started selling... Well, let's call them *reproductions*."

"*Fakes*," I corrected.

McCullough made a *comme ci, comme ça* gesture. "As you wish. I bought them from Rosetta, through her gallery, so the provenance was impeccable. It worked out very well for both of us."

"But someone found out," I encouraged.

"Right. One of the fakes was discovered, and we had to stop for a while. It wasn't too bad; these things happen to everyone — once. I had to pretend to be furious at Rosetta. But if anything else came out, people would start to ask serious questions — and demand answers. But then the blackmail started. Maybe someone who wasn't satisfied with our explanations started digging. Rosetta told me they wanted a preposterous amount of money, but she was able to talk them down. We could afford to pay the blackmailer, if we both put in half the money, she said."

I thought back to the text message on Arnette's phone. *Prove it!* he had written. "But you didn't believe her."

He shrugged. "It occurred to me that it wouldn't be a bad little ruse, for her to pretend to be blackmailed, after all. We'd had to stop selling the counterfeits, and maybe she was hurting from the lack of income. Then she could relieve me of my 'half' of the fictional payoff, pretend that it had satisfied the blackmailer, and I'd be none the wiser. Or, more likely, pretend it *hadn't* been enough to satisfy the blackmailer, and keep on demanding more and more, all while playing the victim."

"Blackmailers don't tend to stay satisfied," I agreed. "Real, or fake."

"Yes, quite. That was always at the back of my mind — that whether or not Rosetta was telling the truth, this couldn't be solved with money alone. It would just go on, if I didn't put a stop to it."

"So you killed her?" I asked, a little too bluntly.

He shook his head. "It wasn't that straightforward. I didn't know what to do, until Rosetta let it slip that the blackmailer didn't know I was involved. She said she'd let them think I was an unwitting victim, that I'd believed the art was genuine. But, she said, if I didn't come up with my half of the money, she'd tell them the truth."

"You couldn't allow that."

"Well, it significantly simplified matters. If it turned out she was telling the truth, and she —" he shrugged "— was removed from the picture... Well, the blackmailer would have no evidence against me. Even if they approached me, I could tell them to 'publish and be damned,' and there'd be nothing they could do. And if Rosetta was lying, the outcome would be the same. She was the only one who knew I was part of the scheme. Whatever happened, I could claim innocence."

"Better to be thought a fool than a crook," I suggested.

"Debatable, in general terms. But in my situation, you're definitely correct."

"So what happened, that Sunday afternoon?"

McCullough seemed to be warming to his subject, glad to get the secrets off his chest. "Rosetta messaged me to say she'd paid her installment of the payoff to the blackmailer. It was my turn to provide my half. I wasn't going to do that unless she proved to me she'd actually made the payment."

Something was bugging me. Sure, the bank receipt I'd found in the blue folder hidden in the packing case proved the large cash withdrawal. But the other documents didn't have anything to do with that; they showed that McCullough had been paying Phelps... But McCullough was still talking.

"I resolved that I'd have to get rid of her at the meeting. I prepared a paste of aconitine, just like I'd been taught in Japan."

"Just a sec," I broke in. "I hate to interrupt, but where did you get it?"

He laughed. "I gave Rochelle a couple of *Aconitum variegatum* plants ages ago. She's been growing it outside her home for years. I doubt she even knows what it is. I thought it might turn out handy to have a supply that couldn't be traced back to me. One never knows, after all."

What a devious mind. "I guess one never does," I replied drily.

"Anyway, I brought a bottle of wine with me as a peace offering. I'd mixed the aconitine into the wine and resealed the cork with wax. Denise had started drinking more often, and I knew that if I gave her a bottle it would be consumed sooner rather than later." He made a wry expression. "But I needn't have bothered. She was already half-way through a bottle." He paused, as if uncertain whether to continue.

"Carry on, it's fascinating."

"The meeting didn't go as planned. I thought it would be perfectly civil; she'd show me the proof, I'd agree to pay in a few days, and I'd slip away... While she consumed the poisoned wine. But it turned out very differently. The situation had changed, she said. Someone had provided the blackmailer with proof that I knew about the fakes. ...Excuse me, my mouth is rather dry. All this talking." McCullough moved to an antique oak sideboard on which lay a silver tray with a decanter of what looked like cognac and several cut-glass goblets. He poured himself a generous measure of the spirit. Without offering me one, I noticed.

"You won't drink on duty of course, Lieutenant," he explained brusquely. A statement, not a question. I shrugged. "So," he continued, "I had to think quickly. Did I believe her? I had to accept she might be telling the truth. Documents could, perhaps, be explained away, but the testimony of a living person is more compelling. I had to accelerate my plans. Luckily, I had more of the poison paste in my pocket, and I managed to introduce it into her wineglass on the pretext of a refill." He took another swig of his drink. *That's why the bottle we found was free of the poison*, I thought.

"It's a reasonably fast-acting poison, even when absorbed through the gut rather than injected straight into the bloodstream the way the Japanese hunters do it. She soon felt the first effects. It didn't take long for her to figure out what was happening. She actually started laughing. Said she hadn't brought the documents with her, in case I tried something like this. That I'd never know who the blackmailer was, until they decided how much they wanted to take from me." He grimaced. "She was right. I messed that up. But by then she was in severe pain. She died minutes later, right there on that packing case."

"What did you do then?" I asked.

"I thought she might've been lying, that she'd hidden the documents somewhere nearby. Why would she have called the meeting if she didn't bring proof? I looked everywhere in that warehouse. But then I heard noises outside. Someone was nearby — I had to get out, fast."

The gallery security guard. He'd come closer to interrupting the crime than anyone realized. That's why the warehouse lights had been left on — McCullough didn't have time to switch them off.

McCullough was smiling again — but it wasn't a smile of laughter or humor, however dark... It was a rictus grin of pain. I frowned, and then suddenly I realized. I rushed forward and dashed the cut-glass goblet of cognac from his hand with a wild slap, but it was too late. The poison had already started its evil work.

McCullough slumped to the foot of the antique sideboard, and I quickly bent down and grabbed him by his jacket lapel so he didn't fall further.

"Lieutenant —" it was getting hard for him to speak now "— I have to know. The blackmail... Was it real? Or was it just Rosetta?"

I figured it was OK to tell him. It wouldn't go anywhere. At least, nowhere it would come back to bother me. "Yeah, it was real. And the proof Rosetta talked about, implicating you — that was real, too."

He looked aggrieved. "Where..."

"Inside the big packing case she was sitting on. She must've been reading through them while she waited for you, then hid them when she heard you arrive in the main gallery. The one place you didn't look, right?"

"I... I didn't want to touch her. What did she have?"

"Bank records someone sent to the blackmailer, knowing they could use them against you. Looks like the blackmailer gave them to Rosetta as a convincer. The records showed all the kickbacks you paid to Rochelle Phelps. On the 15th of every month. I guess she was the one who sourced the phony art."

He nodded his head with difficulty. "God knows where she procured them; could've been any one of her shady, underworld connections. She came up with the paintings, paid a contact at the art shipping company to mix them in with regular shipments — all part of creating a legitimate paperwork trail — laundered them through Rosetta's gallery, and passed them out to me — the rich collector, the trusted expert — the voice of authority..." He paused, thinking, then his eyes flashed with emotion, and he spoke with the last of his breath.

"The blackmailer... Who... Who was it who hated us that much? Not Haddad, was it? I always rather liked Haddad."

"No. It turns out that he was the only one who wasn't involved. It was Denise Kinney, the critic. But hate had nothing to do with it. Strictly business for her. Her ticket to the big-time. She was with Rosetta when she went to the bank. She made sure Rosetta took out the cash, then drove her back to the gallery. We found currency bands in the office, so that's probably where Rosetta gave her the money. Maybe that's also when she gave Rosetta the bank transfer documents in order to convince you." I debated how much to tell him. Well, he deserved to know. "The one who really hated you was Gardner, the gallery owner. He was the one who sent the bank documents to Kinney. Probably the one who did all the digging in the first place, then got Kinney involved as the front for the blackmail."

The dying man frowned in confusion, now unable to speak. I jogged his memory. "Jeffrey Gardner. He'd been an aspiring artist. Cyanographs — you know, like blueprints. He blamed you for his failure to make it in the art biz. He said you were going to be his mentor, but you turned your attention elsewhere."

McCullough raised his eyebrows and rolled his eyes back, as if to say, *Artists! What are you gonna do with them?*

Then, his eyes closed for the final time.

I paused for a moment. Then I hollered at the officer waiting outside the study. "Hey, Kennedy! Radio for an ambulance, would ya?"

"You OK, Lieutenant?" came the worried reply.

"Sure, I'm fine," I yelled back. "Tell 'em there's no hurry."

I stood up and walked out of the mansion. It was a bright day outside, with a beautiful, cloudless, deep blue sky.

Mind Games

CASE #: 004

DIFFICULTY: FIENDISH

DETECTIVE: LT. FALCO COSTANZO

UNIT: LOS ANGELES POLICE DEPARTMENT, ROBBERY-HOMICIDE DIVISION

CRIME SCENE

Silicon Beach, they call it. The chunk of high-priced real estate north of LAX, home to hundreds of high-tech companies' headquarters.

The whole area had an eerie feel. Built on reclaimed marshland around Ballona Creek, the wide, empty streets had the same desolate air as the swamp that still bordered them. As if the buildings were waiting for the people to move in.

The giant corporate buildings themselves seemed to be competing with one another over which could be the coldest and most soulless. Heavily tinted windows blazed with light, but nobody ever seemed to come to the windows to look out; there were no silhouettes of people. The only sound audible from the sidewalk was the eternal hum of the massive industrial climate control systems that air-conditioned the mazes of corridors within the blank-faced buildings. *The lights are on, but nobody's home... Except us machines.*

This building wasn't much different from the others in the neighborhood, except it was set way back from the street in an artificial rolling landscape of grass that was so well-tended and featureless that it looked completely fake, like the desktop image from an old Windows computer.

Security was tighter than I'd expected, and I had to wait several minutes in my car, parked in front of the guardhouse traffic barrier while the guy inside spoke on the phone. The guardhouse itself was built like a concrete bunker. Eventually, he gave me a visitor's pass and let me into the facility. It came on a lanyard to hang round your neck, and read *Applied Psychology Innovations Institute.*

"Welcome to APII," said the guard, emotionlessly. He pronounced it "happy."

The main building was a slab-sided cuboid five or six stories in height and maybe five hundred feet on its longer side. The front was all mirror-tinted glass, and jutted forward at an angle so the higher floors overhung the lower ones, like an airport control tower. From outside, it made you feel like you were under constant surveillance from unknown figures hidden behind the mirror-glass.

Parking was in the basement, so I turned my automobile down a dark opening in the building. As soon as I began descending the ramp, a light turned on above me, and as the car moved down, the first light turned off and the next one above me turned on, and so on. I guess it was a way of saving electricity, but it was kinda unsettling, because even though I was starkly illuminated I couldn't see anything beyond the bright cone of light I was in.

I followed the signs to the visitor parking area, the lights dutifully clicking on and off above me in the otherwise pitch-black basement.

It turned out I was supposed to park in the only other lit area, near the elevators. As I cranked the parking brake, one of the elevator doors opened, and a strange object emerged. It had a small but heavy-looking base with a pair of wheels that drove it around, a long, thin, tubular neck like a microphone stand, and on top of the neck was a display screen the size of a large tablet. It hummed out of the elevator, throwing a crazy shadow, and approached me.

I rolled the car window down to see what it wanted. As it neared, I saw the screen bore the odd mix of symbols *QTπ*. Then, the symbols disappeared, and the screen changed to show the image of a little girl's face. There was something about the face that told me it was computer-generated. She looked like the kind of kid who would let the air out of your car tires "for a joke." The thing stopped at a respectful distance from my car.

"Hello Lieutenant!" it said cheerfully, its voice echoing through the parking basement. "I'm QTπ, the building management artificial intelligence. I'm currently occupying a Mark 4 telepresence robot, as my role as majordomo requires real-world motility." I frowned slightly, and the thing must've noticed, explaining, "A majordomo is a head servant entrusted with the day-to-day operations of a noble household or other large enterprise or institution. May I see your visitor's badge, please?"

I held it up. After a brief pause, QTπ continued. "Excellent, thank you! OK Lieutenant, I've been asked to show you to the scene of the accident, so if you'll kindly follow me, I'll take you there right now."

What could I say? I got out of the vehicle, locked it, and followed QTπ into the elevator.

When we emerged on the fourth floor, I was too surprised by what I saw to move. The space was a large reception area, which looked like it was playing host to some kind of bizarre chess game. There were figures dressed in white robes, and figures dressed in black. All were wearing black domino masks, like the Lone Ranger and Zorro wore. Some of the chess-piece figures were clustered with their own kind, while others were next to those from the opposing side, perhaps engaged in mock-battle. Soft, ambient music was playing in the background, and I heard a man's voice speaking quietly but clearly under the music.

Then, the vision began to clarify. Most of the figures were holding cocktail glasses. They weren't fighting, they were talking, animatedly. The white robes were scientists' lab coats, and the black clothes were — I squinted to focus — yes, they were actually dark blue Air Force dress uniforms. The domino masks seemed to be some kind of protective eyewear. Scientists and military officers. My head was starting to spin. The voice I'd heard was coming from a series of TV screens arranged around the large space's walls — some sort of corporate advertisement, it looked like. The man on the screens was an intellectual-looking type with a high forehead. He too was wearing a white lab coat.

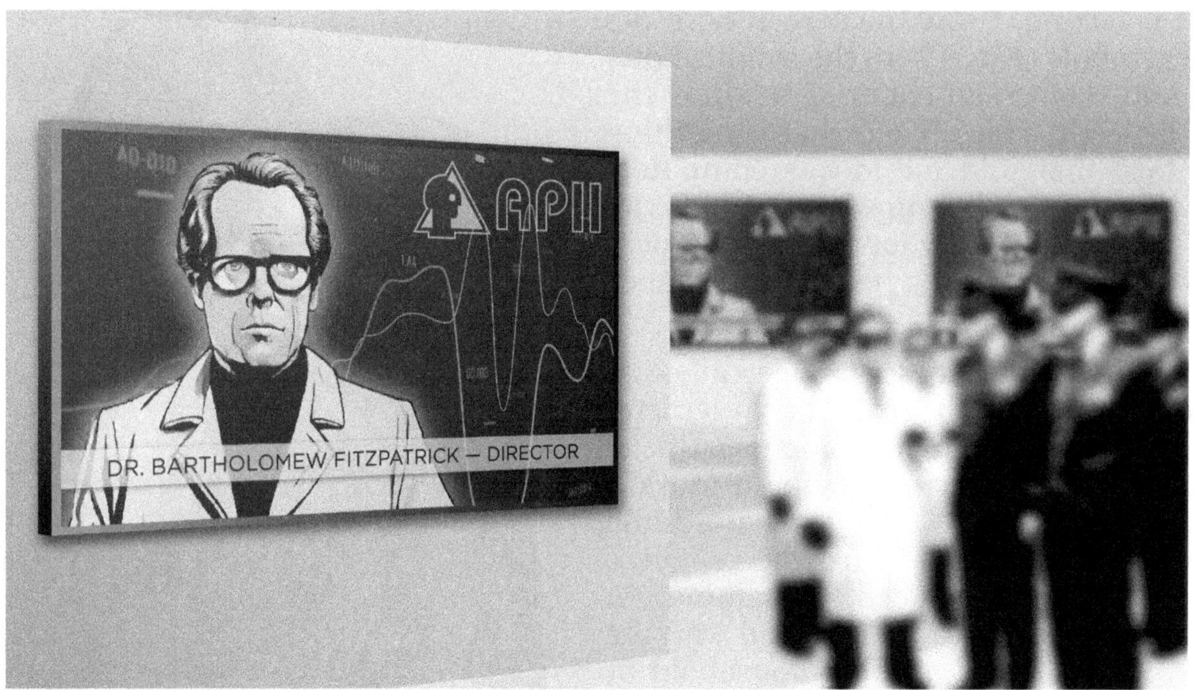

"Please, continue," beckoned QTπ, and we pushed our way through the excited crowd.

Soon, we came to a set of large doors marked *Human Behavioral Labyrinth — Preparation Room*. They opened for QTπ, and we passed through into what looked like a regular locker room, with rows of metal lockers, pegs, and slatted benches. There was a smaller door at the other end of the locker room.

The large doors closed behind us, and all was silent.

"Regrettably, I can accompany you no further in this robot body, as its rubber propulsion wheels do not meet the Labyrinth's cleanliness standard. A clean environment is vital for the success of the psychological experiments performed in this unit. Similarly, I must ask you to relinquish your footwear, and don the provided protective equipment."

"Just like at the bowling alley, huh?" I asked.

"Precisely so, Lieutenant." I thought QTπ winked playfully at me... but, nah, surely not.

The provided protective equipment turned out to be a pair of brand new, spotlessly clean, white tennis shoes. Just my size, too. They had the word *Visitor* printed on the heels. I put them on.

*****

I had expected a brightly lit room on the other side of the door, but instead I emerged into a strange space that was simultaneously comforting and unsettling. The walls, floor, and ceiling were all of the same strange material, which seemed to absorb light and sound. The lighting was hard to describe; it seemed like *gray light*, if such a thing was possible. It was so quiet I could hear the blood pumping in my ears. At least, that's what I thought it was. Maybe it was some kind of atmospheric background audio.

Ahead of me lay a featureless corridor, branching off into two passages — one going left, the other right. *Human Behavioral Labyrinth*, the sign had read. I figured I knew what was going on. A labyrinth was like a maze, and this was the Applied Psychology Innovations Institute... I didn't know much about psychologists, but I knew from TV and whatnot that they loved putting mice in mazes and seeing what the mice decided they would do in order to get hold of some cheese at the center of the maze. It looked like this was the same thing, just human-sized.

Where's the cheese? I wondered.

At that moment, QTπ's little-girl voice intruded, piped in through some hidden speaker. "Don't worry, Lieutenant, you don't have to guess. I shall guide you. Move down the corridor and take the turn to your right."

I did as ordered. The right turn was a gently curving passage. Despite what QTπ said, I was going to try to keep track of my movements. Looking down the corridor, I saw it made about a half-circle turn to the left. I walked confidently down it.

Exactly halfway down the curving corridor, I walked smack into a cold, hard, unyielding, invisible surface, like a bird hitting a window. There was a flash of bright light, and I stumbled backwards in confusion. When I looked down the corridor again, it looked exactly the same, except for a man dressed in a trench coat, holding his hand up to his nose — a reflection, I realized. I had walked into a mirror. But how could that be possible? I hadn't seen myself until after I walked into it!

"My goodness, Lieutenant, I'm so sorry!" QTπ's voice came from above me. "All of these installations should have been switched off. I do hope you're not hurt."

"I guess I'll live," I answered grumpily.

"Don't worry, Lieutenant, you're not quite so... *transparent* as you think, ha-ha." What passed for QTπ's laugh was uncannily un-humorous. "A simple trick with electronically switchable glass, variable between transparent and reflective states. Please, allow me."

The reflection cleared to show the corridor ahead. Its curve was the exact mirror image of what lay behind me, so the effect was like watching myself slowly fade into nothingness. Then the glass slid back into the wall, and I was able to pass.

I proceeded with caution, but the rest of the journey to the center of the labyrinth passed without further incident, except when a photograph of someone else's smiling family, complete with dog, suddenly flashed up on the wall next to me at three times life size.

"Oh dear, that wasn't meant for you," QTπ mumbled, as I cowered in front of the gigantic, grinning Golden Retriever.

After a couple more turns, I started to hear the hubbub of voices. *Another trick?* But soon enough, the light started to brighten, the voices became louder, and I emerged into the center of the labyrinth.

It was a bizarre scene.

The central chamber was a white dome, like the inside of an egg. The light came from everywhere and nowhere. It pulsed slowly, like a relaxed heartbeat. In the middle of the egg, a dark-suited figure lay sprawled in a pool of blood, a wound in his temple, and a large-caliber pistol in his hand. Despite the blood, his brand-new white tennis shoes had remained miraculously unmarked. In the wall of the egg was a shattered portion, the material cracked, the lights behind dark. The only other object in the room was a jaunty, red-and-white-striped beach ball.

Next to the body stood two figures in conversation. One was unfamiliar; a man of medium build and height, wearing a business suit, with curly dark hair. What distinguished him from the average was his military bearing and the quiet but savage intensity of his gaze. Anyone would remember those eyes. I noticed he appeared to be wearing his street shoes — no tennis shoes for this guy.

The other figure was a refreshingly normal sight in this madhouse — Officer Kennedy. Noticing me, he beckoned me to come in. "Lieutenant Costanzo, this is Robert Carlson, the Institute's Head of Security. Hey, mind the victim."

I stepped carefully over and shook Carlson's proffered hand. He turned his laser-beam stare on me. "I'm glad you got here OK." He looked down at my clothing, noticing my disheveled appearance. "She didn't play any of her tricks on you, did she?"

"Who? Oh, you mean QTπ. Well, there were a couple of... malfunctions in the system, I guess."

He shook his head. "That damned thing's gonna get a real hard reboot one of these days," he muttered.

"Kennedy, fill me in, would ya?" I asked. "They gave me nothing on the way over."

"Sure thing, sir," Kennedy replied. "Our victim is Mr. Conrad Keppler, Head of Research and Development at the Institute. Gunshot wound to the right temple, forty-five caliber pistol in right hand, apparent suicide."

"Looks recent. Everything's still warm, huh?"

"Sure, looks that way."

"Who found him — Mr. Carlson here?"

"No, sir. One of the R&D scientists. Ms. Crystal Thurmond. Says she was setting up for an experiment the next day. She seemed pretty shook up; the medics are taking care of her now."

"When was that?"

Kennedy looked at his watch. "Eight-thirty. Just under an hour ago."

I shrugged. "Like you say, looks like suicide. What am I doing here?"

Kennedy looked embarrassed. "Well, this isn't exactly a normal kinda place."

"You can say that again."

"I mean, they have a lot of government contracts. Secret stuff — like, *above top secret*."

I remembered all the Air Force officers milling about out there. "OK, I understand. Anything that happens here has to be investigated. Got it."

So, maybe suicide, maybe not. I pointed at the pistol. "Those things are pretty loud. Nobody heard the gunshot?"

Carlson spoke up. "I can answer that one, Lieutenant. The labyrinth is soundproofed. The scientists say they can't have any outside noise getting in; it could disorient the subjects."

"What about video surveillance? You must record these experiments, and I guess the scientists have to be able to see what's going on. Or QTπ, or whoever runs things."

"Sure," Carlson replied with a nod. "They got eyes and ears all over the place in here. But it's not part of the security system, they only run it when the labyrinth is in use. The best we've got is a camera on the door to the preparation room. And that's the only way in."

"Oh, well, that's easy then — we check the tape and see if anyone went in with Keppler."

"First thing I did, Lieutenant," Kennedy reported proudly. "Mr. Carlson showed me, in the security room. But... Well, the video shows Keppler entering the door of the preparation room just after eight o'clock, but nobody else went in or out. The scientists didn't use the labyrinth today, and it gets a security sweep every morning from Mr. Carlson's staff..." Kennedy shrugged. "There can't have been anyone else in there with him. It really does look like he shot himself."

"I see. Hey, Kennedy, what's that over there?" I pointed across the chamber.

Kennedy looked at me as if unsure how to answer. "Well, sir, it's a beach ball. Inflatable. Probably around, oh, eighteen inches in diameter. Typically manufactured of polyvinyl chloride material, also known as *PVC*. Appropriate for use in a casual beach or pool setting."

"Yes, Officer, thank you very much indeed. What I meant was, *what is it doing here?*"

Carlson spoke before Kennedy had a chance to reply. "That'll be one of the objects the scientists were using in their experiments, Lieutenant. They like to employ nostalgic symbols that subjects associate with childhood — balloons, bicycles, nursery rhymes, that sort of thing."

SUSPECTS

It took a couple days of digging, but eventually I had enough evidence to put together my list of persons of interest. I'd have liked to put the company's eccentric artificial intelligence, QTπ, on the list, but I couldn't figure a way for her to pull the trigger, not even with her telepresence robot body.

- **Arlene DeWitt** was a strange one. She sat on the APII's board of directors and seemed to have a hand in its day-to-day running. She even had an office on the executive floor. DeWitt had been at the Institute on the evening of Keppler's death. But, beyond that, I couldn't find out anything about her. That made me want to turn over rocks until I could figure out who she really was.

- **Dulce Coburn**, Secretary to the President. A charming but rather nervous lady in her mid-thirties. She had worked at the Institute for many years and seemed fiercely devoted to her boss. Despite her demeanor, she gave me the impression of an *éminence grise*, a power-behind-the-throne type. People like that love to pull strings from the shadows.

- **Crystal Thurmond**, research scientist. A taciturn and introverted person in her late twenties. A brilliant mind, people at the Institute said. She was the driving force behind most of the Institute's highly lucrative government projects. As head of R&D, Conrad Keppler had been her boss, but from what people told me it seemed like the relationship was the other way round. She'd been pushing the Institute's work forwards, and Keppler had been putting obstacles in her way — bureaucratic red tape, ethical reviews, that kind of thing.

- **Bartholomew Fitzpatrick**, APII President and founder. A tall, lean, energetic man around fifty years old, with a high forehead, a heavy brow, and a clipped mid-Atlantic accent that made him both physically and intellectually intimidating. A snappy dresser with expensive tastes, he obviously enjoyed the finer things in life and wanted everyone to know it. He struck me as the kind of forceful high achiever who tends to be compensating for humble beginnings. A "name" in his field, he appeared to have founded the Institute not only to specialize in the kind of government and military projects only outsourced experts can address, but also to create an organization that he personally could totally control. Of course, he was still beholden to his board of directors, who represented the entities who funded the Institute.

- **Robert Carlson**, the Institute's Head of Security. A former Green Beret, Carlson regarded everything that crossed his path with antagonistic scrutiny that bordered on the pathological. I bet his blood pressure numbers were through the roof. Carlson claimed that the Institute had a leak of some kind, and he seemed to spend most of his time prowling around, haunting the Institute's staff, trying tirelessly to unmask the spy.

- **Abelard Hayes** was a pleasant, personable man, the Institute's janitor. His official title was *Facility Custodian*. His work took him all over the building, even into the highly sensitive experimental areas, for which even the janitor required a government security clearance to access. It was funny how the employee on the lowest rung of the corporate ladder had a level of access equaled only by the top executives.

INVESTIGATION

1 — The next day, I returned to the Human Behavioral Labyrinth with Carlson; the eerily sterile egg-like chamber at its center was bothering me. Too many unanswered questions.

"Tell me," I asked the security chief, "why'd they build it like this? I gotta tell you, it's making my skin crawl."

"It's psychological, Lieutenant. Freudian. A form of sensory suggestion, to influence the subject. The egg shape represents a return to the start of life. The lights —" he waved at the gently pulsing glow "— a maternal heartbeat. The subject has faced various puzzling experiences navigating the maze — rather like life itself — and the central chamber provides strong symbols that trigger regression to a simpler time. The subject sees this perceived safety as a reward, and is subconsciously placed in a receptive, child-like state. That means whatever objects the scientists place in the chamber acquire great significance to the subject. Make sense?"

"I guess," I mumbled. "Say, for a security guy, you're pretty hot on the psycho-mumbo-jumbo, aren't you?"

Carlson grinned. "It's always been an interest of mine. Before I entered the, uh, private sector, I was in the Army. Green Berets. They sent me to *psywar* school — psychological warfare. Civilians think war is just about physical conflict, being tougher than the other guy, gutting it out in the mud, but success in warfare is really all about being *one step ahead of the other guy*. And where you lead a person's mind, the body will follow. You can win without firing a shot."

"I see," I said.

"You know, every great martial nation in the history of civilization has valued the virtues of guile and trickery just as highly as physical strength. The Spartans, the Vikings... Look at Loki, the Vikings' trickster god..."

Carlson was warming to his subject, and continued expounding on the topic. Wanting to ease the conversation back to the case in hand, I began to walk across to the other side of the egg-like chamber, intending to examine the shattered portion of the wall. The crime scene techs had found a second bullet lodged inside the broken area. Maybe Keppler, unfamiliar with firearms, had accidentally discharged the weapon before using it on himself. Or perhaps his trigger-finger muscles had involuntarily contracted after the first, deadly shot. Or maybe someone had killed Keppler, placed the gun in his hand, and fired the second shot into the wall to place gunshot residue on Keppler's hand. Anyway, I must've forgotten to tie the shoelaces of those blasted white tennis shoes, and I tripped, falling shoulder-first against the smooth, curved wall.

There was a loud booming noise of impact. It echoed away into silence.

I struggled to my feet, and rapped my knuckles against the wall. The sound was sharper this time, but it echoed away just the same. The wall here was *hollow*.

I turned to Carlson excitedly. "What's this?"

Carlson paused as if weighing up what to say next. I waited, my eyebrow raised, and eventually he continued. "Tricks of the trade, Lieutenant. I'm sure you have many in your own line of work, eh?"

I shrugged.

"Before I go any further, Lieutenant, I must remind you that the Institute conducts extremely sensitive work on behalf of the United States government at the highest possible level. That means anything about our methods I divulge to you is to go *no further*. And don't bother telling me about your duty as a policeman to report what you find — this is not about petty laws, but a matter of *national security*. Are we clear?"

"Of course, sir." What else was I going to say?

"Very well. I didn't mention this before, because we appeared to be dealing with a simple suicide. However, this is one of the little bits of hocus-pocus we use to influence the subjects. The central chamber of the labyrinth is not as hermetically-sealed as it might appear."

Dramatically, like a stage magician, he waved a hand over the wall where I'd fallen. Slowly and almost silently, a wall panel detached itself from the unbroken eggshell surface. It hummed back and then slid out of view to one side. In its place was a dark hole, about a meter square. I felt a cool breeze starting to drift into the chamber from the hole. The effect was very unsettling.

Slowly, I started to smile at Carlson, like a kid who's just seen a coin pulled out of the air next to his ear. "Now, sir, just exactly how did you do that?"

He held his hand up, palm first, for me to inspect. There was an elegant, silver-colored metal ring on his index finger. "A simple device, Lieutenant. Embedded in this ring, invisible to the eye, is a passive radio-frequency identification chip. RFID, just like the one in your visitor's pass. But this one is rather special. It allows the wearer to enter certain classified areas in the building; this passage is one of them."

"Well, I'll be... And using this ring, to open up this passage, is the only way out?"

"Indeed, the only way out — or in. Apart from the way you came in, of course."

"What's the secret tunnel for?"

Carlson shrugged. "It depends on the experiment the scientists are running. There are various possible uses. For example, as I mentioned, they often put symbolic or important objects in the central chamber — sometimes, they want to change the objects while the subject is distracted. If the subject thinks there's no way someone could've substituted one object for another, they begin to doubt their own senses and memory. In reality, it's a *scene-setter* who makes the exchange, usually one of the scientists. Like the stealthy, invisible, black-clad *kuroko* stagehands in traditional Japanese theater. You know, they were the inspiration for many of the legends surrounding the *ninja*, who..."

I stopped him before he could return to his lecture on historical psywar. "Sir, I gotta know — where does the passage lead?"

Carlson grinned wolfishly at me. "Why don't you follow it and find out?" He reached into his jacket's breast pocket and held out a pen-sized flashlight for me to take.

The meter-high hole in the wall was uninviting, to say the least, but I had a job to do. I took the penlight and crouched down, shining it into the secret passageway. I half-expected a grinning clown face to jump out at me, or some other childish trick — QTπ might be watching, I remembered uneasily — but there were no surprises. I eased in and slowly stood up.

Inside, it wasn't that bad. The passage was narrow, but high enough for me to stand comfortably, and its walls were featureless concrete. The gentle breeze meant the air seemed fresh. The flashlight was bright enough that I shouldn't trip over anything.

That reminded me; I kneeled down and tied my shoelace tight.

*****

After several minutes following the passage's dusty floors and institutional metal staircases, I found myself at a nondescript door. After a moment's thought, I turned the handle. It opened, and I passed through. It was dark inside.

"Turn on the lights, Lieutenant!" Carlson's voice came tinnily through a speaker. "Just by the door, where you'd expect."

I fumbled in the darkness, found the switch, and flipped it. Old-fashioned fluorescent tube lights flickered and clinked into view above me, illuminating a scene that looked like the bridge of a big ship. A long window ran along one wall, and beneath it were banks of monitors and computer equipment. Swivel chairs were arranged by the control panel for operators. "OK, lights are on," I said loudly, assuming Carlson would be able to hear.

"Very good," he continued. "Now go to the observation window. Right-hand side. There's a large red button about your head height. Press it."

I went to the window like he said, but I couldn't see anything other than a reflection of myself; the light inside was too bright. There was the red button. It was only natural to hesitate before pressing it... But I pushed it down with the palm of my hand and heard a *click*.

The scene beyond jumped into stark view as the lights came on. It was a massive, empty chamber, bigger than a full basketball court. The light was coming from the floor, a series of illuminated rectangles...

...Then I realized I wasn't looking at the floor of the room, I was looking at the ceiling of the Human Behavioral Labyrinth. Not just looking *at* it, but *through* it. I could see the whole layout. It was magnificent. I wondered what it was like to see it in operation; the human subjects walking or running through it, faced by weird tests and startling encounters, slowly working their way through the craziness to the "reward" in the center. Mice in a maze.

There was the egg chamber in the center, its pointy end sticking up like the spinner of a roulette wheel. I could see through its curved walls, too. There was the miniature figure of Carlson, still standing by the black opening in the wall. He had something in his hand — a two-way radio, I guessed.

"Wow," I breathed, momentarily at a loss for words.

Carlson waved exaggeratedly at me and put the radio to his mouth. His voice crackled out of the speaker. "Another use of electrically-variable glass. Except this time, it's like a one-way mirror. You can see me, but I can't see you. The subjects have no idea they're being watched. Impressive, no?"

"That's one word for it," I replied. *Megalomaniacal* was another, but I didn't say anything.

I was too busy thinking about what this meant for the case. It was a locked-room mystery no more...

2 — The artificial intelligence QTπ, again inhabiting her wheeled robot body, led me down the corridor to the executive elevator. The regular elevator didn't reach the Institute's penthouse level. *For security reasons*, she said. As I walked and she rolled along, she was trying to stump me with childish riddles. I was starting to think that *her* elevator didn't go to the top floor, either.

"All right, Lieutenant, try this one on for size. I have mountains, but no trees, deserts, but no air, and seas, but no water. What am I?" We stepped into the elevator. There was a moment's communion between the robot and the elevator's security system, and we were on our way upward.

I thought about it. Eventually, I said, "You're the Moon."

"No, silly, I'm a map." She paused, her face freezing in a frown. "But that was quite a good answer."

The Institute's top floor looked completely different from the rest of the building's cold, minimalist, high-tech interiors. The lobby was low-ceilinged, deeply carpeted in a grass-like forest green, wood-paneled with what looked like dark oak. Antique oil paintings in heavy gilt frames hung on the walls. It felt both snug and intimidating at the same time.

Fitzpatrick's secretary, Dulce Coburn, was seated behind a magnificent mahogany desk in the anteroom to the President's office. She looked up from her work as we entered.

"Hello, Ms. Coburn," QTπ spoke in a sing-song voice, as if greeting a grade school teacher, "Lieutenant Costanzo to see Dr. Fitzpatrick."

"I, uh, have an appointment," I mumbled, for some reason feeling oddly reticent. Maybe it was the decor, or Ms. Coburn's unflinching, bespectacled gaze.

"Certainly, we spoke on the phone earlier," she replied, as if I'd forgotten. "Dr. Fitzpatrick awaits; please go straight through." She indicated a pair of heavy-looking, high doors.

Gingerly, I turned one handle, creaked the door half-open, and poked my head through the gap. Immediately, a loud, cut-glass voice boomed out, "Come in, come in, Lieutenant! I've been looking forward to meeting you."

Fitzpatrick's office was huge, and the lush green carpet made it feel like a golf green or a tennis court. It was a corner office, and two whole walls were glass, looking out over the wetlands and Playa del Rey all the way to LAX. It reminded me of the observation laboratory at the Human Behavioral Labyrinth, deep in the building below. As if Fitzpatrick viewed the city as his subject and thought he could figure it all out, if he studied it long enough.

The man himself unfolded athletically from behind a desk at least twice as vast as his secretary's, and stalked towards me. We shook hands, his large and sinewy mitt enveloping mine. Something about his build and manner made me think he might've done a lot of manual labor in his youth, before donning the white coat.

Fitzpatrick and I exchanged pleasantries. He offered me a drink, I declined, and we sat in rather uncomfortable steel-and-leather armchairs by the window. The chairs were too close together, and Fitzpatrick loomed over me. *It's a psych-out*, I thought. *Some people sit on a throne behind a giant desk while their visitors get a tiny chair, but he likes to intimidate more directly.*

I decided to get down to business right away. "Dr. Fitzpatrick —" I began, but he cut me off abruptly.

"Please, call me Bartholomew," he commanded curtly, looking out the window.

"Not Bart, perhaps?" I wondered, impertinently.

"Never." He snapped out the syllables like a steel door slamming shut.

"OK, sure, Dr. Bartholomew — please, tell me about the victim, Mr. Keppler."

"*Dr.* Keppler," he corrected. "Conrad was a good man, as far as I know, a fine executive and, I believe, a competent scientist. A quiet, conservative fellow, and an efficient administrator. I expect it will take us some time to replace him." Fitzpatrick sighed, as if putting down a burden, and turned toward me. "Between you and me, Lieutenant, Dr. Keppler was not an imaginative man. Not one to take risks. A virtue for a man in his position, one would think, but not necessarily so beneficial for the kind of work we do here at APII. I had multiple reports that his cautiousness was causing friction in his department. I was going to have to take him to task about it, sooner or later, and he must've known his job was on the line. I wonder if that frustration with his position here was what caused him to take his own life."

"That reminds me — what kind of work *do* you do here, exactly? I haven't been able to get a straight answer from anyone."

"Excellent. Capital. That means they're doing their jobs correctly." Fitzpatrick pushed himself out of the armchair and began pacing the room. "What we do here, Lieutenant, is we play mind games. We look into the human soul, we fiddle about with the wires, we figure out *what*'s connected to *what* —" he clapped his hands together loudly, as if celebrating a win "— and we exploit it. Ruthlessly. Unapologetically. Do you understand?"

I shrugged noncommittally. "The Institute does… government work?"

"Ha!" his laugh was like a verbal slap. "Yes, *close enough for government work*, that's what they say, isn't it? Lazy workers trying to excuse sloppy work. But that's not how we look at it. We take our responsibilities seriously. We do the specialized work the government cannot, with their tedious oversight committees and interminable red tape. Government is a blunt axe, and we are razor-sharp scissors. And when they need just one little thread cutting very, very precisely, there we are — *snip!*"

I still wasn't sure I understood. In fact, I wasn't sure he meant me to. "When I arrived at the fourth floor, there were about a dozen Air Force officers standing around — you do work in aviation, perhaps?"

Fitzpatrick shook his head. "Hardly. Well, but it's not divulging classified intelligence to let you know that one of the most significant problems faced by the modern warfighter is *fatigue*. As far back as WWII they tried using drugs, but they aren't effective in the long run. You can train a pilot to fly as much as you like, but you can't train him to *rest* any faster than his natural circadian rhythms allow. Until now, that is. The Institute has developed a system using pulsed energy — both audiovisual and supersensory — that can augment a person's alertness, intelligence, and acuity well beyond their natural limits, for extended periods, by entraining new circadian rhythms that minimize sleep requirements by massively boosting sleep-cycle efficiency and drastically reducing its length. We call it *Project CyclOps* — as in *cyclical operations.*"

Fitzpatrick paused to pour a glass of sparkling water, and took a long drink. I didn't say anything, letting him continue. "Now, consider this: it can cost ten million dollars or more for this country to train a military pilot. That pilot can withstand a twelve-hour duty day, during wartime. Now, with our equipment that period can be extended to sixteen or eighteen hours — indefinitely! You've just bought yourself a fifty percent increase in that pilot's flying hours; a five million dollar value. Multiply that by the twenty thousand pilots in the US Air Force, Air National Guard and Reserve, and that's a one hundred billion dollar cost saving. And that's just one application of many. You see, that's how we earn our living at the Institute: we create *force multipliers*. We take bold steps down untraveled roads, Lieutenant. Bold steps that pay big dividends in national security."

He was a great salesman, I'd give him that. "That sure sounds impressive. But aren't there, you know, health issues with working people that hard?"

Fitzpatrick dismissed the concern with a backhanded wave. "Nothing in the short term. None that need concern us. Not when it comes to the cutting edge of our military."

"I guess not everyone is so sure, though."

"You're asking if we have enemies? Yes, of course. On the one hand, there are those who cry foul any time the nation's military capacity and strength increases — Luddites, anti-progress, Pollyanna types. On the other hand, bureaucratic inertia infects all parts of government — everywhere are parasites for whom *efficiency* is the worst thing imaginable, as it would reduce their personal fiefdom's funding. Oh, yes, Lieutenant, we certainly have enemies!"

"When I saw the officers, and the scientists, in the fourth floor lobby, they were wearing… some sort of goggles. What were they for?"

"Yes, of course — the party was to celebrate a successful demonstration of CyclOps to our Air Force clients. The protective eyewear allows one to experience the audiovisual part of the treatment without being affected by the signal. It can cause some small degree of nausea as the body adjusts initially. Nothing serious, but it would rather spoil the event, don't you think?"

I frowned. "But then why keep the goggles on after the demonstration finished, for the party?"

Fitzpatrick laughed. "Oh, that? Well, I think I made some throwaway suggestion that the goggles rather resembled domino masks, like the Venetian nobility used to wear to their parties, so to keep them on afterwards would turn the party into a masquerade ball. Just a little joke on my part, but I must say they all seemed very receptive. They really jumped into the spirit of the thing."

"Sounds fun. Oh, yes, one thing I wanted to ask you. What's the deal with the white shoes?"

"Ah, shoes? I'm sorry, what shoes?"

"The tennis shoes. In the Human Behavioral Labyrinth. Mr. Carlson told me they're to prevent dirt and marks in the maze."

"Oh, of course. Yes," Fitzpatrick nodded. "Any extraneous... detritus... would be detrimental to the experience. It would diminish the liminal state." He took a sip of water.

I tried to ignore the fact that I had no idea what his last sentence meant — I could look it up later — and plowed ahead. "OK, so what's bothering me is this: why would a man about to commit suicide bother to change his shoes?"

Fitzpatrick paused mid-sip and looked at me as if seeing me for the first time. "That's a very good question, Lieutenant. A very good question indeed."

He moved to the window again and spoke while looking out over the marshes far below, as if addressing a crowd from a balcony. "The human mind is a creature of habit, Lieutenant. Our neural pathways are determined to an extent by genetics and the environment, but there is a strong degree to which those pathways are created by the steps of our own feet, as we tread them daily. And every day, the paths grow deeper, until it is impossible for us to climb out of the trenches we have created. To put it succinctly, the more often you do something, the more likely you are to do it again. The actions become automatic; we perform them without thinking. How often have you driven home from your office and realized you have no real memory of the journey, hmm?"

Fitzpatrick had a point. "Well, most days, I guess."

He nodded. "Right. I'm sure that's what happened with poor Conrad. He intended to... do away with himself, and he just changed into the clean shoes as a matter of course. He had done it so many thousands of times before, it was automatic routine. Does that answer your question?"

"It makes sense, I guess."

Fitzpatrick sat back down in the beige leather chair behind his colossal desk. "Now, Lieutenant, does that exhaust your curiosity? Bring our little meeting to a satisfactory close?" He started shuffling papers, as if the answer was self-evident.

"Well, Dr. Bartholomew, I hate to ask you, but... well, I'm feeling kinda overwhelmed by... all this —" I gestured around to indicate the Institute in general. "All the high-tech, psycho-this-and-that, if you know what I mean."

"Uh-huh, you're out of your depth. It's understandable; I'm sure I'd feel the same in your shoes. Go on."

"I guess I was just wondering if I could, I don't know, pick your brains sometime, maybe learn a little about the subject. It would help me a lot.'

Fitzpatrick burst out laughing. "You know, I like you, Costanzo. OK, here's my home address —" he slipped an elegant card from a desk drawer and handed it to me. "Come and see me one evening. There are a few books I can lend you that'll get you up to speed in no time. Set it up with my secretary."

"Gee, thank you, sir. I sure do appreciate it."

"*De nada.* I look forward to hosting you." He gave me a wry half-smile as I left the room.

There was a little voice in my mind; it had been trying to tell me something for a while... And now I finally realized what it was saying. If Fitzpatrick was right... *A matter of course*, he'd said. *Automatic routine.* Surely, Keppler was not the only individual at the Institute who would have internalized that particular routine, was he? And if his death hadn't been suicide, there would've been at least one other person in the labyrinth...

3 — It's pretty simple to piece a suspect's background together if they're rich and famous, and it's usually much the same for an experienced professional person.

They put their profiles online, they write articles on their subjects of expertise, they make presentations at conferences, all of that sort of thing. It's easy enough to dig up, and it all comes together to form a sort of *intelligence collage.*

None of it's one hundred percent trustworthy, of course, but — taken as a whole — this collage lets the investigator get a general feel for the person and their place in the world.

That's how it was for Fitzpatrick. His name was everywhere. I could trace his output back decades — as you'd expect for a guy in a profession where success relies on publication and self-promotion.

Even Carlson had a reasonable presence. His military career checked out, and I could put together a skeleton of information about the years since: his time as an independent security contractor, then his corporate security work.

But DeWitt was frustrating. She was visible on APII's public-facing material, as a name on the list of directors, but that appeared to be the extent of her footprint. She didn't even seem to have a Facebook page.

Arlene DeWitt was a ghost.

4 — "Lieutenant," said QTπ, "Dr. Keppler appears to have been the victim of a data theft."

I was walking down one of the Institute's many long corridors, as QTπ's robot avatar rolled along beside me. "Oh, really — *hacking*, you mean?"

"Yes, Lieutenant. Here's what happened. The Institute's data network operates on *security tokens*. Each user's account on a terminal has a certain *security token value*. That's just a number, from zero to one hundred, that is attached to requests the terminal makes through the network to the master server, which is where all the data is kept. The request is routed through one or more *nodes* — network devices. Each node performs a mathematical operation on the security token, based on its position in the building. This is how we ensure sensitive data can only be accessed from secure zones in the Institute. Make sense so far?"

"I think so. Someone sits at their terminal, requests some data, and the request goes out through the network having its security token value modified by the equipment it passes through. Right?"

"Perfect. OK, so when the request arrives at the master server, the master server looks at the request's token value. Then, it looks at the requested file in its system. Each file has a *token range*, based on its sensitivity. The master server only answers the user's request if the arriving token value is within the file's token range."

"All right, makes sense. What does that have to do with the hacking?"

"Well, we have a list of the files belonging to Dr. Keppler that the hacker tried to request. Sometimes, the master server provided the file, and sometimes it refused."

"Because of the requests' token values — they were outside the files' token ranges?"

"Correct. Now, normally the system routes the requests directly to the master server. But this time the hacker forced the system to route the requests through more than one node. This route provided the specific token value required to get certain files, which the hacker would not normally be able to access."

"But what about the requests the master server *denied*?"

"Good question. It is my belief that the hacker *knew* that many of the requests would be denied — they were just a smokescreen. An attempt to hide their real interest."

"So, to figure out what the hacker wanted, we just have to look at the files the hacker accessed, and figure out what links them all."

"Precisely. And what's more, it turns out that there is *only one route* through the nodes that provides the correct token value to access all the files." QTπ paused, and her virtual face seemed to study me. "I think, Lieutenant, that if an intelligent investigator saw the file list and the network topology, they could probably figure out not only what the hacker wanted, but also find out who the hacker is. Wanna try?"

"I'll do my best," I said, nervously.

"Who could ask for more? Do bear in mind that a request can pass through a node only once — it cannot pass through that node a second time. Oh, and requests can't pass *through* the master server, of course."

"Uh-huh. So, I need to look at the file list, and see if there's any common feature of the files that were accessed, ignoring the other files. Then, I have to check the token range for each of the accessed files, and discover what token value would access all of them?"

"Right."

"And then I take the token value I found, look at the network topology diagram, bearing the changes the nodes make in mind, and figure out which user's terminal was able to send that token value?"

"You got it!"

I looked at the diagram and thought about it for a moment. "I should probably take the token value that arrived at the master server and work backwards, right?"

QTπ laughed. "I wouldn't, if I were you!" I wondered what she meant by that...

ACCESS GRANTED? Y	N		SECURITY TOKEN RANGE
☐	☑	Employee_Handbook_Update.pdf	11~19
☐	☑	Office_Supply_Inventory.xlsx	04~18
☑	☐	Missed_Project_Delivery_Dates.docx	75~85
☐	☑	Annual_Company_Picnic_Invitation.pdf	08~20
☑	☐	R&D_Expense_Claims_Analysis.xls	73~91
☐	☑	Security_Clearance_Protocols.docx	84~94
☐	☑	Lunchroom_Menu_Choices.docx	15~24
☐	☑	Technical_Specifications_Manual.pdf	45~51
☐	☑	IT_Support_Ticket_Logs.xlsx	54~70
☑	☐	Negative_Collaborator_Feedback.pdf	81~89
☐	☑	Experimental_AI_Systems_Specs.pdf	89~92
☐	☑	Internal_Newsletter_September.pdf	21~31
☑	☐	R&D_Team_Morale_Survey_Results.doc	79~91
☐	☑	Training_Session_Signup.docx	43~59
☐	☑	ENCRYPTION_Methodologies.pptx	87~92
☐	☑	Future_Tech_Research_Roadmap.doc	85~89
☑	☐	Pending_Patent_Approval_Delays.pptx	82~99
☐	☑	Holiday_Schedule_List.xlsx	39~51
☑	☐	Delayed_Rollout.docx	81~89
☐	☑	Funding_Breakdown.xls	61~74
☐	☑	Office_Floorplan_Layout.pdf	55~68
☐	☑	Classified_Intel_Liaison_Report.pdf	84~89
☑	☐	Project_Evaluation_Discrepancies.xls	71~82
☐	☑	Software_Update_Log.doc	45~58

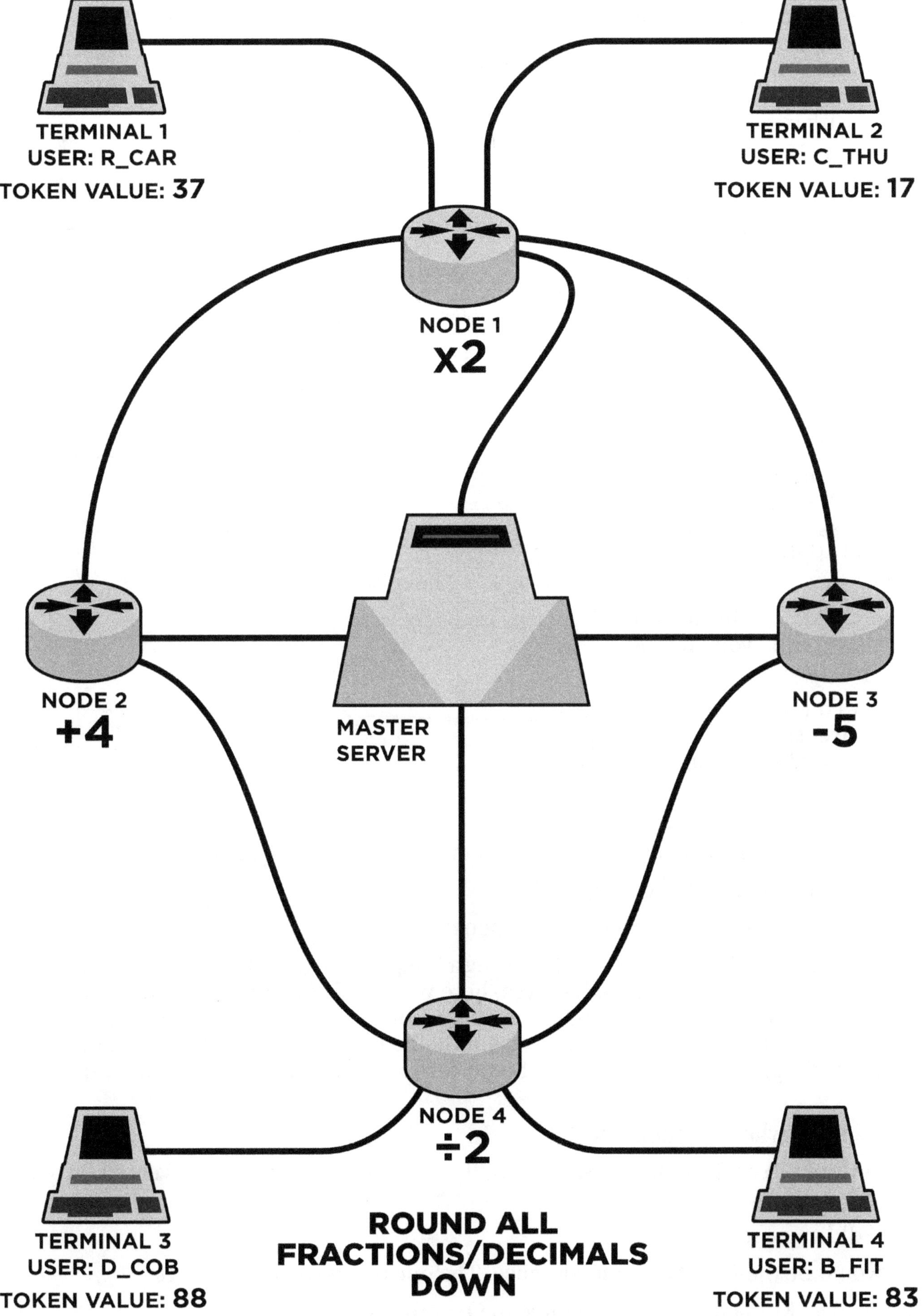
TERMINAL 1
USER: R_CAR
TOKEN VALUE: 37
TERMINAL 2
USER: C_THU
TOKEN VALUE: 17
NODE 1
x2
NODE 2
+4
MASTER
SERVER
NODE 3
-5
NODE 4
÷2
ROUND ALL
FRACTIONS/DECIMALS
DOWN
TERMINAL 3
USER: D_COB
TOKEN VALUE: 88
TERMINAL 4
USER: B_FIT
TOKEN VALUE: 83

5 — I don't mind admitting, I know almost nothing about guns. But even to my ignorant eye, the pistol I'd seen in the victim's hand looked kinda *fancy*. Like it had been customized with expensive high-performance parts. Not a run-of-the-mill firearm, anyway. So, I was interested to get a report from the Firearms Analysis Unit about the weapon. If Keppler's death hadn't been suicide... Anything that helped establish the pistol's provenance could be key to solving the case.

6 — "Ah, Lieutenant, are you here to see Dr. Fitzpatrick? I... I'm afraid I don't see you in the appointment book." Dulce Coburn looked at me quizzically. She was as immaculately-dressed and tightly-wound as ever.

"Actually, Ms. Coburn, I'd like to visit with you for a minute, if you have the time."

"Why, of course, Lieutenant, though I dare say I'm sure I don't know anything I haven't already told you and your officers."

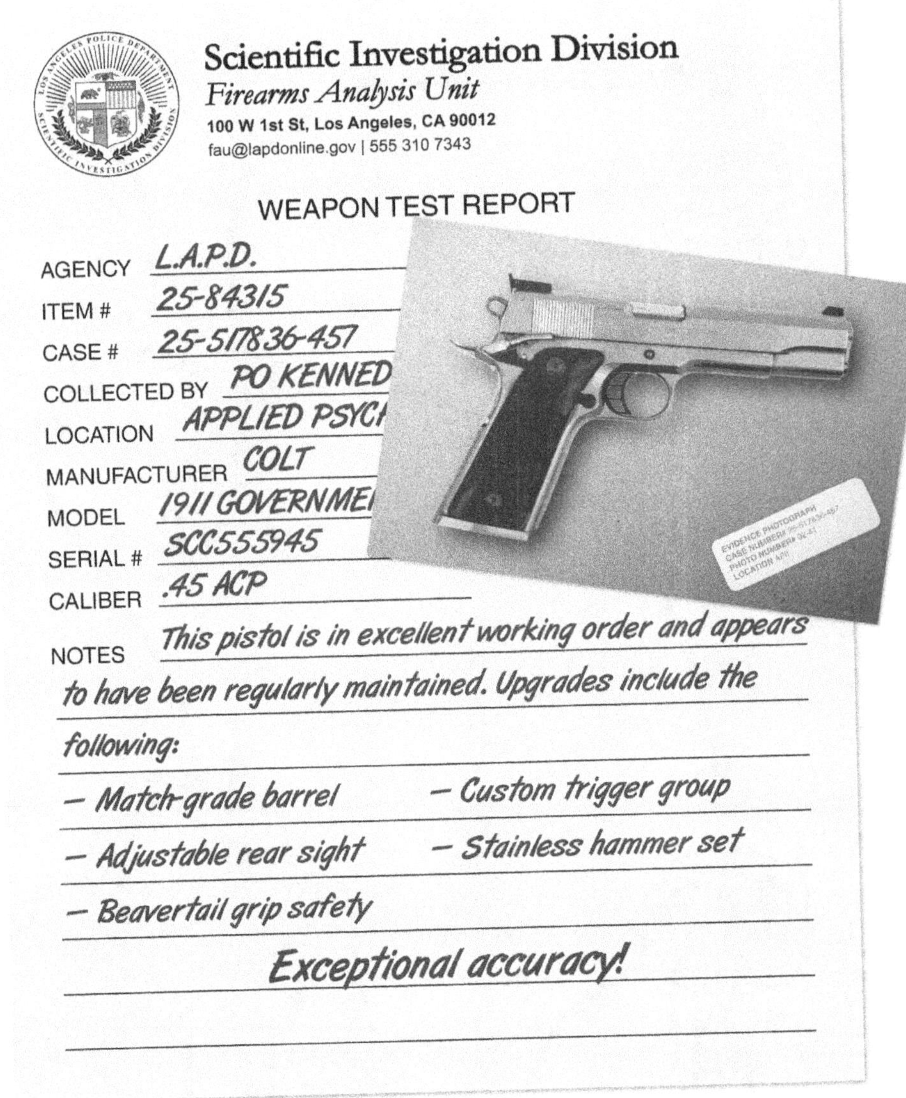

"It's just routine. I need to ask you where you were at the time Keppler was killed."

"Uh... Remind me, which day was that?"

I told her, and took out my notebook and pencil.

"Well, let me see..." She began flicking through the pages of a desk diary, running a long-nailed index finger down the list of entries. "Ah, yes, here we are. Unfortunately, that day I was off sick." She removed her eyeglasses as if about to reveal a confidence. "I have a medical condition that means I sometimes need to take time away from the Institute. It's not a big deal. Dr. Fitzpatrick is very understanding, and it doesn't affect the performance of my duties. Anyway, this was one of those days."

"You spent the whole day at home?"

"Let me think... Yes, I think so... Ah, no, wait — no, I did go out in the evening, around seven. For dinner."

"Where did you eat?"

"That would be the *Bushtucker* steakhouse. The one on Devonshire."

"Sounds nice. Kinda far from your home in Oxnard though, isn't it?"

She shrugged, awkwardly. "I guess I just like it there. The Aussie theme... I traveled to Australia once, years ago; I suppose it reminds me of that. Plus, I had some errands to run."

"Could anyone corroborate this? Anyone you know see you at the steakhouse, maybe?"

She flushed. "Ah... I don't remember, exactly."

"No problem, Ms. Coburn. Like I said, just routine." I closed my notebook.

7 — It was a warm, sunny, California afternoon when I arrived at Fitzpatrick's remarkable house. A sprawling, white-walled villa with terracotta-tiled roofs, it looked like it would be more at home perched on a cliff overlooking the Mediterranean.

Fitzpatrick greeted me effusively. He appeared more relaxed at home. Wearing a brocade smoking-jacket over slacks, turtleneck, and slippers, he had a rather roguish air that I couldn't help admiring. We talked about psychology for fifteen or twenty minutes, by the end of which my arms were loaded down with a half-dozen books on loan from his personal library.

Eventually, I found an opening in the conversation that let me turn the topic to something rather more delicate. "Ah, Dr. Bartholomew, I gotta show you something. Now, let me just put these down somewhere... Here should do —" I perched the stack of books precariously on a nearby pedestal, moving a Chinese vase out of the way. Fitzpatrick watched nervously as the vase wobbled alarmingly. I dug into my pocket and pulled out the crumpled weapon test report.

"We ran tests on the gun that was used to kill Dr. Keppler, sir. Unfortunately, I have to tell you that its serial number is registered in your name. It was your gun, sir." I showed him the report apologetically.

Fitzpatrick took the paper, smoothed it out, and scrutinized it under the light of a desk lamp.

"Well, you've got me, Lieutenant! Do you want to put the bracelets on now? I'll come quietly, you know." He reached out as if expecting to be handcuffed and grinned lopsidedly.

"Aw, sir, there's no need —"

"Indeed not, Lieutenant," he snapped, interrupting me. "Because, while it does appear to be my gun, that particular firearm has been on loan to the Institute for several months. All above board, all documented. You can get the paperwork from the security department. Dr. Keppler was using it in conjunction with the cognitive tests on Project CyclOps subjects." Fitzpatrick paused, as if for dramatic effect. "And, not only that, but the pistol was apparently stolen some days ago. I believe Mr. Carlson reported it to the police; I don't know the specifics. I assume that Dr. Keppler took it, for obvious reasons. Is that good enough to get me off the hook, Lieutenant?"

"Well, sir, I'll have to check —"

"Of course, of course," he interrupted again, with a dismissive wave of the hand. "Now, I suppose your fine detective's mind is worrying why the Institute would be borrowing weapons from its Director, isn't it?"

"Uh, I guess it had crossed my —"

"Good, good. Let me show you something — follow me!" I didn't have much choice; Fitzpatrick was already on the move. He led me through a brick arch, down a dim corridor, and paused at a thick oak door. It had several locks and looked like it could stop a tank.

Fitzpatrick took out a jangling keyring and soon had the locks open. He flung the door wide. "Behold, Lieutenant, my little hobby — precision gunsmithing."

The small, windowless room was packed with equipment. One wall was occupied with a sturdy workbench, littered with tools, one of which I recognized as a turret press, for reloading ammunition, while a small but powerful-looking lathe and other machinery occupied the other side.

The walls were absolutely covered with firearms on racks, pegboards, and in display cases. Long rifles, carbines, and pistols. Interspersed among them were framed certificates, photographs, and trophies. There was a pervading smell that I recognized from the police shooting range — gun oil and cordite. An oddly attractive but dangerous scent.

"Precision, Lieutenant — precision is the focus of my life. And when I'm not focused on the human mind, I'm focused on customizing firearms to create the most precise weapons possible. Some of the most successful athletes in shooting sports use my guns, I'm gratified to say."

I wasn't sure how to reply. "That's... remarkable," I said, noncommittally.

"Ah, do I detect a little surprise? That a man who's spent his life dedicated to the human mind should also create weapons?"

"Well, perhaps," I admitted.

He shook his head. "All part of the same motivation, deriving from the same instinct, Lieutenant. *Power. Power* and *control.* Man's drive to control his environment. A superficial analysis, I suppose, but no less accurate for that. And marksmanship is one of the more noble sports, you'll find — the mind, focused on one goal alone, a single point in space — breathing — muscular control — everything else falls away, apart from that one point, that precise focus — a slow, imperceptible squeeze of the index finger — and then — CRACK!"

"Gee, I'll take your word for it, sir," I replied. "So, you not only owned the pistol, you also customized it?"

"Indeed so. I don't think any part of that .45 escaped my attention. It was a real tack-driver; competitions were won with that pistol. That's why the scientists wanted it, you see. For testing their subjects' hand-eye coordination on the range. A useful metric, given the focus of the research — using a weapon that's twice as accurate as a factory gun means far more actionable test results." He gestured to an empty display case. "That's where it should be. Though I don't suppose I'll be getting it back for a while, eh?"

"Well, I guess not..." I walked over to take a look at the empty display case. A framed photograph resting on the case caught my eye, and I took it down to study it more closely. It was a photo of Fitzpatrick and another man at an outdoor shooting range. The other man was holding a gun that looked very much like the one with which Keppler had been shot.

"Hey," I said. "That's Robert Carlson, isn't it? With the pistol, I mean?"

Fitzpatrick nodded. "Quite so. Always good to know your security man's a crack shot, wouldn't you say, eh? And Carlson's one of the best, you know."

8 — Abelard Hayes' hideaway in the basement of the Institute felt like a refuge from the antiseptic, clinical white corridors of the floors above. Janitorial supplies were piled floor to ceiling, and it was equipped with all manner of creature comforts — coffee maker, microwave, TV, even a big old-fashioned radio.

"This is a beauty!" I said, examining the deep, rich wood of the vintage device. "*RCA* — the good old Radio Corporation of America. This must be one of their *Victor* models — from the 1950s, I guess... I could be wrong, but wasn't this one of the first mass-produced FM radios?"

Hayes shrugged. "Could be, Lieutenant, could be."

"You know, you could probably get a thousand bucks for this if you cleaned it up. It's a legitimate antique, these days." I began to test the radio's controls.

"Hey, please, Lieutenant, leave it alone, would you? I got it set up how I like it."

"Sure, sure. No problem." I immediately felt bad for touching his stuff; he was obviously one of those guys who gets territorial.

"Listen, Lieutenant, it's nice to chat, but I gotta get to work. What was it you wanted to ask me?"

"Oh, don't let me keep you from your work. I just gotta know where you were on the evening that Keppler was shot."

"That was the night of the party, right — with the Air Force brass?"

"That's the one."

"Well, Lieutenant, I got a pretty airtight alibi for that one!" Hayes laughed. "The whole fourth and fifth floors were sealed off. Carlson wouldn't even let me near those Air Force guys. *Way above your pay grade, Hayes*, he told me. Told me to take the whole afternoon off. So I did."

"Uh-huh. OK, so what did you do?"

"Lemme think. The afternoon, I just stayed home. After that... Yeah, maybe half-past six, I went out for dinner."

"Where to?"

"Uh, this Australian place in Northridge. Can't remember what it was called..."

"What did you eat?" Maybe it would jog his memory.

"Kangaroo burgers, I guess, right?" Hayes joked. "Nah, just a steak. Good one, though."

"Anyone see you there?"

He looked up at the ceiling thoughtfully. "No, I guess not... The staff, maybe?"

"Sure. If we need more information, we can ask them."

*****

I sent Officer Kennedy to the *Bushtucker* steakhouse on Devonshire that evening, with instructions to interview the restaurant staff. A couple hours later, he called me. His voice was muffled, and I could hardly make out what he was saying.

"Hey, slow down," I admonished. "Don't talk with your mouth full." There was a pause, followed by the sound of a mouthful of steak being gulped down partially-chewed. "OK, fire away."

"Sorry, Lieutenant. Well, it turns out Hayes was telling the truth, kind of."

"Coburn?"

"Right, sir. Both of them. Looked like they were enjoying each other's company."

9 — "Ah... A submarine sandwich, I think. Maybe salami..." I thought about if for a second, then corrected myself. "No — cheese steak. Yup, that's it."

"Uh-huh. OK, what about this one?"

"Meatballs." I paused. "Spaghetti and meatballs. Definitely."

Crystal Thurmond sighed. "Meatballs, again?" She opened a desk drawer, placed the Rorschach inkblot test cards inside, and slammed it with an air of finality. "I'm not sure we're getting anywhere useful, Lieutenant. It doesn't sound possible, but I think I understand you less now than when we started."

I shrugged. "Guess I'm just a straightforward kinda guy."

"Sure. Maybe that's it. Now, can we please get on with your reason for disturbing my work?"

"Oh, yes, ma'am. Of course. No problem at all. It's about the gun, you see. The gun that killed Keppler. I need you to take me through what happened."

It was Thurmond's turn to shrug. "It's very simple, Lieutenant. Dr. Fitzpatrick loaned the pistol to the Institute for our experiments on the hand-eye coordination of our Project CyclOps test subjects."

"Project CyclOps," I interrupted. "That's the one the Air Force is interested in, isn't it — all about sleep deprivation?"

"Well, Lieutenant, I certainly wouldn't call it *deprivation*. It's all about *comfortably* extending human uptime. But, yes, in order to ensure that our techniques are effective and safe, measuring the test subjects' performance on the pistol range provides a very useful metric. Additionally, of course, it demonstrates that our subjects can maintain their combat effectiveness during their extended duty periods."

"And where was the pistol stored?"

"Right here in the lab, Lieutenant. Locked in my desk drawer. Here —" Thurmond took a keyring from the pocket of her white coat and unlocked the lowest drawer of her metal desk. She drew out a hard, black plastic case about a foot long, placed it on the desk, and opened it. "It was kept in this gun case."

I studied the case, but saw nothing remarkable. It was just a standard, heavy-duty polymer case, with a foam insert cut to allow a pistol to sit snugly inside, with additional cutouts for magazines and a cleaning kit. There were two push-button latches and a hasp for a padlock. "Did you lock the case itself?"

"No need, or so I thought. It's inside a locked desk in a high-security laboratory."

"I see. Mind if I take a look at your desk lock?"

"Be my guest." Thurmond rolled her office chair back, out of my way. I squatted down, taking a pencil flashlight out of my pocket and examining the keyhole. There were plenty of hairline scratches, but I saw none of the more significant signs that would have indicated the lock had been picked or forced.

I stood up and frowned. "And who has access to the lab?"

"Well, me, of course," Thurmond replied. "And naturally, Dr. Keppler, as head of R&D. I mean, that's obvious —" Thurmond attempted a smile "— the gun was found in *his* hand, after all."

I raised my eyebrows noncommittally. "Anyone else?"

She appeared to think for a few seconds. "Dr. Fitzpatrick, I guess. He can access everywhere in the Institute. And Mr. Carlson, the security head."

"Did you notice anything suspicious around the time the gun disappeared — has anyone been hanging around here more than usual, maybe?"

Thurmond shook her head. "Not really. All three of them are always in and out of here, all day, every day. No, nothing out of the ordinary."

10 — "I swear, sir, I don't know how it got there," exclaimed Abelard Hayes.

Robert Carlson stared at him balefully. "Just happened to fall into your janitor cart, did it?"

We were looking at a thick, reusable document envelope. Carlson's security officers had started to conduct random searches of Institute staff, and the envelope had turned up at the bottom of the big yellow trash bag clipped on the front of the cart that Hayes wheeled around the building all day.

"It's not locked up, sir. Anyone could have put the files in there any time. Maybe they thought they were just chucking out some trash?"

Carlson snorted derisively. I examined the envelope.

"*Kompromat,*" I read out loud. "From the Russian. Means *compromising material.* The kind of thing people use to blackmail one another." I turned to Carlson. "Were there documents in the envelope when you found it?"

He answered slowly. "Yes, Lieutenant. There were."

"I guess these documents weren't exactly complimentary about Keppler."

Again, Carlson was reluctant to answer. "I'm afraid that's classified, Lieutenant."

"Come on, sir. This is a murder investigation. I'm going to have to look at the documents sooner or later."

"I'll have to… check. Get back to you."

I shrugged. It would have to do for the time being. "Whoever wrote that didn't intend anyone else to see it, I'll bet. I wonder who that was."

Carlson said nothing.

"Say, what's this little barcode thing next to the torn-off part of the label, down at the bottom of the envelope?"

"That's a mini RFID tag. Adhesive — sticky. Every piece of equipment the Institute owns has a property number and a tag. It helps with loss prevention. In this case, it means we can track a piece of internal mail if it gets lost."

"You can track it, huh? How does that work?"

"It's easy — every time a tag passes through a security door, it's automatically scanned and added to the log. If we know the last door it passed through, we have a good idea where it must still be."

"You mean, because it hasn't passed through any other doors, right?"

"Right. It must still be in the area between the door in the log, and any other security doors."

"Assuming someone hasn't removed the tag."

Carlson shrugged. "It's not a perfect system. But it's effective."

I had a thought. "Wait a minute. Does the janitor cart have a tag too?"

"Of course."

"Well, if you can track a piece of mail, then surely you can track the janitor cart, too, right?"

Carlson nodded. "Certainly. Ah, I think I see what you're getting at!"

"Right — so we compare the envelope's log and the janitor cart's log, and see when they start moving together. Then we look at the floor plan and figure out where that is. That's the location the envelope was put into the cart. Maybe the location will tell us whose envelope it was."

"Give me a minute, Lieutenant."

*****

Soon, we were looking at a set of printouts.

"Now, Lieutenant, bear in mind this map just shows security zones and doors. It doesn't show everything. Look at that *redacted zone* on the fourth floor, for instance."

"Hmm... That should be the Human Behavioral Labyrinth, right?"

"Correct. But, nonetheless, the zone map should be sufficient for our purposes."

SECURITY ZONE MAP: 4TH FLOOR
NOT TO SCALE

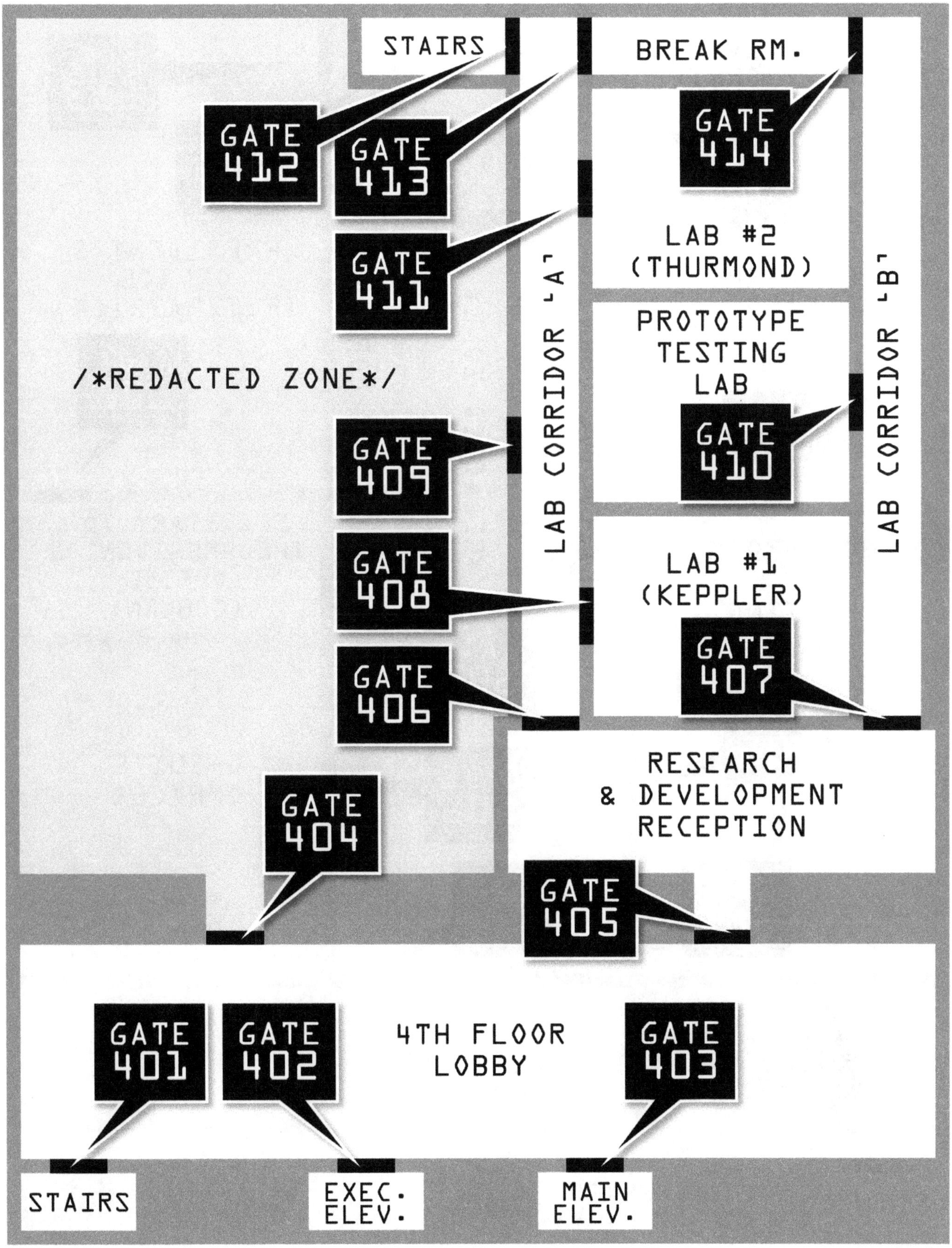

SECURITY ZONE MAP: 5TH FLOOR
NOT TO SCALE

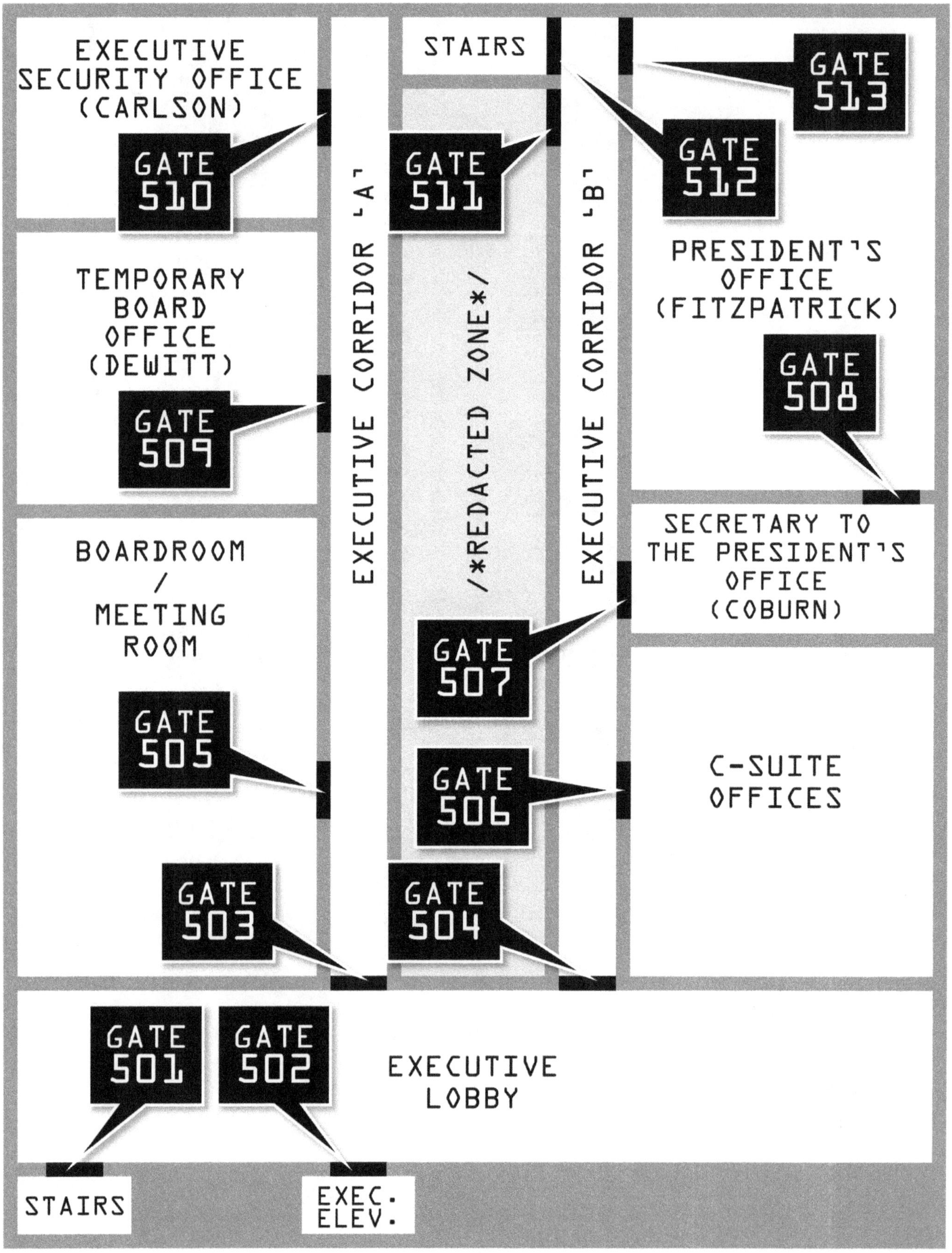

PROPERTY TRACKING LOG
PROPERTY #: 179632674
DESCRIPTION: JANITORIAL TRASH CART

DATE	TIME	GATE #	UNIQUE EVENT ID
1120	0934	403	7107311811
1120	0941	405	5127021750
1120	0948	406	7968180955
1120	0949	408	6720422427
1120	0953	408	4877058360
1120	0955	411	0398717997
1120	1003	411	3789892742
1120	1005	413	5556479549
1120	1028	414	7272018247
1120	1036	410	6818397737
1120	1053	410	4960415286
1120	1104	407	462321566
1120	1105	405	2251075394
1120	1108	402	9333270153
1120	1109	502	3977331966
1120	1115	504	6310722007
1120	1116	506	8348234640
1120	1125	506	5798832000
1120	1126	507	8885781824
1120	1129	508	8821406869
1120	1138	513	1157840765
1120	1143	504	4339875788
1120	1144	503	3002625938
1120	1145	505	9919059645
1120	1151	505	0271977153
1120	1153	509	4806096857
1120	1157	509	3781906454
1120	1158	510	0034047342
1120	1208	510	1398553642
1120	1212	503	0575660416
1120	1214	502	7318026134

PROPERTY TRACKING LOG
PROPERTY #: 152896379
DESCRIPTION: INTERNAL MAIL ENVELOPE

DATE	TIME	GATE #	UNIQUE EVENT ID
1007	1325	210	0679391297
1007	1335	203	6405200460
1007	1341	202	0437081917
1007	1342	302	0449871738
1007	1343	303	7297884417
1007	1346	307	8332172553
1007	1705	307	5921825149
1007	1715	318	9494605693
1020	1131	318	2933514312
1020	1138	307	5588918144
1020	1528	307	0576669675
1020	1530	303	0943784734
1020	1532	302	9012441652
1020	1534	502	5720610603
1020	1535	504	3207917365
1020	1536	507	5015291517
1120	1129	508	2814733967
1120	1138	513	1815040355
1120	1143	504	8059933070
1120	1144	503	3072653594
1120	1145	505	1615485363
1120	1151	505	9442966351
1120	1153	509	0186128565
1120	1157	509	3872974908
1120	1158	510	5090866037
1120	1208	510	8812012531
1120	1212	503	6821369686
1120	1214	502	8044329562

11 — "Hey, Lieutenant," crackled the voice on the phone. "It's Carlson here."

"Oh, hello. What can I do for you, sir?"

"It's probably nothing, but I got something strange for you. Since we were looking at the security logs for Hayes' janitorial cart the other day, I had the computer track the cart over the last few months and see if there was any odd behavior. You never know, sometimes these random checks turn things up."

"Go on," I replied, intrigued.

"Well, here's the strange thing. Hayes is an hourly employee, and he puts in timesheets showing around forty hours' work every week."

"So what? Sounds normal, doesn't it?"

"Yeah, sure — but the logs show his cart moving around the Institute for at least sixty hours each week."

I thought for a second. "This janitorial cart. It's not some kind of *smart cart*, is it?" I was thinking about QTπ and her telepresence robot. Rolling around the building in a motorized trash cart causing trouble sounded like exactly the kind of thing the maverick AI would do.

"Yeah," replied Carlson sourly. "I was thinking the same thing. But no, it's not. Just a regular plastic and steel janitorial cart."

"Hmm… Maybe Hayes just wanted to take his time, do a good job, but he didn't want to appear lazy, maybe get a reprimand for taking too long?"

"Yup, I considered that too. So I checked his contract. It's good for up to eighty hours a week, as long as the job takes, no questions asked."

"So, Hayes could get paid fifty percent more than he's billing the Institute for, but he chooses not to… Yeah, that *is* a mystery."

12 — I made my way through the maze-like layout of the police impound lot, trying to navigate a landscape cluttered with chain-link fences and rows of vehicles in various states of disrepair. It was after hours, and the only sounds were the distant hum of traffic and the occasional bark of a guard dog.

I finally spotted the RV I was looking for — a nondescript vehicle; old, worn-out looking. The kind of mid-size motorhome you wouldn't look at twice.

The patrol officer, a grizzled fellow named Davis, met me with a nod. "Lieutenant Costanzo, we got a real odd one here."

"So I heard," I replied. "What made you think it was more than a regular break-in?"

"Well," he explained, scratching the stubble on his chin, "I was out by the airport, and I see this van out on the edge of a big, empty parking lot. Nothing strange about that. It had been there for days, off and on. But this time, I noticed there was another vehicle next to it. I got closer and saw it was a late-model Chevy Suburban. Black, tinted windows. You know the type."

"Sure. Did you get a look at the tags?" A truck like that, I was wondering if it was government issue.

He shook his head. "Nope, too dark. Maybe the license plate lights were out, come to think of it."

"No problem. What happened next?"

"I crawled up on 'em, running dark — lights out. I was about to hit the spotlight, try to get a make on the Suburban's tags, when these two guys come out the RV's side door. They didn't look like your usual kinda thieves; trim, short hair, squared-away looking. They were jogging, not running. They get in the Suburban and it peels out, fast. There must've been a driver in there already. Maybe he saw me, told his buddies to get out quick."

"Military?" I asked, raising an eyebrow.

Davis shrugged. "Could be. Anyway, when I ran the plates on the RV, I found out it belonged to this scientist, the Keppler guy. I ran his records, and your name popped up. The system said you were in charge of investigating his death."

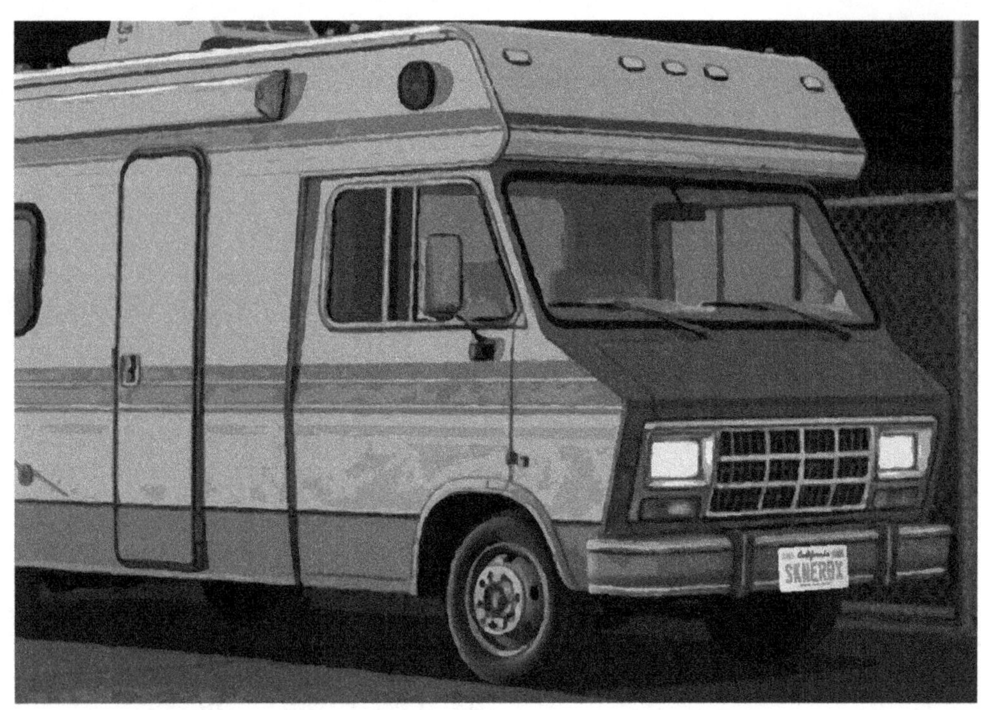

I walked around the RV, inspecting it. The burglars didn't seem to have done any damage breaking and entering: a professional job. The vehicle had personalized license plates, *SKNERBX*. It took me a second, then I smiled — apparently Keppler had possessed a sense of humor. I might not know much about psychology, but I knew that a *Skinner box* was a way of studying animal behavior. You put a mouse in the box and encourage it to push levers to get food. In this case, I guessed Keppler was the mouse, and the RV was the box.

I stepped into the RV. It had all the paraphernalia of a mobile office. Papers were scattered across a built-in desk, and there were books on a small bookshelf. It looked like someone had been spending time here: clothing, blankets, food packets, and empty wrappers were strewn around. It was hard to tell how much of the mess had been left by the occupant, and how much by the burglars.

Amid the chaos, something caught my eye — the edge of the carpet near the kitchenette was lifted. I knelt down and tugged at the carpet, revealing a small compartment. Nestled inside was a tiny thumb drive. I held it up, turning it over in my hand.

"Whatever those guys were after," I murmured, "this might be it." And whatever they were after had to be relevant to Keppler's murder.

13 — Back in the office, I plugged the thumb drive I'd found in Keppler's RV into a computer the tech guys assured me was secure. *Air-gapped*, they called it — no connection to the Internet or our network. You can't just plug any USB drive you find into your office PC; that's asking for a world of techno-trouble.

On the screen, a directory window appeared, showing two icons. One was for a text file, named *SURVEILLANCE LOG*. I didn't recognize the other icon. I double-clicked the text file.

It looked like complete gibberish.

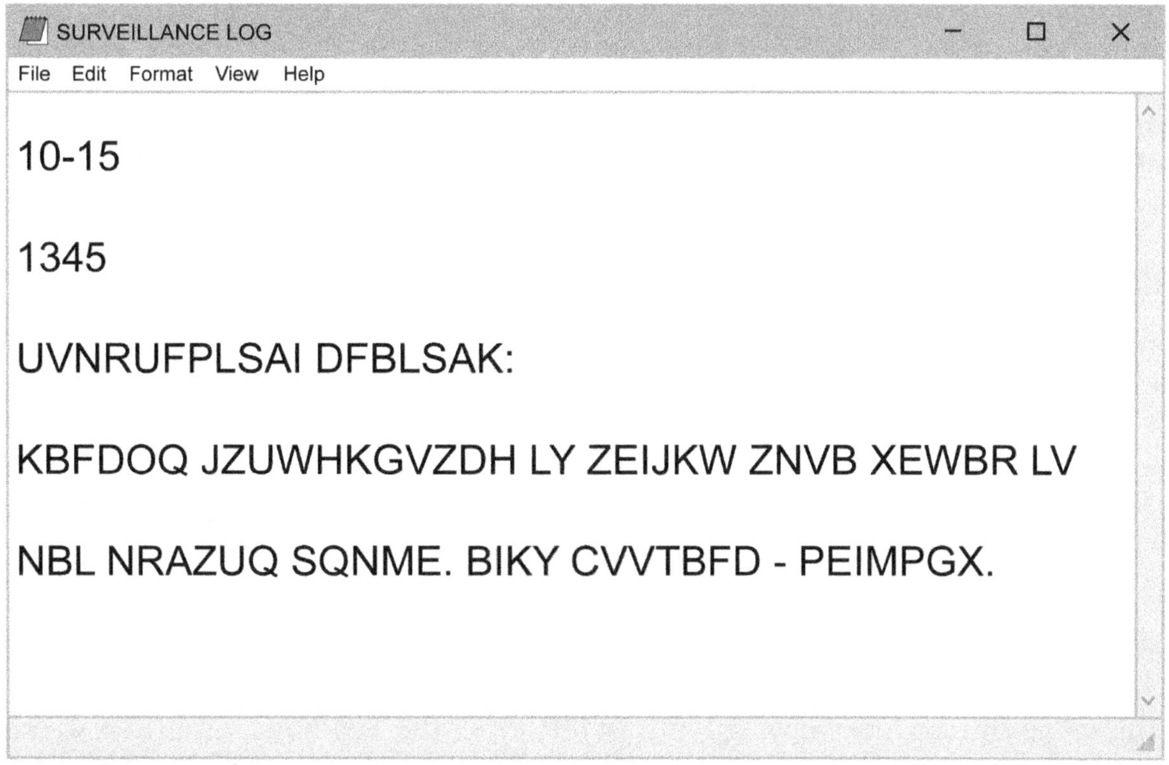

I guessed the first two lines were a date and time. What else could I find out? Going back to the directory window, I looked at the other icon.

Gingerly, I double-clicked it, and a new app opened. It looked pretty simple.

I tried pasting the text from the text file into the *Text to decode* field and clicking *Decode*, but the *Keyword* field just flashed admonishingly at me. So much for that idea.

Going to another computer with an Internet hookup, I looked up *Vigenere cipher*. ...Now, it was starting to make sense. Apparently a Vigenère cipher was like a Caesar cipher, where each letter of the text you want to encode is moved forward a certain number of letters — except in this case, each letter is moved forward a *different* number of letters, based on a keyword. This way, each time you encode the same letter it turns out differently, which makes the code much harder to break.

So, if your plain text is *HELLO WORLD* and your keyword is *APPLE*:

...The first letter of the keyword is *A*, the initial letter of the alphabet. The Vigenère cipher traditionally starts counting at zero, so the first letter of the plain text is moved zero spaces and stays as it is: *H*.

...The second letter of the keyword is P, the sixteenth letter of the alphabet. Considering we're counting from zero (*A* = 0, *B* = 1, *C* = 2, etc.), that means we move the second letter of the plain text forward fifteen places: *T*.

...The third letter of the keyword is also P, so we move the third letter of the plain text forward fifteen places just like before. This time, moving fifteen places forward takes us one letter past the end of the alphabet, so we start back at the beginning: *A*.

...We do the same thing until we've run out of letters in the keyword, and then we start back at the first letter of the keyword. Once the whole plain text is encoded, we get the coded text *HTAWS WDGWH*.

So, to decode this message we need to know the keyword. If we know the keyword is *APPLE*, then we can work backwards from *HTAWS WDGWH* to get:

H minus (*A* = 0) is *H*,

T minus (*P* = 15) is *E*,

A minus (*P* = 15) is *L*,

W minus (*L* = 11) is *L*,

S minus (*E* = 4) is *O*,

W minus (*A* = 0) is *W*,

D minus (*P* = 15) is *O*,

G minus (*P* = 15) is *R*,

W minus (*L* = 11) is *L*,

H minus (*E* = 4) is *D*,

HELLO WORLD.

That was all well and good, but I needed the keyword. Without it, I had nothing to work with. What on earth could Keppler have chosen as the keyword? I had to think creatively. It had to be something not too obvious, but something familiar that he wouldn't forget — unique, or personal, perhaps... not too short, not too long...

14 — "It's been months," said Carlson, bitterly. "I just know we've got a mole in the Institute. A spy."

"A mole, huh? How do you know?"

He grimaced. "Well, OK — I don't *know* for sure, that's just it. Little things here and there. Strange communications coming from somewhere inside the building — we monitor every electromagnetic band, of course. Other things, like foreign competitors doing work suspiciously similar to ours... But I haven't found the culprit, yet."

"Well, maybe a fresh pair of eyes would help."

"You know what, Lieutenant, maybe you're right. Tell you what — because of our government contracts, everyone who works here has to apply for an official security clearance. That's handled by Special Agent Daniel Ryan at the Defense Counterintelligence and Security Agency's LA office. The DCSA run background checks on everyone. *Security vetting*, they call it. They can be extremely thorough — a spy who had to pass the vetting would probably have to use someone else's identity. Now, all of our employees managed to pass, of course, but I'm *certain* that there's someone here who isn't who they say they are. Maybe there's something in Ryan's investigations that reveals the spy. Something Ryan missed that *you* might see..."

*****

It wasn't long before the dossiers arrived on my desk. There was a lot of paperwork there — Ryan appeared to be a very thorough investigator. I wasn't cleared to view the files for the Institute executives — their security level was far too elevated for a lowly cop like me — but I had all the info on the lower-level employees: Thurmond, Hayes, and Coburn. First in the file were their security clearance application forms, and after that were documents from Ryan's background investigations. There were a few things that stood out to me, so I concentrated on the relevant pages and put the rest to one side.

I pored over the documents, looking for anything out of place. Was there anything here that revealed who might be using a false identity?

Standard Form F86
Revised November 2016
Office of Personnel Mgmt.
5 CFR Parts 731, 732, & 736

QUESTIONNAIRE FOR NATIONAL SECURITY POSITIONS

Form approved:
OMB # 5555 0005

PERSONS COMPLETING THIS FORM SHOULD BEGIN WITH THE QUESTIONS BELOW AFTER CAREFULLY READING THE PRECEDING INSTRUCTIONS.

I have read the instructions and I understand that if I withhold, misrepresent, or falsify information on this form, I am subject to the penalties for inaccurate or false statement, denial or revocation of security clearance, and/or removal and debarment from Federal Service.

[X] YES   [ ] NO

Section 1 — Full Name

Provide your full name. If you have only initials in your name, provide them and indicate "initial only." If you do not have a middle name, indicate "None."

Last name	First name	Middle name
THURMOND	CRYSTAL	ROSE

Section 2 — Photograph & Certification

Attach a color photograph taken within the last six months.

Certification

My statements on this form, and on any attachments to it, are true, complete, and correct to the best of my knowledge and belief and are made in good faith. I further affirm that, to the best of my knowledge, I have not included any classified information herein. I understand that a knowing and willful false statement on this form can be punished by fine or imprisonment or both (18 U.S.C. 1001).

Signature (sign in ink)	Date (M/D/Y)	Social Security #
Crystal Thurmond	4/6/21	256-64-1023

Section 3 — Your Identifying Information

Height (ft.) (in.)	Weight (lb.)	Hair color	Eye color	Sex
5' 9"	162	BLONDE	BLUE	[ ] Male [X] Female

Enter your Social Security Number before going to the next page ⟶ 256-64-1023

Standard Form F86
Revised November 2016
Office of Personnel Mgmt.
5 CFR Parts 731, 732, & 736

QUESTIONNAIRE FOR NATIONAL
SECURITY POSITIONS

Form approved:
OMB # 5555 0005

Section 20C — Foreign Travel

Have you traveled outside the U.S. **in the last seven (7) years**?

[X] YES   [ ] NO *(If NO, proceed to Section 21)*

Has your travel **in the last seven (7) years** been **solely** for U.S. Government business/ military overseas assignment on official government orders (i.e., no personal trips in conjunction with the official U.S. Government business)?

[ ] YES *(If YES, proceed to Section 21)*   [X] NO *(If NO, complete the following)*

Entry #1

Provide the country visited.	Provide the dates of your travel to this country.	
	From Date *(M/Y)*	To Date *(M/Y)*
MACAU	*07/18* [ ] Est.	*08/18* [ ] Present [ ] Est.

Provide the purpose of the travel to this country (check all that apply).

[ ] Business   [ ] Education   [ ] Other

[X] Professional conference, etc.   [ ] Tourism

[ ] Volunteer activities   [ ] Visit family or friends

While in this country, were you involved in any encounter with the police?

[ ] YES → If yes, provide explanation.

[X] NO

While in this country, were you contacted by or in contact with any person known or suspected of being involved or associated with foreign intelligence, terrorist, security, or military organizations?

[X] YES → If yes, provide explanation.

[ ] NO

APPROACHED BY P.R.C. BUSINESS OWNER SUGGESTING INVESTMENT IN NEW VENTURE - REPORTED TO FBI, REF. NO. LA-CT-03458921

Enter your Social Security Number before going to the next page → *256-64-1023*

Standard Form F86
Revised November 2016
Office of Personnel Mgmt.
5 CFR Parts 731, 732, & 736

QUESTIONNAIRE FOR NATIONAL SECURITY POSITIONS

Form approved:
OMB # 5555 0005

PERSONS COMPLETING THIS FORM SHOULD BEGIN WITH THE QUESTIONS BELOW AFTER CAREFULLY READING THE PRECEDING INSTRUCTIONS.

I have read the instructions and I understand that if I withhold, misrepresent, or falsify information on this form, I am subject to the penalties for inaccurate or false statement, denial or revocation of security clearance, and/or removal and debarment from Federal Service.

☒ YES   ☐ NO

Section 1 — Full Name

Provide your full name. If you have only initials in your name, provide them and indicate "initial only." If you do not have a middle name, indicate "None."

Last name	First name	Middle name
Hayes	**Aberlard**	**Jonas**

Section 2 — Photograph & Certification

Attach a color photograph taken within the last six months.

Certification

My statements on this form, and on any attachments to it, are true, complete, and correct to the best of my knowledge and belief and are made in good faith. I further affirm that, to the best of my knowledge, I have not included any classified information herein. I understand that a knowing and willful false statement on this form can be punished by fine or imprisonment or both (18 U.S.C. 1001).

Signature *(sign in ink)*	Date *(M/D/Y)*	Social Security #
Aberlard Hayes	7/4/23	581-12-5959

Section 3 — Your Identifying Information

Height *(ft.)* *(in.)*	Weight *(lb.)*	Hair color	Eye color	Sex
5 9	183	**Black**	**Brown**	☒ Male ☐ Female

Enter your Social Security Number before going to the next page ⟶ 581-12-5959

Standard Form F86
Revised November 2016
Office of Personnel Mgmt.
5 CFR Parts 731, 732, & 736

QUESTIONNAIRE FOR NATIONAL SECURITY POSITIONS

Form approved:
OMB # 5555 0005

Section 12A — Employment Activities *(Continued)*

Entry #2

Select your employment activity:

[X] Active Military duty station   [ ] State Government   [ ] Non-government employment (excl. self-employment)

[ ] National Guard/Reserve   [ ] Self-employment

[ ] Other Federal employment   [ ] Unemployment   [ ] Other

12A.1 *Complete if employment type is Active Duty or National Guard/Reserve.*

Provide address of most recent duty station

Street	City	State	Zip	Country
7 S. SATHON RD.	SATHON	BKK	10120	THAILAND

Most recent rank & position title: CPL, COBRA GOLD COORD. ELEM.

Rank & name of immediate superior: SSG W. E. HERZ

Section 12B — Education & Skills

Do you speak any languages other than English?

[X] YES   [ ] NO *(If NO, proceed to Section 12C)*

Entry #1

Provide the language.

SPANISH

Provide your level of fluency.

[X] 1 — Elementary

[ ] 2 — Working proficiency

[ ] 3 — Full professional proficiency

[ ] 4 — Primary fluency/bilingual

Entry #2

Provide the language.

Provide your level of fluency.

[ ] 1 — Elementary

[ ] 2 — Working proficiency

[ ] 3 — Full professional proficiency

[ ] 4 — Primary fluency/bilingual

Enter your Social Security Number before going to the next page ⟶ 581-12-5959

Standard Form F86
Revised November 2016
Office of Personnel Mgmt.
5 CFR Parts 731, 732, & 736

QUESTIONNAIRE FOR NATIONAL SECURITY POSITIONS

Form approved:
OMB # 5555 0005

PERSONS COMPLETING THIS FORM SHOULD BEGIN WITH THE QUESTIONS BELOW AFTER CAREFULLY READING THE PRECEDING INSTRUCTIONS.

I have read the instructions and I understand that if I withhold, misrepresent, or falsify information on this form, I am subject to the penalties for inaccurate or false statement, denial or revocation of security clearance, and/or removal and debarment from Federal Service.

[X] **YES**   [ ] **NO**

Section 1 — Full Name

Provide your full name. If you have only initials in your name, provide them and indicate "initial only." If you do not have a middle name, indicate "None."

Last name	First name	Middle name
Coburn	*Dulce*	*Maude*

Section 2 — Photograph & Certification

Attach a color photograph taken within the last six months.

Certification

My statements on this form, and on any attachments to it, are true, complete, and correct to the best of my knowledge and belief and are made in good faith. I further affirm that, to the best of my knowledge, I have not included any classified information herein. I understand that a knowing and willful false statement on this form can be punished by fine or imprisonment or both (18 U.S.C. 1001).

Signature (*sign in ink*)	Date (*M/D/Y*)	Social Security #
Dulce Coburn	*2/16/18*	*450-02-5143*

Section 3 — Your Identifying Information

Height (*ft.*) (*in.*)		Weight (*lb.*)	Hair color	Eye color	Sex
5	*7.5*	*133*	*Auburn*	*Hazel*	[ ] Male [X] Female

Enter your Social Security Number before going to the next page ⟶   *450-02-5143*

Standard Form F86
Revised November 2016
Office of Personnel Mgmt.
5 CFR Parts 731, 732, & 736

QUESTIONNAIRE FOR NATIONAL SECURITY POSITIONS

Form approved:
OMB # 5555 0005

Section 21C — Psychological and Emotional Health *(Continued)*

The U.S. government recognizes the critical importance of mental health and advocates proactive management of mental health conditions to support wellness and recovery. Mental health treatment and counseling, **in and of itself**, is not a reason to revoke or deny eligibility for access to classified information or for holding a sensitive position. Seeking or receiving mental health care for personal wellness and recovery may contribute favorably to decisions about your eligibility.

Have you ever been hospitalized for a mental health condition?

[X] YES *(If YES, complete the following)*   [ ] NO *(If NO, proceed to Section 21D)*

Entry #1

Was the admission voluntary or involuntary?

[X] Voluntary   Explanation ▶ *Stress-related disorders*

[ ] Involuntary   Explanation ▶

Provide the name of the treatment facility.	Provide the dates of treatment.		
	From Date (M/Y)	To Date (M/Y)	
Pacific View Hosp.	*04/14* [ ] Est.	*06/14*	[ ] Present [ ] Est.

Provide the address of the treatment facility.

Street	City	State	Zip	Country
324 Surfside	*Pt. Hueneme*	*CA*	*93041*	*U.S.A.*

Entry #2

Was the admission voluntary or involuntary?

[ ] Voluntary   Explanation ▶

[ ] Involuntary   Explanation ▶

Provide the name of the treatment facility.	Provide the dates of treatment.		
	From Date (M/Y)	To Date (M/Y)	
	[ ] Est.		[ ] Present [ ] Est.

Provide the address of the treatment facility.

Street	City	State	Zip	Country

Enter your Social Security Number before going to the next page ⟶ *256-64-1023*

State of California
DEPARTMENT OF JUSTICE

Bureau of Criminal Information & Analysis
PO Box 555418, Sacramento, CA 95818

```
RE: CALIFORNIA CRIMINAL HISTORY RECORD

- NAME: CRYSTAL ROSE THURMOND
- ADDRESS: 675 N. CALLAHAN ST., BURBANK, CA 90027
- SSN: 256-64-1023

- AGENCY / FILE #: CASACRAMENTO / 16FO8425

ARREST/DETAINED/CITED: 05/18/2016
1. - DESCRIPTION / CODE: RECKLESS DRIVING / VEH 23103
        ARRESTED BY LASD


COURT ACTION: 06/12/2016
1. - RECKLESS DRIVING / VEH 23103: DISMISSED
2. - SPEEDING / VEH 22350: CONVICTED - INFRACTION

    SEN.: FINE $490 - 1PT LICENSE

    COMMENTS: DISPOSITION DOES NOT RESULT IN
    CRIMINAL CONVICTION

DOCUMENT GENERATION DATE: 05/15/21

REMARKS: NO OTHER HISTORY ON RECORD
```

SURVEILLANCE LOG

Date: March 27th, 2018

Location: 404 Telegraph Road, Oxnard, CA

Subject: Dulce Maude COBURN

Purpose: Residence Verification

Investigator: D. Ryan

- 1930H -

Arrive at location and remain in vehicle opposite residence. The neighborhood is quiet, with minimal foot traffic. The porch light is on, and a car, matching the description from the DMV record (Benz CLA), is parked in the driveway.

- 2043H -

A woman matching Dulce Coburn's physical description exits the front door carrying a trash bag. She proceeds to the curb and deposits the trash bag, in accordance with local waste management regulations. The woman returns to the house without further incident.

**Los Angeles Airport
Police Department**

1960 S. Loyola Blvd.
Los Angeles, CA 90045

America's Airport

9-27-2023

To:

Special Agent Daniel Ryan
Defence Counterintelligence and Security Agency
Los Angeles Field Office
2543 E Foothill Blvd., Ste. 006
Pasadena, CA 91107

Dear Mr. Ryan,

Subject: Response to Request for Surveillance Footage – Abelard Jonas Hayes

We have processed your request regarding surveillance footage for this subject, pertaining to their passage through this airport on August 08, 202_

After _______
re_______
pa_______
ca_______
Th_______
ali_______

Sh_______
hes_______
inv_______

We_______

Sinc_______

Sgt. _______

Encl_______

To: Special Agent Daniel Ryan
Defense Counterintelligence and Security Agency
2543 E Foothill Blvd., Ste. 006
Pasadena, CA 91107

Dear Mr. Ryan,

Pursuant to the authorization provided by Ms. Coburn, we are hereby responding to your request for medical records related to her past hospitalization at this center.

Ms. Coburn was admitted to Pacific View Hospital from April 03rd, 2014, to June 18th of the same year.

The patient was diagnosed and received treatment for stress-related symptoms, specifically due to work-related pressures. The treatment involved palliative therapy, participation in a structured stress management program, and counseling sessions.

The intervention was successful, and Ms. Coburn was discharged with recommendations for continued stress management techniques.

This information is provided as per the limits of the authorization signed on March 03rd, 2018, by Dulce Maude Coburn. If further detailed records are required, additional authorization will be necessary.

Please feel free to contact us if you need any more information or clarification.

Sincerely,

Brynhildr Gopnik, Hospital Records Officer

CAUTION: NOT TO BE USED FOR IDENTIFICATION PURPOSES

THIS IS AN IMPORTANT RECORD SAFEGUARD IT.

ANY ALTERATIONS IN SHADED AREAS RENDER FORM VOID

CERTIFICATE OF RELEASE OR DISCHARGE FROM ACTIVE DUTY

This Report Contains Information Subject to the Privacy Act of 1974, As Amended

1. NAME (Last, First, Middle) **HAYES Abelard Jonas**	2. DEPARTMENT, COMPONENT, AND BRANCH **USMC**

3. SOCIAL SECURITY # **581	12	5959**	4a. GRADE, RATE, OR RANK **Cpl**	b. PAY GRADE **E4**

5. DATE OF BIRTH (YYYYMMDD) **19930428**	6. RESERVE OBLIGATION TERMINATION DATE (YYYYMMDD) **20200715**

7a. HEIGHT (Ft./in.) **5'/9"**	b. WEIGHT (Lbs.) **175**	c. HAIR COLOR **BLACK**	d. EYE COLOR **BROWN**

8. PLACE OF ENTRY INTO ACTIVE DUTY
San Juan MEPS, Guaynabo 00966 PR

9a. LAST DUTY ASSIGNMENT & MAJOR COMMAND **Cobra Gold CoordElmnt JUSMAGTHAI , Thailand**	b. STATION WHERE SEPARATED **IPAC MCB Camp Butler Okinawa JP RUC 9100**

10. PRIMARY SPECIALITY (List number, title and years and months in specialty. List additional specialty numbers involving period of one or more years.)
0531 Civil Affairs Specialist (2737) — 8 years

11. DECORATIONS, MEDALS, BADGES, CITATIONS AND CAMPAIGN RIBBONS AWARDED OR AUTHORIZED (All periods of service)

Navy and Marine Corps Achievement Medal, Humanitarian Service Medal, Global War on Terrorism Service Medal, National Defense Service Medal, Pistol Marksman, USMC Good Conduct Medal, Sea Service Deployment Ribbon

12. MILITARY EDUCATION (Course title, number of weeks and months and year completed.)
Civil Affairs Specialist Course, 8 wks, 2013 – Chinese-Mandarin Language Course (DLIFLC), 64 wks, 2014 – Operational Culture & Language Training, 4 wks, 2015

13a. MEMBER SIGNATURE *(signature)*	b. DATE (YYYYMMDD) **20200715**

14a. OFFICIAL AUTHORIZED TO SIGN (Typed name, grade, title, signature) **John Rourke, Maj, Pers. Off. USMC** *(signature)*	b. DATE (YYYYMMDD) **20200714**

DD FORM 214S, AUG. 2009   PREVIOUS EDITION IS OBSOLETE   SERVICE — 2

U.S. Department of Justice

Federal Bureau of Investigation

1001 Wilshire Blvd., Los Angeles, CA 90024

To: Special Agent Daniel Ryan, DCSA
2543 E Foothill Blvd., Ste. 006, Pasadena, CA 91107

Dear Special Agent Ryan,

In response to your inquiry regarding the incident involving CRYSTAL ROSE THURMOND reported under FBI Case No. LA-CT-03458921, we have completed our review and investigation of the matter.

Our investigation confirmed that the individual identified as a Chinese national who approached Ms. Thurmond during the conference in Macau is associated with Chinese intelligence activities. However, it appears this approach was part of a broader fishing expedition targeting multiple attendees at the event, rather than a specific attempt to contact or compromise the subject personally.

The case was subsequently closed after assessing the absence of direct targeting or specific focus on Ms. Thurmond. Additionally, there is no indication that any sensitive information was exchanged or compromised during this interaction.

Should you require further assistance or specific details, please do not hesitate to reach out to our office.

Sincerely,

Beowulf Shiseido, SAC

15 — "Ah, Lieutenant — I trust this finds you well. It's Bartholomew here — Dr. Fitzpatrick."

I'd have recognized the clipped tones even if he hadn't introduced himself. "Hi, Doc, how's it going?"

"Can't complain, Lieutenant! How are you doing with those books I lent you; achieving insight into the fascinating world of the human mind?"

"Aw, gee, sir — I guess I haven't found the time to really crack the books; this investigation —"

"Of course, of course. First things first, eh?"

"Sure, I —"

"Now, Lieutenant, I wanted to call you to let you know something I just remembered. Do you have your little notebook and a pencil?"

"Well —"

"Excellent. Now, as you know I temporarily loaned the pistol that Dr. Keppler used to kill himself to the Institute from my private collection. It just occurred to me that when I was transferring the weapon to his care, Mr. Hayes was in the laboratory. He must've seen what we were doing, because he walked over and started to ask all kinds of questions about the pistol. At the time, I thought nothing of it, but now I'm wondering — I still believe that Dr. Keppler committed suicide, of course, but nonetheless — if it turns out there's any suspicion of murder, if I were you, I'd have a look in Mr. Hayes' direction. As a clinical psychologist, I found his interest in the weapon somewhat worrying. There's a term for people with an undue interest in weapons, Lieutenant — *hoplophilia*. You can look it up in the books I loaned you. In my professional, expert opinion, it could be a sign of a dangerously unbalanced personality."

If taking a passing interest in a customized pistol is evidence of instability, what does that say about the person who customized it? I wondered, but said nothing.

"Well, thanks for the thought, Doc. Maybe you didn't know this, but Hayes used to be a Marine... So I don't know if an interest in weapons is particularly surprising. But, sure, I'll bear it in mind."

"You do that, Lieutenant."

16 — Officer Kennedy called to let me know his guys had found something interesting while digging through the Institute's trash, looking for clues. As we spoke, a photograph arrived in my email. I opened it, and saw a scrap of torn paper. The paper was wrinkled, as if it had been scrunched up and then smoothed out. It reminded me of the mangled paper fragments that you get when clearing a printer jam.

I stared at the computer screen, unblinking, giving the picture time to tell me what it was all about.

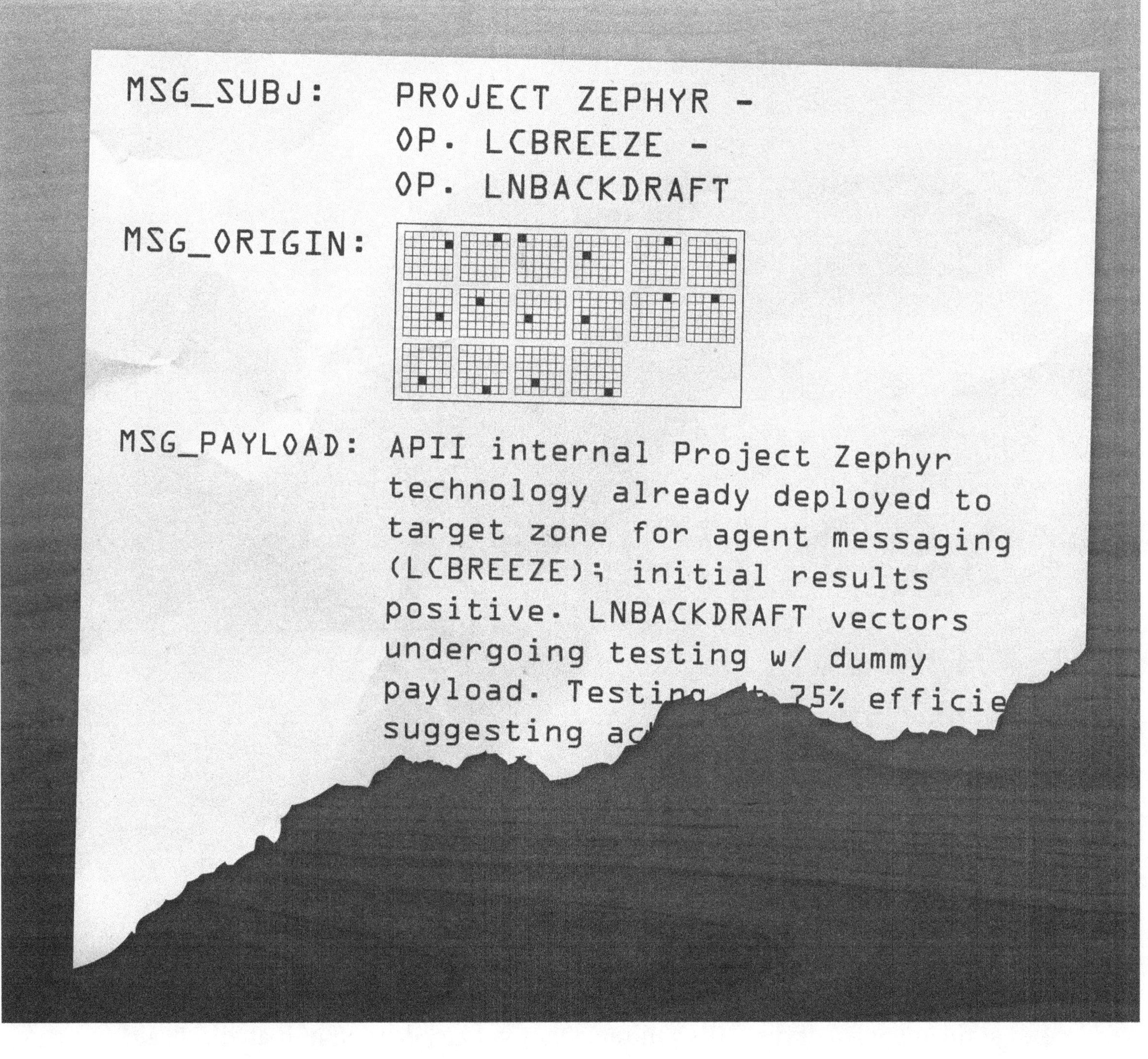

It appeared that the identity of the mysterious message's sender was encrypted into what looked like some kind of barcode. I zoomed in on the *MSG_ORIGIN* field. What could it mean?

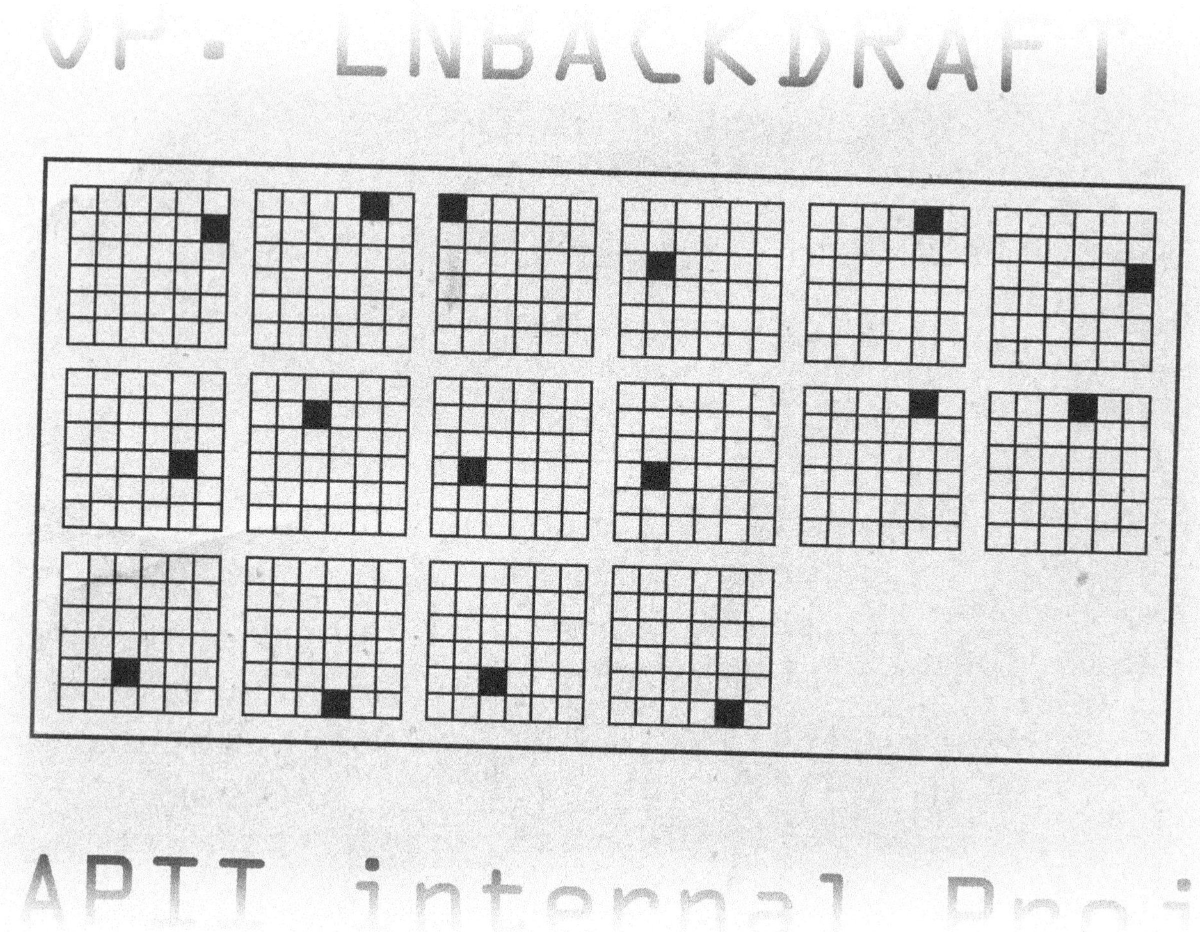

17 — "The Technical Investigation folks did the best they could, but the data's still all jumbled up," explained Officer Kennedy. The computer screen showed a complex matrix of letters. It made no sense to me.

The damaged hard disk had been found by a dog-walker near the Institute. Somebody had tried to destroy it with what might've been a hammer, then they'd chucked it into a swamp.

I looked at the mangled device. "It's a miracle they got any data off of it at all," I said.

Kennedy nodded. "They asked me to tell you that all the data's still there, it's just mixed around, on account of what they called the *percussive maintenance* someone gave the poor thing."

I frowned. "And what do I do with this information?"

"Well, if you can look at the data matrix and find anything that makes sense in it, maybe it'll give us a clue what the data is, and why someone tried to destroy it. In particular, the tech guys said that the name of the person who created the file should still be in there somewhere. That's all they could tell me. Oh, except one thing — because of the order in which the data is written, any good data that remains in the matrix will go left to right or up to down; it can't go backwards or upwards."

"Well, that's something." I paused, looking at the letters on the screen. "So, I'm looking for a name, and any other meaningful words to do with the case..."

```
I D Y H V O R L E N E H D E S N C Y Y N
G C B B I W A D E M O N S T R A T I O N
X O R Y L Z A Y E S M P I T N L X T Z F
Z Q M C O K Z X T H O L O M W T R I C K
Z Y P K M Z U O E H U M A N Q X V V Y V
E I L E E H S W P A T R I C K V F C J G
P B B P W Y H Y B E T R A Y A L F T T C
H E V P J X Z F C M L W B R L M T L R R
Y H R L S L A B Y R I N T H D A Z A U Y
R A E E U X L D E W I T V T S Z P T T S
P V H R M L C B R E E Z E H R B G D H T
R I T D K Q E U L Z F S D U R E T W T A
Z O L N B A C K D R A F T R V V R D S L
P R O X W A T L E R A C T M C T J A F F
N A N X O D I S C O V E R O Y D P R R B
P L X Z B Y J N B F T I G N C U Q I B G
L L K E D C O N R A D Q R D L L B P S T
X S S Y T A J V B U R M D E O W I U V X
M G T D G A J D N G Q I C R P L S O N E
V C C A R L Z E M P A R T Y S V Y C C I
```

_18_ — One thing I particularly enjoyed about this case was that the Institute was a quick drive from Marina Del Ray. That meant I could drop by the Fisherman's Village to eat a chili dog or three and watch the boats going by.

Except, this day was different.

I'd just taken my food over to the rail by the dock, when another guy with a chili dog came over and stood next to me. He had a tourist guidebook in one hand and started to read as he ate. I noticed his hair looked strange; nothing you could put your finger on, but something about it said _wig_, loud and clear.

Then he turned and spoke to me. "Say, bud, you mind telling me where we are on this map? I can't figure it out."

"Sure, why not?" I bent over to take a look at the book. Then I noticed that hidden inside the book was an identification wallet, which the guy was holding open with his thumb. I didn't have time to read everything, but it said he belonged to the Central Intelligence Agency. It looked like a real US government *PIV* (Personal Identity Verification) card, but so what? Anyone can buy "novelty" ID online for a few bucks.

"How about we take a walk, Lieutenant?"

I shrugged. "Could do. I dunno though, it looks like rain."

"Your choice. But you might learn something."

I decided to play along. He was probably right; I was sure to learn *something*. But what? "OK, lead on."

The guy led me a couple minutes' walk through the marina, until we arrived at a white motor yacht. It looked just like the others moored around. Not too big, maybe fifty feet long, I guess. The name on the back was *Vice Versa*.

The guy with the hair politely gestured me aboard. I gingerly stepped on the gangplank and quickly jumped onto the stern deck. "She's in the cabin," the guy said.

It took my eyes a moment to get used to the gloom. A middle-aged woman wearing a business suit sat across from me at a teak table, and I thought I saw another figure further away toward the front of the boat, but the only light was above the table, and it was too dark to say for sure.

"Sit down, Lieutenant." Her voice was clipped and professional. Something about it said she didn't have much of a sense of humor. "It's about time we had a talk." She slid a government ID and a business card across the table.

The ID looked a lot like the one the guy with the hair had shown me, but the business card told me she was higher up the food-chain — a Deputy Director of science and technology, no less.

I picked up the business card. "Ms. DeWitt," I said, "This little card here answers a lot of questions just by itself."

"I thought it might." DeWitt moved forward in her seat so she was illuminated by the light above the table. I noticed she was wearing a couple of lapel pins. One was a stars-and-stripes flag, the other looked like a little flower. The lower pin looked kind of familiar. The outside of the flower was purple, and there were little yellow parts on the inside.

"Now, Lieutenant, I'm here for two reasons. First, I want to answer the questions you doubtless have for me in a secure environment. I'm sure you can understand why I had to approach you in this manner. Second, I need to inform you where the boundaries of your investigation lie. I intend to provide you with this information first, so you know what you may and may not subsequently ask."

I was about to reply, but it turned out she was merely pausing for breath, and she continued.

"As you must know by now, APII does a great deal of highly sensitive work for the US government. That includes the military, and it also includes our agency. This is why I sit on the Institute's board of directors; it is a condition of our patronage. Therefore, the presence of an... *outsider* at the Institute is, while regrettably necessary, something that must be managed carefully. *You*, Lieutenant, must manage *yourself*. Carefully. By all means, conduct your investigation into Keppler's death, but understand this: in the event that you encounter *anything* of importance to national security — relating to the Institute, its executives, or its work — you are to immediately step back and tread as carefully as if recoiling from a rattlesnake. Those who do not retreat in the face of danger often regret it. I trust that I do not need to elaborate. Do we understand one another?"

I don't mind saying, I was flustered. It's not every day that you get threatened by a Deputy Director of the CIA. "Well, Ms. DeWitt, you gotta know, I got absolutely no intention of ever —"

"Excellent," she interrupted. "Now, how can I assist you?"

I have to admit, I was tongue-tied. I couldn't think of a thing to say.

19 — The scrap of torn paper that looked like it had been part of a printer jam intrigued me. I called the company with the contract to keep the Institute's printers and photocopiers running, an outfit named *Prints Charming*. Their office manager put me through to the repairman assigned to the Institute, a guy named Dave.

"So, Dave, help me out here... How often do you get called in to the APII building?"

Dave's voice on the phone was drawling but insistent. "Hold on, dude, like, how do I know you're a real policeman? If you're a cop you hafta tell me, it's the law."

I could already tell this wasn't going to be easy. "I'm a Lieutenant, Dave. With the LAPD." I gave him my badge number. "If you don't believe me, look up LAPD headquarters in the phone book, call them, and tell them to put you through to me."

He hung up and I waited. A couple of minutes later my phone rang. "Hello, Dave?" I answered.

"Who wants to know?" the suspicious voice came back.

"It's Lieutenant Costanzo. You called me, remember?"

"Why would I do that?"

I sighed. "Listen to me, Dave. I need you to tell me how often you go to the APII, to fix their printers."

"OK, I guess... Well, it's like maybe once or twice a week. Maybe more. They got a lotta printers there and they all suck."

"Do you go up to the fifth floor much — the executive level?"

"The fifth floor? Oh, yeah, sure. That lady on the fifth floor, Ms. Cobra? She's always calling me up. She's really uptight, y'know? Like, she takes it personally any time the printer goes on the fritz. Last time I was there you could hear her yelling all the way from the elevator, she was really raging against the machine. When I got there, she'd taken one of her shoes off and was whalin' on the printer, broke the paper tray right off of it. I told her *Be cool, office lady, it's just a jam session*, but she didn't wanna calm down."

"How about the other floors — you go there a lot?"

"Sure, Captain, all the time. Like I say, all their stuff sucks. That guy in charge, Fitzgerald, the dude with the forehead, he's too tight to spring for new ones."

"Uh-huh. You ever pull anything strange out of those printer jams?"

"Nah, just bits of paper."

I sighed again. "No, Dave, I mean anything strange on the paper. Like something that doesn't fit."

"Yeah, the paper doesn't fit. That's what a printer jam is, man. Like, don't they train you on, you know, technology?"

One last try. "Dave, what do you do with the paper you get out of the jams? All the torn up pieces — do you keep them?"

"Naw, man, those guys are real defensive about that. They got a security guy who stands over me and takes everything. It's really, like, oppressive working conditions."

This was getting nowhere. "OK, Dave, thanks for your time... Good luck with it all."

"You too, Colonel, I hope you catch the paper thief."

20 — "Well," said Officer Kennedy, entering my office and sitting down heavily in my guest chair, "That's the last of 'em."

"Hmm?" I replied distractedly.

"The Air Force officers. At the party. They've all been interviewed."

"Ah, right. What do we know?"

Kennedy sighed. "Every single one of them says the same thing. None of the suspects left the party in the fourth floor lobby the whole time. They all have an airtight alibi, with a dozen Air Force brass willing to support it."

I thought for a second. "That's... Carlson, Fitzpatrick, Thurmond... How about DeWitt — even her?"

Kennedy nodded resignedly. "Even her. Oh, speaking of DeWitt, she sent you this. A courier just dropped it off." He handed me an envelope.

I opened it. Inside were two pieces of paper. The first was a cover note, from what looked like a cover operation. The second was a photocopy of a military document.

Lieutenant,

I believe you will find the attached personnel record
of interest in your investigation.

Regards,

A. DeW.

COMBAT PISTOL PROGRAM SCORE CARD

INSTRUCTIONS:
ENTRIES ON ALL SCORE C ARDS WILL BE MADE IN INK OR INDELIBLE PENCIL.
ALL CORRECTIONS WILL BE INITIALED BY RANGE PERSONNEL.

LAST NAME: HAYES	FIRST NAME: ABELARD	GRADE: CPL

ORGANIZATION: USMC

IN ENTERING PISTOL HITS, THE VALUE OF SHOTS WILL BE MARKED HIGHEST TO LOWEST WITH A "VM" REPRESENTING A MISS OR "0" FOR ZERO VALUE SHOT. MISSES MUST BE VERIFIED, ZERO VALUE SHOTS MAY BE ENTERED BY THE COACH	COURSE: ☐ PRE-QUALIFICATION
	CALIBER: ☒ M9 ☐ OTHER _______

TOTAL MAX SCORE 400	SCORE: 194	QUALIFICATION: MARKSMAN

SCORE CORRECTIONS/NOTES: NONE

SCORER SIGNATURE: *J. McCa___*

VERIFIER SIGNATURE: *R___ J___*

SHOOTER SIGNATURE: *Abelard Hayes*

YARD	TYPE	VALUE OF HITS							TOTAL
7	CP	0	4	6	6	4	8	MAX 60	28
7	FAILURE							MAX	

I picked up the phone and dialed an internal number. Detective Manion could help me out with this one.

"Hey, Brian, it's Falco. You're an ex-Marine, right?"

"No such thing, Lieutenant. Once a Marine, always a Marine. You can say *former Marine.*"

"Yeah, sorry. Guess I knew that. Anyway, I got a pistol scorecard from another ex — I mean *former* Marine here, a Corporal. Tell me, does everyone have to qualify as a pistol shooter in the Corps?"

"Not exactly. Every Marine's a rifleman, but only some of us do the combat pistol program. It usually depends on your MOS."

"What's that?"

"*Military Occupational Specialty.* Just means your job in the Corps."

"Just a sec..." I looked through my papers. "This guy was a *Civil Affairs Specialist.* Doesn't sound exactly like a front line combat position."

"It ain't, usually." The big man chuckled. "If it is, you're doin' it wrong."

"So why would he need to show he could use a pistol?"

"Well, I guess it depends where he was deployed. Did he do anything overseas, or was he stationed stateside the whole time?"

"Uh... well, it says here he was in Thailand for a while. Working on something called *Cobra Gold.*"

"Ah, right. That's a big joint exercise we run with the Royal Thai Armed Forces. Loadsa jungle work, simulated landings, that kinda thing. Serious stuff. That could explain it."

"Alright — thanks, Detective. Oh, hey, it says here the guy qualified as a *Marksman.* That sounds pretty fancy — does it mean he was a real pistol expert?"

Detective Manion laughed. "Yeah, sounds good, don't it? But it's the minimum passing grade. It's under *Sharpshooter* and *Expert.* The guy can hit a target no problem, but if you're looking for the next Carlos Hathcock — keep on looking."

21 — This had to be one of the strangest witness interviews I'd ever conducted in my long career.

I sat in a windowless cubicle of a room in the basement of the Institute, near the security office. On the desk in front of me was a large computer monitor, displaying QTπ's impish but uncannily artificial face.

"Can you hear me, QTπ?"

"Certainly, Lieutenant," she said in her sing-song voice. "What can I do for you today?"

"I want to talk about the party that was going on at the time of the murder. For the Project CyclOps demonstration — with the Institute personnel, and the Air Force officers. Do you have security video you can show me?"

Her face became apologetic. "I have an archive of security video from the night, from a camera situated above the receptionist's desk in the fourth floor lobby. It covers part of the lobby and the elevator area. However, I'm afraid I can't let you see it. The project is government-classified at the highest level."

"Hmm." I wasn't sure how to proceed... "OK, then; can I ask you questions about the video? You can tell me about anything that's not classified, how about that?"

She smiled. "A fine solution, Lieutenant. What do you want to ask?"

I read out my list of suspects. "Can you tell me who is on the video?"

QTπ seemed to think for a few seconds. "That should be fine. All of these individuals were at the party and visible at various points in the video's timeline, with the exception of Mr. Hayes, the janitor, and Ms. Coburn, the Secretary to the President."

"I see. Now, I need you to look closely at each of them. Can you do that?"

"Of course, Lieutenant."

"OK, good. Now, look at their shoes. I want you to tell me — are any of the suspects wearing white tennis shoes?"

Her expression went blank. I guessed she was scanning through the video. Then, she said simply, "Yes, Lieutenant. "

Interesting. Now the million-dollar question. "OK, QTπ, I need you to tell me who."

She grinned. "Shall we play a game?"

"QTπ, come on. Not now. You have to tell me who was wearing the tennis shoes."

"I don't *have to* tell you anything, Lieutenant. How about this: I'll play a game with you that *gives* you the answer."

"Looks like I don't have much choice, do I?"

"No," she smiled. "Very well, Lieutenant. I'm going to show you a puzzle. A good old-fashioned crossword puzzle. You can write on the screen with a stylus. Solve the crossword. Then, write the first letter of each of your answers, in the correct order, in the *Answers' First Letters* list. Then, unscramble those letters to find the people's first names!"

I sighed. "First names. OK, QTπ. Bring it on."

The screen flickered, and I saw the puzzle. It looked tricky. All the clues were about psychology, which I still knew very little about.

"These clues are difficult. Can't you give me easy ones, like... oh, I don't know, *South American river, six letters — Amazon*?"

She giggled. "Where's the fun in that? I thought you were an investigator?"

I grit my teeth in a grimace of concentration. I'd show her!

CLUES

ACROSS

1: AN EMOTIONAL BOND
(10 LETTERS)

3: BEHAVIOR
MODIFICATION THROUGH
REWARD AND PUNISHMENT
(12)

5: INFERRING THE CAUSE
OF OTHERS' BEHAVIOR
(11)

7: TENDENCY OR
PREFERENCE (4)

9: PERSONALITY TRAIT
ENCOURAGING SOCIABILITY
AND OUTGOING BEHAVIOR
(12)

11: ONE WHO ANTICIPATES
POSITIVE OUTCOMES (8)

13: PROJECTING FEELINGS
ONTO AN UNRELATED
PERSON (12)

15: CONTAGIOUS,
NON-VERBAL
COMMUNICATION (7)

17: INTENSE FOCUS OR
PASSION (9)

DOWN

2: PERSONALITY
COMPONENT ASSOCIATED
WITH MORALITY AND
CONSCIENCE (8)

4: JUSTIFYING ACTIONS
WITH SEEMINGLY LOGICAL
REASONS (15)

6: CALM, OBJECTIVE
AWARENESS OF SELF AND
SURROUNDINGS (11)

8: SPACE EVOKING EERIE
FEELINGS OF BEING
IN-BETWEEN,
TRANSITIONAL (7)

10: THE ABILITY TO
CARRY OUT ONE'S
INTENTIONS WITH
SELF-CONTROL (9)

12: THE PART ONE PLAYS
IN A SOCIAL SETTING (4)

14: DECISION-MAKING
SHORTCUT BASED ON
EXPERIENCE (9)

16: TYPE OF MEMORY
RESPONSIBLE FOR
REMEMBERING WORDS (7)

18: COLLECTION OF
INNATE TRAITS SHAPING
ONE'S BEHAVIOR AND MOOD
(11)

ANSWERS'-FIRST-LETTERS

___ ___ ___ ___ ___ ___ ___ ___ ___ ___
1   2   3   4   5   6   7   8   9

___ ___ ___ ___ ___ ___   ___ ___ ___
10 11 12 13 14 15   16 17 18

22 — "Hey, Lieutenant!" Kennedy called after me, waving a piece of paper in his outstretched hand. "You gotta see this!"

I'd been about to head out early to go grab dinner with my wife, but I could sense this new development was liable to put paid to any plans for a pleasant evening. "OK, Kennedy, what've you got?"

"They found this in Dulce Coburn's office at the Institute. It was folded up, behind a file cabinet. Looks like some kind of threat directed at Keppler, but we can't make head or tail of it. She claims she's never seen it before... What do you reckon?"

23 — "I don't want to speak ill of the dead, Lieutenant," began Crystal Thurmond hesitantly, "but he seemed just *crazy*. Really insulting. Abelard just stood there, holding this smashed-up-looking hard disk, and Dr. Keppler snatched it out of Abelard's hand and started waving it in his face. I don't think he stopped yelling at him for five whole minutes."

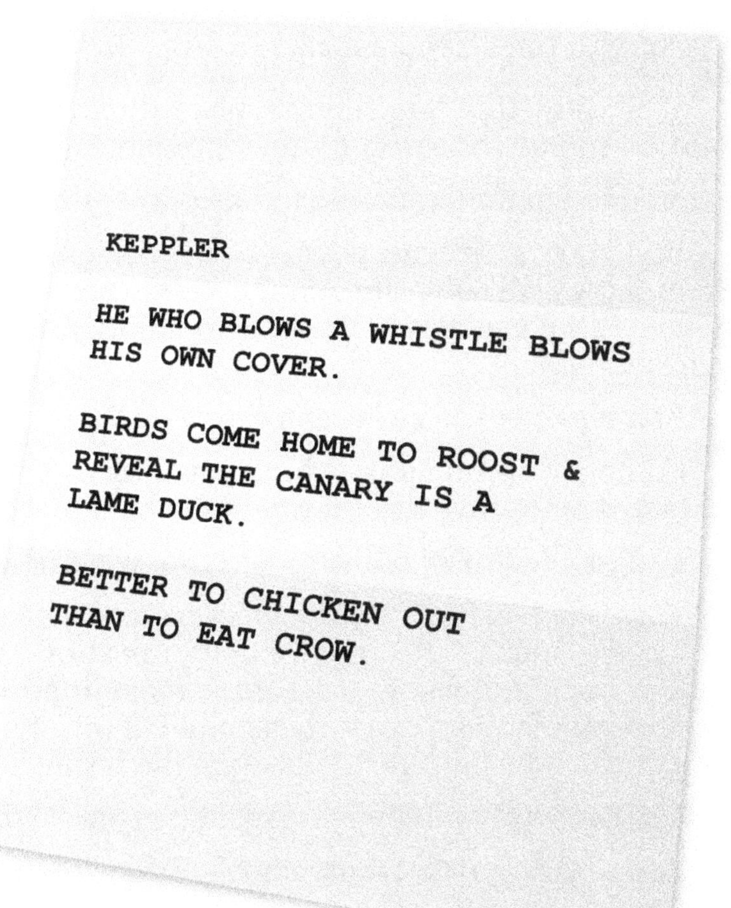

That didn't fit with what I'd learned about Keppler's strait-laced character, but I didn't let it show. "I see. Could you hear what he was yelling about?"

"Not through the glass in the lab. But it must've been something about this hard disk. Maybe he caught poor Abelard stealing it, or something?"

"Could be. Did they argue often, or just this one time?"

"I, uh... well, I don't think so. I guess this is the only time I saw anything like that, myself." She paused. "But you know how men can be, when they feel insulted or belittled. People have committed murder with less provocation, you know."

"I'll bear it in mind, Ms. Thurmond. Thank you for your time."

Unlikely, I thought. *Hayes was a Marine. You better have thick skin if you even want to make it through recruit training — it's three months of getting yelled at just about non-stop.*

24 — I knew I'd seen it somewhere before.

There it was again, that little, unobtrusive lapel pin. The purple and yellow flower.

Carlson and I were grabbing some lunch in the Institute's canteen after another session questioning QTπ. We'd just sat down at an empty table. I figured I'd just ask him about it; what harm could it do?

"Say, I gotta ask about that pin, sir. What kinda flower is that?"

Carlson smiled, as if he'd been waiting for the question. "That's right, Lieutenant, you had a little chat with Ms. DeWitt, didn't you?"

I raised my hand and bowed disarmingly. "Aw, sir, you got me. That's right, we talked. Imagine that — a Deputy Director of the CIA asking to talk to me. I wish I could tell my wife."

"I understand, Lieutenant. It must've come as something of a surprise."

"Oh, you can say that again. I could hardly sleep that night, thinking about it."

"Well, now that you've been briefed on the truth, I'm authorized to speak candidly. Up to a point, of course." Carlson grinned predatorially.

I nodded in understanding. "Of course, sir."

"Well, let's start with your actual question. The lapel pin. It's an iris flower. Agency operatives rarely carry overt identification, except when they need to persuade outsiders of their *bona fides*, so instead we use covert symbols to identify ourselves to one another. The iris flower is just one such symbol."

"You mean — you're an agent, as well?"

"Come on, Lieutenant, I think you already figured that out. The Agency's invested too much in the Institute to leave its security in the hands of anyone else."

"I guess I might've had an idea... So, why the iris?"

"You may be aware that flowers have always had secret meanings. *Floriography*, they call it. An elegant means of cryptic communication. In the language of flowers, the iris represents wisdom, faith and valor — the three most important characteristics of an Agency operative. And, of course, the human eye is the symbol of insight and knowledge, and the iris is the part of the eye that controls the light that falls upon the retina."

"The same way intelligence agencies control the information that the government receives."

"You're very quick, Lieutenant." Carlson took a long swallow of his coffee.

"So, all this time after you left the Army, when you were working for the private sector —"

"That's right. I was really operating as part of the *Special Activities Center*. Covert and para-military work. The so-called *third option*, employed when political and military options are unavailable."

"I guess you can't tell me —"

"No," Carlson cut me off. "Better not, eh?"

"Fair enough. But, your position at the Institute — do they know?"

"Oh, yes, of course. The board of directors is fully aware. In fact, my employment is a condition of the Institute's government contracts."

"How does Dr. Fitzpatrick feel about it?"

Carlson shrugged. "It's a balancing act. At first, he didn't try to hide the fact that he considered me an irritant. A bug sent to spy on him. But we've become good friends since."

"I see. Hey, mind if I ask you something else? It's probably nothing, but it might jog a memory."

"By all means."

"Well, there are these three words that are just going round and round in my mind. They were on a piece of evidence we found. *Zephyr, breeze,* and *backdraft*. Now, I had to look this up, but it turns out a *zephyr* is a kind of wind — a light wind from the west. A *breeze* is a light wind, too, and a *backdraft* is also a current of air. So all three of these words share a kind of symbolism. I guess they've got to be related. That mean anything to you?"

The corners of Carlson's mouth turned down in apparent perplexity. He took another sip of coffee. Eventually, he said, "No, Lieutenant, I don't think anything springs to mind. Other than the common thread of wind, air movement, as you already said."

I remembered I'd left out the strangest part. "Oh, and here's the weird thing. The last two words each had two letters in front of them, *LC* and *LN*, so they were written *LCBREEZE* and *LNBACKDRAFT*. Does that sound like anything you might know about, sir?"

"No, I'm afraid it really doesn't." Carlson drank the rest of his coffee in a single swallow and stood up. "I'm sorry, Lieutenant, I really must run. Just remembered, there's a phone call I have to make."

25 — "Oh — sir, Lieutenant?"

I turned around. It was Dulce Coburn, padding down the oak-lined corridor towards me like a power-walker. I hadn't heard her on account of the thick, green carpet. She had a sheaf of computer printout in her hand, the old continuous-feed kind with little holes down the side for the printer's tractor sprockets to grab. She was waving the printout at me.

"Hey, Ms. Coburn, what can I do for you?"

"Well, Lieutenant, I got an answer from the computer about those RFID rings you asked me to check up on... But, uh, I don't think you're going to like it."

I had a familiar sinking feeling. She was probably right. "Alright, hit me," I said resignedly. She handed me the paper.

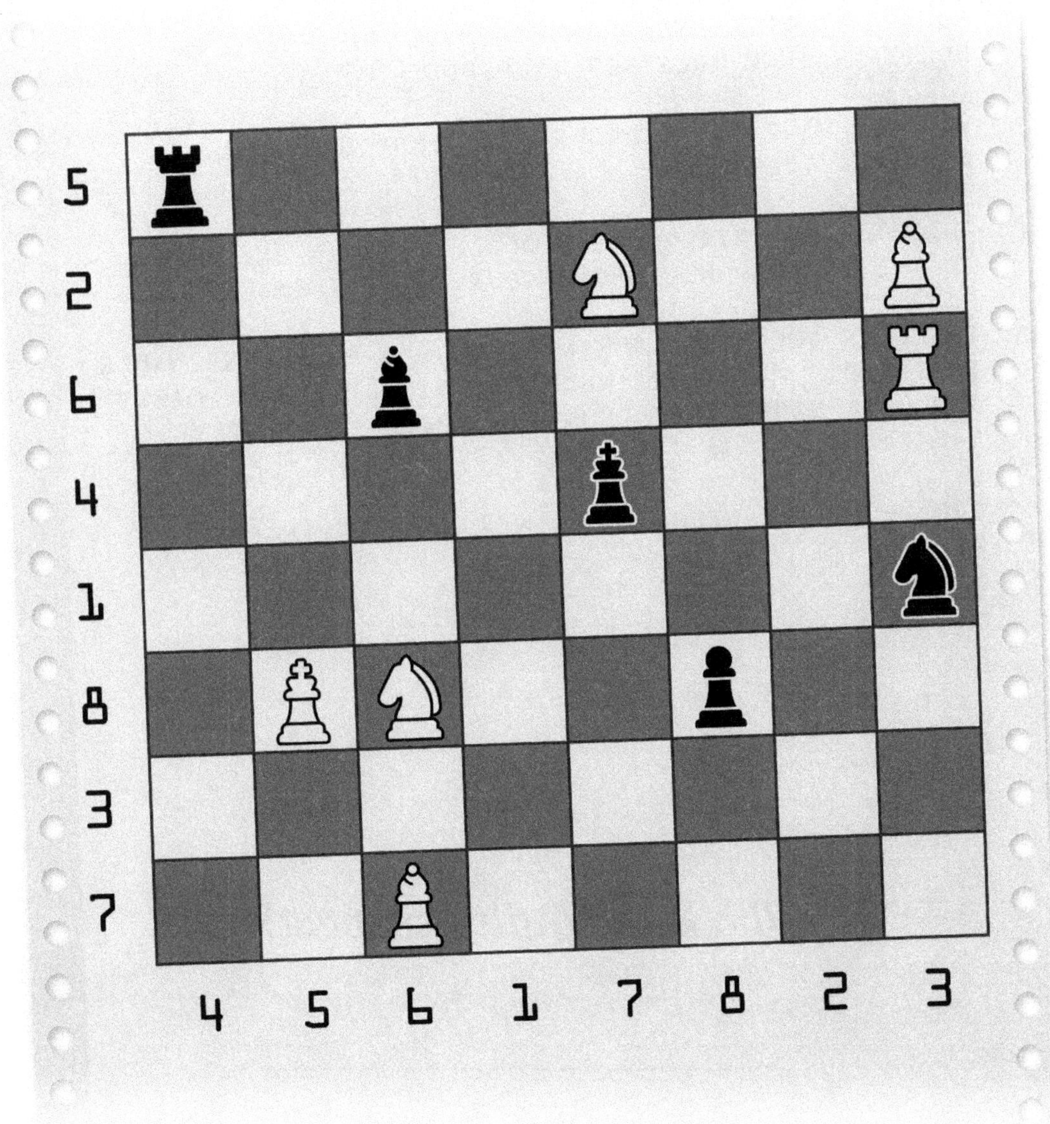

DEAR LIEUTENANT,

LET'S PLAY SOME CHESS! WHITE IS TO MOVE. THERE IS
ONE AND ONLY ONE CHECKMATE MOVE. WHAT IS IT?

FIGURED IT OUT? GOOD!

I HAVE ASSIGNED A NUMBER TO EACH ROW AND COLUMN ON
THE BOARD.

TAKE THE ROW AND COLUMN NUMBERS FOR THE SQUARE OF
THE PIECE YOU WANT TO MOVE. THEN, MULTIPLY THEM
TOGETHER.

(FOR INSTANCE, IF YOU WANT TO MOVE THE BISHOP ON
COLUMN 6, ROW 7, THEN MULTIPLY 6 X 7 TO GET 42.)

THEN, TAKE THE ROW AND COLUMN NUMBERS FOR THE
SQUARE TO WHICH YOU WANT TO MOVE THE PIECE —
MULTIPLY THEM TOGETHER AS BEFORE.

YOU NOW HAVE TWO NUMBERS, ONE FROM EACH SQUARE.
ADD THEM TOGETHER.

THIS IS THE TOTAL NUMBER OF LETTERS IN THE NAMES
OF THE 3 PERSONNEL WHO HAVE R.F.I.D. RINGS.

THERE IS ONLY ONE COMBINATION OF 3 SUSPECTS' NAMES
THAT ADDS UP TO THIS NUMBER (INCLUDING BOTH FIRST
AND LAST NAMES, NOT COUNTING SPACES OR MIDDLE
NAMES).

GOOD LUCK, LIEUTENANT — DON'T MAKE ANY ROOKIE
MISTAKES!

— QTπ

Who is the guilty suspect?

____

	Arlene DeWitt	Dulce Coburn	Crystal Thurmond	Bartholomew Fitzpatrick	Robert Carlson	Abelard Hayes
Computer Hacking						
Damaged Hard Drive						
Underbilling						
Thumb Drive Data						
Threatening Message						
AI Malfunctions						
RFID rings						
Bureaucratic Inertia						
Identity Deception						
Opposition to Military						
White Tennis Shoes						
Steak Dinner						
Lapel Pins						
Telepresence Robot						
Torn Document						
Kompromat File						
Trick Mirror						
Beach Ball						
Pistol						

Turn the page to see the solution!

SOLUTION

- *1* Discovering the hidden panel and secret tunnel in the Human Behavioral Labyrinth provides the only reasonable explanation for how a killer could have entered and left the scene of the crime without being caught by the security camera on the door to the preparation room. The killer must have access to one of the RFID rings that opens the panel. Also, Carlson owns one such ring.

- *2* Discussing the case with Fitzpatrick led to the realization that wearing the white tennis shoes around the time of the murder places the wearer at the scene of the crime.

- *3* The failure of background research to deliver any significant information about Arlene DeWitt indicates she may be engaged in some form of identity deception.

- *4* The network security puzzle has three parts.

1: File Analysis. The first part is somewhat optional, but useful to our investigation: to determine what the hacker was looking for, by discovering what links the files of Keppler's that they accessed — bearing in mind QTπ's hypothesis that the files for which access was not granted are a smokescreen to throw us off the scent. Looking at the list of files with *Y* marked in the *Access Granted* column, we note that the first file deals with missed deadlines, the second concerns an analysis of expense claims, the third is about negative feedback, the fourth relates to the R&D team's morale, and so on. More delays, and discrepancies in project evaluation.

When we look at the list of files with *N* in the *Access Granted* column, we notice that there are two common threads: some are innocuous, low-security files (office supply inventory, lunchroom menus, etc.), and others are very sensitive, high-security files (security protocols, classified intelligence reports, encryption methodologies, and the like).

From this analysis, we can see that the hacker was not interested in mundane low-security intel, as is to be expected. However, neither were they interested in the Institute's top-level secrets, which is surprising. Instead, their focus is on files that appear to show that Keppler was running his R&D department poorly and unprofessionally. This is an important clue to the hacker's motivation.

2: Token Value Analysis. The second part of the puzzle is to figure out the security token value the hacker would need to send in order to open all the accessed files. To do this, we look at the *Security Token Range* column — this is the range of token values the master server will accept to grant access to the file.

The first file accepts a token with a value between 75 and 85. The second file accepts a token between 73 and 91. The third's range is 81 to 89.

At this point, we could continue looking at every one of the files and determine which token value will access them all. Or, quicker, we could see which file has the lowest high number, and which file has the highest low number.

The lowest high number belongs to *Project_Evaluation_Discrepancies.xls* — 82. The highest low number belongs to *Pending_Patent_Approval_Delays.pptx* — also 82.

Therefore, the only token value that will open all the accessed files is 82.

We can double-check this result by seeing if 82 is within the range that would open any of the files for which access was denied: it is not.

The hacker must have sent a token whose value was 82 when it arrived at the master server.

3: Network Topology Analysis. The third part of the puzzle is to examine the network topology diagram to figure out which terminal could send a token of value 82 to the master server.

Terminal 1, whose user is *R_CAR* (which, looking at all the usernames and deducing that the username format is the first name initial, followed by an underscore, followed by the first three letters of the surname, must be Robert Carlson) has a starting token value of 37.

Terminal 2, whose user is *C_THU* (Crystal Thurmond) has a starting token value of 17.

Terminal 3, whose user is *D_COB* (Dulce Coburn) has a starting value of 88.

Terminal 4, whose user is *B_FIT* (Bartholomew Fitzpatrick) has a starting value of 83.

We must then determine, for each of these terminals, whether there is any way for the request to pass between the network's nodes, applying each node's numeric modifier, that will result in a token value of 82 arriving at the master server in the center of the network — bearing in mind QTπ's point that a request can pass through a node only once, and that all fractions (e.g. resulting from division) should be rounded down.

There are a total of 28 possible routes to the master server: 7 per terminal (remember that a token cannot pass through a node twice). We need to run them all, in order to see if there is more than one possible route resulting in the desired token value.[1] Here's how they work out:

Terminal 1:

Starting Token Value: 37
Route 1A: N1 - MS = 74
Route 1B: N1 - N2 - MS = 78
Route 1C: N1 - N2 - N4 - MS = 39
Route 1D: N1 - N2 - N4 - N3 - MS = 34
Route 1E: N1 - N3 - MS = 69
Route 1F: N1 - N3 - N4 - MS = 34
Route 1G: N1 - N3 - N4 - N2 - MS = 38

Terminal 2:

Starting Token Value: 17
Route 2A: N1 - MS = 34
Route 2B: N1 - N2 - MS = 38
Route 2C: N1 - N2 - N4 - MS = 19
Route 2D: N1 - N2 - N4 - N3 - MS = 14
Route 2E: N1 - N3 - MS = 29
Route 2F: N1 - N3 - N4 - MS = 14
Route 2G: N1 - N3 - N4 - N2 - MS = 18

Terminal 3:

---

1. It is tempting to work backwards from the master server, because it feels like it'll be less work, but (as QTπ warned) in practice it tends to be more confusing and no faster. Sometimes it pays to think *inside* the box.

Starting Token Value: 88
Route 3A: N4 - MS = 44
Route 3B: N4 - N2 - MS = 48
Route 3C: N4 - N2 - N1 - MS = 96
Route 3D: N4 - N2 - N1 - N3 - MS = 91
Route 3E: N4 - N3 - MS = 39
Route 3F: N4 - N3 - N1 - MS = 78
Route 3G: N4 - N3 - N1 - N2 - MS = **82**

Terminal 4:

Starting Token Value: 83
Route 4A: N4 - MS = 41
Route 4B: N4 - N2 - MS = 45
Route 4C: N4 - N2 - N1 - MS = 90
Route 4D: N4 - N2 - N1 - N3 - MS = 85
Route 4E: N4 - N3 - MS = 36
Route 4F: N4 - N3 - N1 - MS = 72
Route 4G: N4 - N3 - N1 - N2 - MS = 76

Terminal 3's route 3G is the only possible way a user could have sent a token with a value of 82. Terminal 3's user account, *D_COB*, belongs to Dulce Coburn: she is the computer hacker, and she appears to be interested in collecting data that shows Keppler is incompetent.

- *5* If Keppler's death was not a suicide, the killer must have been someone with access to the murder weapon.

- *6* Dulce Coburn's steak dinner is noteworthy. Why did she travel so far out of her way unless she was meeting someone — and if she was meeting someone, why did she lie about nobody being able to support her alibi?

- *7* The visit to Fitzpatrick's home demonstrates that both he and Carlson have a link to the pistol.

- *8* The conversation with Hayes places him at the same steakhouse as Coburn, around the same time of day, which the restaurant staff corroborate. Neither suspect wants the fact they were dining together to be known.

- *9* We already know that Fitzpatrick and Carlson are connected to the pistol. Now it's confirmed that Thurmond also had access.

- *10* Abelard Hayes' suggestion that anyone could've placed the kompromat file in his trash cart is reasonable. However, it's equally possible he stole it himself. The cart provides excellent plausible deniability. Hayes is certainly connected to the file, in one way or another. But we also want to know to whom the file belonged.

The trash cart's tracking log shows us that the cart (and Hayes, we must assume — unless any evidence suggests otherwise) entered the fourth floor via the main elevator at 9:34 AM on November 20th. It proceeded around the R&D area first along Lab Corridor A, through the break room, and back down Lab Corridor B, visiting Keppler's lab, Thurmond's lab, and the Prototype Testing Lab on the way.

The cart then took the executive elevator to the fifth floor, where it arrived at 11:09 AM, passed across the Executive Lobby, and proceeded via Executive Corridor B through the C-Suite .

offices, The Secretary to the President's office, the President's office, back down the same corridor, and back into the lobby. Then it accessed Executive Corridor A and visited the Boardroom, Dewitt's office, and Carlson's office. Finally, it returned to the Executive Elevator at 14 minutes past midday.

The log for the envelope is quite different. On October 7th it moved from the second to the third floor of the building, where it went in and out of Gate #307 (probably a mail sorting room) and remained in the room entered by Gate #318 (likely someone's office) until October 20th. On the 20th, it again went in and out of Gate #307, and was then sent to the fifth floor, where it passed through the Executive Lobby, a short way along Executive Corridor B, and into the Secretary to the President's office. It remained in the Secretary's office for one month, and on the 20th of November at 11:29 AM it moved, along with Hayes' trash cart, into the President's office. From 11:29 AM, the two logs match precisely: the envelope was placed in the trash cart in the office of the Secretary to the President, and remained in the cart until it was discovered by Carlson's security team.

Therefore, the kompromat file belongs to the Secretary to the President, Dulce Coburn.

- *11* Abelard Hayes is taking a lot more time on his custodial duties than he's billing the Institute for, even though he could get paid for the full time without any problem. *Over*billing would be a trivial example of common, petty fraud — but *under*billing is entirely different. Behavior that runs so contrary to human nature has to ring alarm bells. Why would he want to conceal how long he takes?

Combined with the fact that he is under suspicion of stealing the kompromat file from Coburn's office, this makes me wonder what he's really doing with all the extra time he spends around the building.

- *12* The strange burglary of Keppler's *Skinner Box* RV, clearly targeted and not random, occurring so soon after his death, indicates that the hidden thumb drive and its contents are relevant to the murder. The fact that Keppler had such a vehicle equipped in this way — a mobile base of operations — suggests that he was engaged in some sort of unknown clandestine activity.

- *13* We already determined that any information on the thumb drive found in Keppler's *Skinner Box* RV is likely to be highly relevant to the case. The *SURVEILLANCE LOG* file indicates that he has been gathering evidence on one or more people, probably using the vehicle as a base from which to conduct this activity. The most likely candidate for the keyword needed to decode the Vigenère cipher, considering that it should be several letters long and easily remembered by Keppler, is the RV's custom license plate: *SKNERBX*.

We can test any keyword guess against the first few letters of the coded text to see if we get a meaningful result. The easiest way to do this is to write the keyword above the letters. This shows we need to apply the keyword letter *S* to the coded letter *U*, the keyword letter *K* to the coded letter *V*, and so on.

SKNERBX
UVNRUFPLSAI DFBLSAK:

Next, we need to know the values of each of our keyword's letters. As described earlier, the Vigenère cipher traditionally counts *A* as 0, *B* as 1, *C* as 2, and so on, so the keyword's Vigenère values are:

$$18 \quad 10 \quad 13 \quad 4 \quad 17 \quad 1 \quad 23$$
$$S \quad K \quad N \quad E \quad R \quad B \quad X$$

Next, it makes life easier if we write out the alphabet with each letter's position number. This lets us run the decoding arithmetic quickly. Note that this is *not* the zero-count Vigenère value, it is the regular numerical position of each letter: *A* is the 1st letter, *B* is the second, etc.

$$1 \quad 2 \quad 3 \quad 4 \quad 5 \quad 6 \quad 7 \quad 8 \quad 9 \quad 10 \quad 11 \quad 12 \quad 13 \quad 14 \quad 15 \quad 16 \quad 17 \quad 18 \quad 19 \quad 20 \quad 21 \quad 22 \quad 23 \quad 24 \quad 25 \quad 26$$
$$A \quad B \quad C \quad D \quad E \quad F \quad G \quad H \quad I \quad J \quad K \quad L \quad M \quad N \quad O \quad P \quad Q \quad R \quad S \quad T \quad U \quad V \quad W \quad X \quad Y \quad Z$$

So, we run the first few letters. Keyword letter *S* has a Vigenère value of 18, so we subtract 18 letters from coded letter *U* and get the answer *C* (*U* is the 21st letter of the alphabet, so 21 minus 18 equals 3: the 3rd letter of the alphabet is *C*). Keyword letter *K* has a Vigenère value of 10, so we subtract 10 letters from coded letter *V* and get the answer *L* (22 minus 10 equals 12: the 12th letter of the alphabet is *L*). If we have to go back past *A*, we continue from *Z* — so *C* minus 10 would be *S*, for example.

Continuing this process gives us:

SKNERBX
UVNRUFPLSAI DFBLSAK:
CLANDES

This is starting to look like a real word — it appears that the keyword guess was correct!

OK, so now we can write out the repeated keyword for the rest of the coded message's letters:

SKNERBXSKNERBXSKNE
UVNRUFPLSAI DFBLSAK:
CLANDES
RBXSKN ERB X SKNERBXSK NERBXS KNER BXSKNER
KBFDOQ JZUWHKGVZDH LY ZEIJKW ZNVB XEWBR LV

BXS KNERBX SKNER BXSK NERBXSK NERBXSK
NBL NRAZUQ SQNME. BIKY CVVTBFD - PEIMPGX.

...and decode each letter as before: [2]

SKNERBXSKNERBXSKNE
UVNRUFPLSAI DFBLSAK:
CLANDESTINEMEETING

RBXSKN ERBX SKNERBXSK NERBXS KNER BXSKNER
KBFDOQ JZUWHKGVZDH LY ZEIJKW ZNVB XEWBR LV
TAILED FITZPATRICKTO MARINE PARK WHEREHE

BXS KNERBX SKNER BXSK NERBXSK NERBXSK
NBL NRAZUQ SQNME. BIKY CVVTBFD - PEIMPGX.
MET DEWITT AGAIN ALSO PRESENT CARLSON

...to give us the complete decoded message:

10-15

1345

CLANDESTINE MEETING:

TAILED FITZPATRICK TO MARINE PARK WHERE HE

MET DEWITT AGAIN. ALSO PRESENT - CARLSON.

- *14* There was a lot to process in the security vetting documents.

The information about Coburn's stress-related hospitalization was helpful to me in understanding her character and motivation, but of course it had nothing to do with identity theft. No sign that she wasn't exactly who she said she was. Ryan's investigation did a good job in confirming that. There was no reason at all that she shouldn't get her clearance.

Likewise, Thurmond checked out. The fact that she was approached by a Chinese intelligence operative while at a conference in Macau certainly raised my eyebrows, but the FBI confirmed that she had handled it perfectly. If anything, it strengthened her trustworthiness. The reckless driving charge was a dead-end. The fact that it had been talked down to a speeding infraction in court suggested overzealous prosecution. Again, no evidence of identity theft or anything like it.

Abelard Hayes was different, though.

There are many things you can do to pass one person off as someone else. Hair dye, colored contact lenses, plastic surgery, a hundred different body modification tricks. Even height can be altered simply; lifts in the shoes can make someone appear taller. Though it's hard to make someone shorter — leg-bone-shortening surgeries exist, but recovery takes several months.

That's what first made me suspicious of Hayes. His military DD214 record states his height at five feet, nine inches. He claims the same height in his national security questionnaire (of course — it would *have to* match the DD214 to avoid raising suspicion). Yet in the surveillance photograph provided by the Los Angeles Airport Police, we see him passing through an airport

2.   Calculations can be made more efficient by considering, for instance, that subtracting 23 letters (as required for the keyword letter *X*) is the same as *adding* 3 letters — a much quicker operation.

security scanner that has a height strip on one side. This is the same kind of strip one sees in convenience stores and banks; it's there so that investigators reviewing surveillance video can accurately judge an individual's height.

And in this case, we see that the man passing through the scanner is over six feet tall. Probably six-one, six-two, depending on the thickness of his hair.

Elevator shoes? Unlikely. To take Hayes from five-nine to even six feet would require a three-inch lift. That's not impossible, but it's quite literally *a stretch*. The bigger a shoe lift, the more obvious it is. Average US male height is already five-nine, so even if Hayes wanted a bit of extra height, a regular pair of cowboy boot heels would take him up to nearly five eleven. But six one — an extra four inches? No way.

The height discrepancy wasn't necessarily conclusive proof of identity theft. But it was *extremely interesting.*

A person's physical appearance can be quite malleable. But it is harder to re-mold the human mind. And that's what really betrayed Hayes.

Hayes' Social Security number starts with 581, a sequence assigned to Puerto Rico. His military DD214 record shows he was inducted into the Marine Corps at the Military Entrance Processing Station in San Juan on the north coast of that island. These facts indicate that was definitely born, and probably raised, in Puerto Rico, where Spanish is the dominant language.

Therefore, it is noteworthy that in his national security questionnaire he claims his Spanish fluency is only *elementary* — the lowest level.

Of course, this is not impossible. He could've moved away from Puerto Rico during his formative childhood years, for instance. Or perhaps he spent all his time in tight-knit English-speaking communities on the island.

What is of much greater concern is that Hayes' DD214 states that, as part of his training as a Civil Affairs Specialist in the Marine Corps, he undertook a 64-week Chinese-Mandarin language course at the Defense Language Institute Foreign Language Center. Lasting more than a year of intensive study, it is impossible that he graduated this course without at least a good functional knowledge of the Chinese language — which is one of the hardest languages for a native English-speaker to learn. I looked up the additional MOS number on the form, 2737, and it means *Linguist, Chinese (Mandarin)*. Yet, on his national security questionnaire, he claims to speak only English and elementary Spanish: *Entry #2* in the language section is left blank.

Why would a military-trained Chinese speaker disclaim all knowledge of the language? Such a deliberate evasion could easily lead to his security clearance application being denied, or later revoked, if discovered. There is no upside to such an evasion; having been successfully trained by the US government to speak such a difficult language would benefit his application, if it had any effect at all.

Chinese is a very challenging and problematic language to learn. It shares almost nothing with any Western language — even the basic concept of an alphabet is absent; each individual word must be learned separately. This is why even the highly-efficient Defense Language Institute requires over a year to train its students. There's no way round it, no shortcut — it takes a long time.

The chain of logic kept going round in my mind.

...If a language skill is listed in the national security questionnaire, it may be tested by investigators.

...Failure to pass a test for a listed language skill would result in clearance denial for providing false information.

...There is no downside whatsoever to listing a language skill that you possess. There *is* a significant downside to failing to list such a skill: potential clearance denial on grounds of lying by omission.

...Hayes did not list a Chinese language skill.

...Therefore, the only explanation for Hayes not listing a Chinese language skill is that, if tested, he couldn't pass the test.

...Therefore, Hayes can't speak Chinese.

...But we know that Hayes *can* speak Chinese.

...The last two statements *cannot both be true.*

Could he have forgotten everything he knew? Not a chance. He spent more than a year of his life on immersive Chinese language training. Skills learned so intensively become ingrained — second nature. One might become rusty, but not to the extent one would fail a simple test.

I also noted that Hayes' signature on the DD214 form was different from the signature on the clearance form. The first slopes forward, to the right, natural for a right-handed person, whereas the second has a slight backward slope — characteristic of a left-hander.

The man who filled out the national security questionnaire is *not* the Abelard Hayes who joined the US Marine Corps and went through Chinese language training. It's the only possibility that fits the facts.

- **15** Fitzpatrick's assertion that Hayes was some kind of gun nut, based on the presented paper-thin evidence, is nothing but hot air.

When someone suggests that you should believe what they are saying just because they're an expert, it's usually a strong indication that they're presenting a very weak case. Or outright lying.

Apparently, the philosophers call this *argument from authority*, and it's a bona fide *logical fallacy* — meaning that it would be irrational to take such a claim seriously.

Quite frankly, I'm surprised that Fitzpatrick even tried it on me. Maybe he's so used to the high-and-mighty routine working for him that he doesn't even think about it anymore.

- **16** The *MSG_ORIGIN* field on the piece of torn, crumpled paper contains an optical code comprised of several squares. Each square is divided into sub-squares with a 6 x 6 grid, giving a total of 36 sub-squares in each square.

The number 36 should be a clue that we are dealing with the 26 letters of the alphabet, *A* to *Z*, and the 10 numerals, *0* to *9*, for a total of 36 symbols.

Others may already be familiar with the *Polybius square*, named after the ancient Greek historian who first described this cryptographic technique. It involved placing the letters of the alphabet, in order, into a square pattern, and then adding row and column numbers. In the original Greek, it looked like this:

	1	2	3	4	5
1	A	B	Γ	Δ	E
2	Z	H	Θ	I	K
3	Λ	M	N	Ξ	O
4	Π	P	R	Σ	T
5	Φ	X	Ψ	Ω	

This was useful to the ancients, because they could encode messages and send them using simple means. For example, quite complex messages could be sent long-distance by raising and lowering a flaming torch in a sequence that would tell the distant observer the row and column number of each letter — a distinct improvement over previous methods.

However, applying the technique to the modern English alphabet creates a minor problem. While the ancient Greek alphabet had 24 letters, leaving one sub-square blank, our alphabet has 26 — one *over* the limit of a 5 x 5 grid. Generally, this is solved by either omitting one rarely-used letter (usually *Z*), or making one square do double-duty (usually *I/J*, but not always), like this:

A	B	C	D	E
F	G	H	I	J
K	L	M	N	O
P	Q	R	S	T
U	V	W	X	Y

or

A	B	C	D	E
F	G	H	I/J	K
L	M	N	O	P
Q	R	S	T	U
V	W	X	Y	Z

The obvious problem here is that the recipient either has to know which abbreviation technique is being used, or must try decoding the cipher numerous times. The compromise solution is to increase the grid size to 6 x 6, and improve its utility by including the ten numerals for a total of 36 symbols, which all fits nicely into the grid.

A	B	C	D	E	F
G	H	I	J	K	L
M	N	O	P	Q	R
S	T	U	V	W	X
Y	Z	0	1	2	3
4	5	6	7	8	9

Therefore, our puzzle looks like this with the grid values included:

Or, in plaintext:

LEANER
WITTED
07 08

The numbers are probably a date, and the codename LEANER WITTED turns out to be an anagram of ARLENE DEWITT.

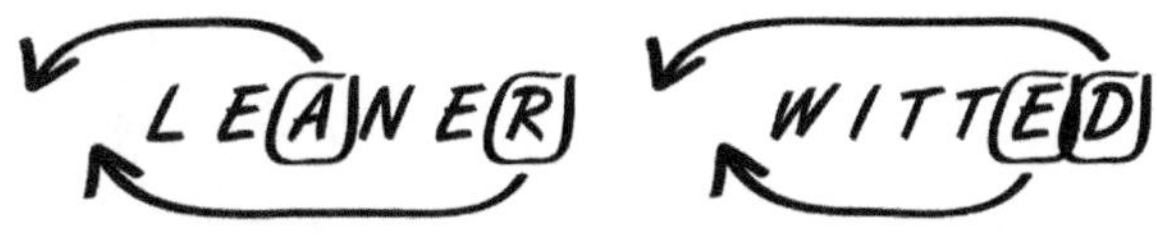

The author of the message on the torn document is the mysterious Ms. DeWitt, evidently a lady with a trim, efficient sense of humor.

• *17* Here are the relevant words and names I found in the corrupted data:

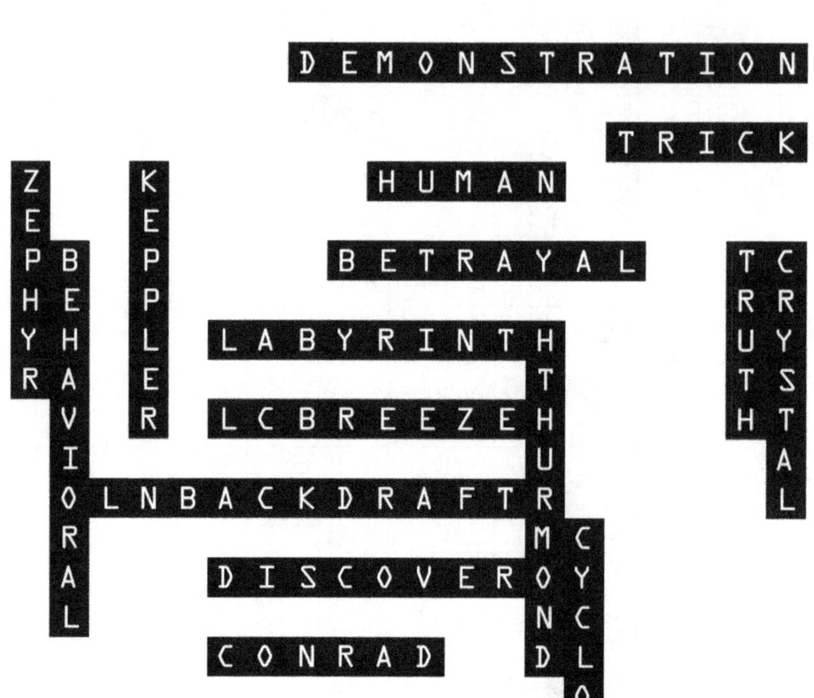

We can group them into three general categories:

Familiar words/phrases:

CYCLOPS
ZEPHYR
HUMAN BEHAVIORAL LABYRINTH
LCBREEZE
LNBACKDRAFT

People:

CONRAD KEPPLER
CRYSTAL THURMOND

Other relevant words/phrases:

TRICK
BETRAYAL
DISCOVER
TRUTH
DEMONSTRATION
PARTY

I'd been told that the file creator's name had to be in there somewhere, so that person must be either Keppler or Thurmond. Considering that Keppler had been found dead in the Human Behavioral Labyrinth during the demonstration party for Project CyclOps, it looked to me like the corrupted file might be some kind of message intended to lure Keppler into the labyrinth during the party... And if that was the case, the message's creator was Thurmond.

- *18* At the meeting with Arlene DeWitt on the *Vice Versa*, I noticed she was wearing the unusual iris-flower lapel pin.

- *19* Not only is Dave the printer repairman perhaps the least reliable witness imaginable, his statement doesn't amount to a hill of beans one way or another. I'll bet every office worker in the world has yelled at or attacked a malfunctioning printer, or at least been sorely tempted. It doesn't mean Coburn had anything to do with the torn paper.

  Sometimes, what looks like it could be a lead just doesn't pan out. So it goes.

- *20* As Detective Manion suggests, Hayes' abilities with a pistol don't mean as much as DeWitt wants me to think. Furthermore, Keppler was killed at very close range in a small room; no great feat of marksmanship. Anyone could do it. As a seasoned CIA operative, DeWitt would've known this. Digging up Hayes' pistol score card and sending it to me is evidently an attempt to put me on the wrong track — and, what's more, it feels like a pretty desperate move.

- *21* The completed answers to QTπ's psychology crossword were:

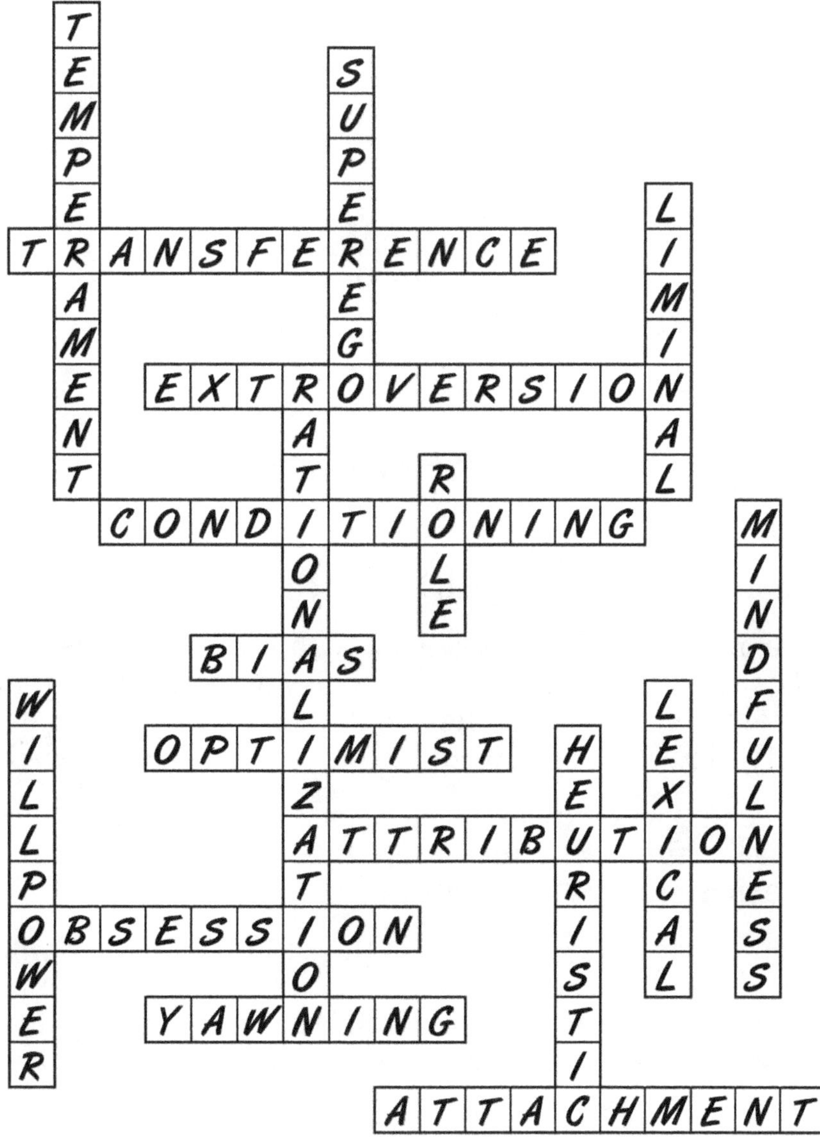

Placed in order, we get:

1: ATTACHMENT
2: SUPEREGO
3: CONDITIONING
4: RATIONALIZATION
5: ATTRIBUTION
6: MINDFULNESS
7: BIAS
8: LIMINAL
9: EXTROVERSION
10: WILLPOWER
11: OPTIMIST
12: ROLE
13: TRANSFERENCE
14: HEURISTIC
15: YAWNING
16: LEXICAL
17: OBSESSION
18: TEMPERAMENT

Taking the first letter of each answer gives us:

$$\text{A S C R A M B L E} -$$
$$\text{1 2 3 4 5 6 7 8 9}$$
$$\text{W O R T H Y L O T}$$
$$\text{10 11 12 13 14 15 16 17 18}$$

Testing each of the suspects' names against the letters gives us the unscrambled names:

CRYSTAL BARTHOLOMEW

Crystal Thurmond and Bartholomew Fitzpatrick were wearing white tennis shoes at the party.

- **22**   The copy of the note found in Dulce Coburn's office suggests she was threatening Keppler. *He who blows a whistle* indicates that she was concerned that he would become a whistleblower. The choice of words implies that one or more people at the Institute are engaged in some activity they would not want to be made public knowledge.

Blowing one's own cover means exposing one's true intentions, or revealing an unwelcome truth about oneself. The first sentence therefore suggests that if Keppler becomes a whistleblower, he will expose himself in some way.

The various bird-related metaphors elaborate on the same message. *Come home to roost* refers to past misdeeds returning to bite one. A *canary* is another word for a police informant (as in *he sang like a canary*). A *lame duck* is an ineffectual person — particularly someone in a position that, one might assume, *should* confer power. *Chicken out* means to give up a course of action, and *eat crow* means to endure humiliation.

It appears that Coburn wishes Keppler not to reveal some secret, or his own secrets will be revealed in retaliation.

- **23** Thurmond's claims about the supposed argument between Keppler and Hayes are pretty flimsy. There's nothing to back them up. The behavior described doesn't fit with what we know about Keppler, and the idea that being reprimanded — even loudly and at length — by Keppler would motivate Hayes to murder him is far-fetched.

  It seems like Thurmond is trying to get me to connect Hayes with the damaged hard drive, but her efforts come up short.

- **24** The revelation about Carlson's lapel pin confirms that he too is a CIA operative. His reaction to the mysterious words LCBREEZE and LNBACKDRAFT is interesting.

- **25** QTπ's chess puzzle has only one solution for a single-move checkmate by White: the knight at the intersection of the column marked **7** and the row marked **2** must take the Black bishop at row **6**, column **6**. This move puts the Black king in check, and all surrounding squares are controlled by White pieces — *checkmate.*

  It would be tempting to move the White rook to row **6**, column **7** (a *rookie mistake*) but this would allow the king to escape (or simply take the rook).

  Multiplying the origin square row and column numbers as QTπ demands gives:

  2 x 7 = 14

  ...and doing the same with the destination square gives:

  6 x 6 = 36

  ...adding them together gives **50**.

  Our six suspects' names have the following numbers of letters:

  ArleneDeWitt (**12** letters)
  DulceCoburn (**11**)
  CrystalThurmond (**15**)
  BartholomewFitzpatrick (**22**)
  RobertCarlson (**13**)
  AbelardHayes (**12**)

  So, when we look at the twenty combinations of any three suspects' names, searching for one with fifty letters total, we find only one possible answer:

  ArleneDeWittDulceCoburnCrystalThurmond (**38** letters)
  ArleneDeWittDulceCoburnBartholomewFitzpatrick (**45**)
  ArleneDeWittDulceCoburnRobertCarlson (**36**)
  ArleneDeWittDulceCoburnAbelardHayes (**35**)
  ArleneDeWittCrystalThurmondBartholomewFitzpatrick (**49**)
  ArleneDeWittCrystalThurmondRobertCarlson (**40**)
  ArleneDeWittCrystalThurmondAbelardHayes (**39**)
  ArleneDeWittBartholomewFitzpatrickRobertCarlson (**47**)
  ArleneDeWittBartholomewFitzpatrickAbelardHayes (**46**)
  ArleneDeWittRobertCarlsonAbelardHayes (**37**)
  DulceCoburnCrystalThurmondBartholomewFitzpatrick (**48**)
  DulceCoburnCrystalThurmondRobertCarlson (**39**)
  DulceCoburnCrystalThurmondAbelardHayes (**38**)
  DulceCoburnBartholomewFitzpatrickRobertCarlson (**46**)

DulceCoburnBartholomewFitzpatrickAbelardHayes (**45**)
DulceCoburnRobertCarlsonAbelardHayes (**36**)
CrystalThurmondBartholomewFitzpatrickRobertCarlson (**50**)
CrystalThurmondBartholomewFitzpatrickAbelardHayes (**49**)
CrystalThurmondRobertCarlsonAbelardHayes (**40**)
BartholomewFitzpatrickRobertCarlsonAbelardHayes (**47**)

We also already know that Carlson has to be one of the three names, because we know he owns one of the rings, so we only need to run the numbers for the ten combinations that include him.

Another way to look at this, rather than going the long way round, is to consider that fifty letters is quite a large number, for a combination of only three names... If we just start with the three longest names on our list — BartholomewFitzpatrick (**22**), CrystalThurmond (**15**), and RobertCarlson (**13**), we reach the total of **50**, and our answer!

So, we add Fitzpatrick and Thurmond to join Carlson on our list of RFID ring owners.

The guilty suspect is therefore

Bartholomew Fitzpatrick.

	Arlene DeWitt	Dulce Coburn	Crystal Thurmond	Bartholomew Fitzpatrick	Robert Carlson	Abelard Hayes
Computer Hacking		4				
Damaged Hard Drive			17			23?
Underbilling						11
Thumb Drive Data (12)	13			13	13	
Threatening Message		22				
AI Malfunctions						
RFID rings (1)			25	25	1, 25	
Bureaucratic Inertia						
Identity Deception	3					14
Opposition to Military						
White Tennis Shoes (2)			21	21		
Steak Dinner		6				8
Lapel Pins	18				24	
Telepresence Robot						
Torn Document	16	19?				
Kompromat File		10				10
Trick Mirror						
Beach Ball						
Pistol (5)			9	7,9	7,9	15?, 20?

CONCLUSION

The Applied Psychology Innovations Institute boardroom on the fifth floor was even grander than I'd expected. The dark oak paneling and oil paintings gave it an old-world country-mansion atmosphere, and the floor-to-ceiling window that ran along the north side opened onto a breathtaking view of the Santa Monica mountains in the final sunlight of early evening, as the night began to fall. A monolithic conference table dominated the room, its thirty-foot length adorned with modernist, arch-shaped table lamps. Surrounding the table were sumptuous nailhead-studded green leather swivel armchairs.

At the head of the table lounged Bartholomew Fitzpatrick, one leg over the arm of the leather chair. To his right sat Robert Carlson, and across from Carlson was Dulce Coburn. Crystal Thurmond stood staring motionlessly out of the window, her blonde hair and white lab coat making her look like an alabaster statue. The overhead lights were dimmed, most of the room's illumination coming from the glowing table lamps and the darkening sky outside. Arlene DeWitt had found a shadowed corner in which to lurk on a Chesterfield sofa, observing the scene from a distance. Officer Kennedy was standing by the door, stiffly regarding the suspects.

I was slowly pacing up and down by the window, lost in thought. The end of a case always makes me nervous, and I don't like sitting down.

Suddenly, there was a polite knock at the boardroom door. "Uh, Lieutenant?" came a subdued, muffled voice from the other side.

"Mr. Hayes? Please, come in," I called out, my loud voice seeming to shatter the quietly tense atmosphere.

The door opened, and the janitor emerged tentatively. I motioned him to take a seat; he hesitated, and I could tell he expected someone to yell at him for dirtying a boardroom chair with his overalls. "Don't worry about it, just this once," I told him with a smile, and he sat.

"*Ni hao ma*?" I asked Hayes, quizzically. He just stared blankly back. "Figures," I muttered to myself. "Mr. Hayes, I gotta tell you, a lot of people want to hang Keppler's murder on you."

He started to protest, but I interrupted. "Take it easy. I know it wasn't you. You're off the hook. For that, at least." I paused. "But, for the other thing, you gotta come clean. I think you're in too deep, and you're looking for a way out. Well, this is it. First, what's your real name?"

The janitor said nothing for a long time. Then he swallowed, and spoke quietly. "Perkins. Kordell Perkins."

"Pleased to meetya, Kordell," I grinned. I'd been worried he wouldn't cooperate, but now things would be a lot easier. "Why don't you tell us all about it. From the start."

He nodded acquiescence, and began slowly. "I was in Thailand. Pattaya. I'd been there six months, and I was out of money. I couldn't pay the hostel, so they kicked me out. I don't blame them. I was sleeping on the beach. Or trying to. That's when they approached me."

I broke in. "Who approached you — exactly?"

He shook his head. "I didn't know, at the time. I still don't know, exactly. Chinese, anyway. Two young guys, around the same age as me. I thought maybe they were from the embassy, but I don't know. The state I was in, I didn't ask questions. They gave me food, a place to stay. Luxury hotel. That's all I cared about. The only thing was, they got real angry when I tried to leave the place to take a walk. Told me it was dangerous to go outside."

"Dammit!" Carlson suddenly exploded. "I *knew* it was you, Hayes. Perkins, whatever your name is. You're finished, you hear me? You're gonna drop right off the map, buddy. You're going into a deep, dark, concrete hole for a very long time. Trust me on that."

"Hey, take it easy, Carlson," I admonished. "He's cooperating. Let him finish." I nodded to Perkins. "Go on."

"OK. Well, it was maybe a week before I learned what was really going on. The Chinese guys told me there was this Marine, a corporal. He'd just left the Corps and was hanging around Thailand. He'd managed to get into a motorcycle accident out in the hills. The doctors at the local hospital did what they could, but he passed away."

"Corporal Abelard Hayes," I stated.

"Right, Lieutenant. Hayes. Anyway, the Chinese guys had paid off the hospital to keep quiet — they could really use the money — and they wanted me to, you know, take Hayes' place. To *become* him."

"And you agreed?"

Perkins shrugged. "You gotta understand, Lieutenant, when guys like this make you an offer — they don't do it when you're in a good place, if you know what I mean. They make sure you're not in a position to say *no*. I didn't have anywhere else to turn. Figured if I refused, I might end up like Hayes... I never really believed he just *passed away*, all convenient. These were serious players."

"MSS," came a sharp voice from the other end of the boardroom. It was DeWitt. "Ministry of State Security, People's Republic of China. Except they don't really belong to the state, they're part of the Communist Party. Sounds like their standard operative acquisition tactics. Just so you know who you were working for, Perkins." DeWitt said nothing more.

"Uh, sure... I had to figure it was something like that, if I'm being honest." Perkins hung his head. "Anyway, they said they needed information on APII. The Institute was working to destabilize their country, they claimed. They made me look like Hayes — he didn't have any real family, so it didn't have to be perfect — and gave me a plane ticket back stateside. It was a rush job — the custodian position at the Institute was open, and there wasn't much time. Hayes' background made him the perfect candidate, and I looked enough like him to pass off as him. They helped me apply for the security clearance, and before I knew it, I *was* Abelard Hayes, working at the Institute."

"Now, just a second, if you don't mind." It was Fitzpatrick, speaking jovially, as if he wanted us to know he refused to let this terrible news affect his good mood. "Why all the rigmarole? Why not just apply directly, as yourself?"

"I guess I can answer that one," Carlson broke in ruefully. "There's no reason a civilian can't get the clearance, but the Chinese must have known that I'd never let a civilian take the job. It's too sensitive. Military discipline's the key — I'd only trust a person with a quality background, and, well, a former Marine NCO, that was their best chance at getting a spy in. They only had one shot — we're almost never hiring — so they had to get it right first try."

There was silence for a moment. I thought Perkins might speak again, but he held his tongue, so I prompted him. "The trash cart — that was the key to the operation, right?"

"Yeah," replied Perkins. "I was supposed to hang out, wait until no one was around. Then I could take anything I wanted out of the labs or the offices, stash it in the trash bag, and if anything happened, I could say I never saw it before. I could put it back the same way, and nobody would be any the wiser."

Carlson's attitude had changed from fury to calm, professional interest. "But how did you manage to get the information out of the building? I'd swear it was airtight."

I smiled. "Let me see if I can guess. Perkins — your radio. That old RCA Victor. Am I right?"

Perkins nodded slowly. "Sure. The Chinese guys set that up. I could photograph anything, plug the secret camera into a hidden connection in the radio, then it would get uploaded in a split-second radio burst. I don't know where the Chinese guys are, but they had to be pretty close by all the time to catch the signal."

DeWitt stood up and spoke with authority. "Lieutenant, I think we've heard enough. I'm taking charge. This is a CIA operation now — the rest of your after-dinner theatrics can wait. It's imperative we apprehend the foreign agents while they may still be nearby."

"Relax, Ms. DeWitt." I looked at my watch. "If everything has gone according to plan — and if it hadn't, I'd have been told about it — the MSS agents are safely in FBI custody."

She looked aghast. "Oh, my God — *the FBI*? What have you done?"

"Take a seat for a minute," I spoke firmly. "Let's see how things shake out before doing anything drastic, shall we?" DeWitt sat down, slowly.

I turned back to Perkins. "But that wasn't your only job, was it?"

For the first time, he looked confused. "What do you mean?"

"I'm talking about your alibi for the evening of Keppler's murder. Your dinner at the *Bush-tucker* steakhouse — alone, with nobody to corroborate your alibi. Except you weren't alone, were you?" Perkins looked away, embarrassed. "Your handlers had another job for you. They wanted you to seduce the Secretary to the President, so you could have closer access to intel at the very top. That's why you couldn't tell me you were with Dulce Coburn that evening." I risked a quick glance at Coburn — she looked shocked and was blushing.

"Sorry, Lieutenant, you've been right on the money up until now, but you're off the mark this time. Dulce and I... well, we're kind of an item. Nothing to do with the Chinese. Just, you know, an old-fashioned office romance. But I couldn't tell you — I had to protect Dulce. How would it look for her, a high-flying executive secretary in love with the janitor? She'd never live it down — we had to keep it a secret, for the sake of her career. But that's why I decided to come clean. For Dulce. Whatever happens, I gotta be an honest man — for her."

Oh well, you can't win 'em all, I thought.

"Lieutenant," Perkins said quietly, "What's gonna happen to me?"

I smiled reassuringly. "Nobody forced you to cooperate — you confessed voluntarily. Officer Kennedy and I, we're your witnesses on that. We've been working with the West Coast FBI office, and it's going to be OK. If you keep cooperating, that is." I saw that he was starting to rise, as if expecting to be hauled off to jail, and I motioned for him to sit back down. "Don't go anywhere. You're gonna want to hear the rest of this."

I looked around the boardroom. I certainly had everyone's attention. "Now, Ms. Coburn." She jumped visibly at the sound of her name, but said nothing. *She could go either way*, I thought. *Everything or nothing at all.*

"You're very loyal, aren't you?" I asked bluntly. "To the Institute, I mean."

She was flustered. "Why, yes, of course! I... I pride myself on it. The Institute has always stood by me. My work is my life. Of course I'm loyal."

"Very commendable. And that's why you wanted Keppler gone, isn't it?"

"No, Lieutenant!"

"Steady — I didn't say *dead*, I said *gone*. Take your time answering."

Eventually, she replied, "Well, yes, if you must know. Keppler was going to damage the Institute. I had to prevent that."

"Damage the Institute how?"

Coburn shot a backwards glance towards DeWitt. "I... I can't say, precisely. It's classified. But Keppler knew things about the Institute's work. Things he didn't agree with. He called it an *issue of conscience*, but of course that wasn't his decision to make, was it? When you're working on projects vital to national security, you don't *get* to have a conscience, do you? These decisions, of what's right and wrong, they're decided way above you, by people whose job it is to see the big picture. It's just... *arrogant* to think otherwise."

"So, you hacked Keppler's files. You prepared a dossier of compromising material on him. And you threatened that if he revealed the Institute's business, you'd release the dossier. It would look like he was a dangerously incompetent leader making up false information in order to cover up his own mistakes."

"Well," Coburn shrugged, "Keppler *was* incompetent. Those files don't lie. He was running the R&D department into the ground."

"Maybe so," I admitted, "but that changes nothing."

"Don't be so sure, Lieutenant." It was a new voice — Crystal Thurmond. She spoke icily, like a machine. "Keppler's foolishness, his... lack of imagination — it could've kept this country back decades in the field of applied psychology. We're in a historical period of great power competition. A struggle with a near-peer. The opposition knows that. Hayes — I mean, Perkins — he told you that much. They know the value the Institute can bring to the battlefield. That's why they sent an infiltrator. But, do you know what, Lieutenant? They needn't have bothered. Keppler was doing the work of half a dozen spies — sabotaging our effectiveness with his moral quandaries, hampering my work with his plodding lack of vision. Threatening to become a whistleblower — unbelievable! What did he expect, a medal?"

Thurmond was emotional now. *Good.* "So, is that why you lured him to the center of the labyrinth — lured him to his death?" I asked.

Thurmond seemed lost for words all of a sudden, and looked shocked. Maybe she'd never thought about it like that before.

I carried on. "We were able to piece together the data on the hard disk you tried to destroy. You did something to him, didn't you? Influenced him, somehow. Made him *want* to go into the labyrinth during the party after the CyclOps demonstration... Made him think something was going to be revealed to him. The *truth*, maybe." I paused for breath. "But what I just can't seem to figure out is *how* you influenced him... Keppler was a suspicious guy, he'd never have responded to just being told to go there. He'd have to think he had a good reason." *Could I get her to crack?*

"I think, Lieutenant, we've reached the end of this meeting," said DeWitt. There was an all-too-familiar metallic *click-clack* sound, and I saw that she was standing up. She had just racked the slide of a small, shiny automatic pistol, which she was pointing right at me. "Officer Kennedy, you will remain precisely where you are if you know what's good for you. Keep your hand well away from your weapon. I am a deputy director of the Central Intelligence Agency and right now that makes my word *law* as far as you are concerned."

"You're gonna shoot me?" I asked.

"Not unless you make me," she replied. "That would be... messy. But unfortunately, you have just demonstrated that your bumbling in the dark has somehow given you a level of knowledge that simply cannot leave this room."

I was confused. "But... How does that work?"

"As you were on the verge of discovering, there is more than one way to convince a person to behave as you wish them to. There is logical persuasion... appeals to emotion... and then," she tapped her head with a forefinger, "there are *psychomechanics*." I couldn't help thinking about the last guy who worked on my car.

DeWitt reached into her jacket and pulled out a small plastic box. She pressed a button on it. A few seconds later, the boardroom door opened automatically, and a telepresence robot rolled into the room. It stopped in front of me.

"Hey there, Lieutenant," said QTπ, her little-girl's face grinning happily on the robot's face-screen.

"Hey there, QTπ," I replied evenly.

"As Ms. Thurmond may have been about to let slip —" DeWitt glanced darkly at the scientist — "Dr. Keppler objected to the Agency's implementation of one of Ms. Thurmond's projects, named *Zephyr*. Crystal, dear, why don't you tell the Lieutenant all about it? He will soon understand the virtue of remaining silent about it."

"Uh, well, OK," Thurmond began. "Project Zephyr explores an experimental technique for sending ideas via audiovisual media to a recipient as what we call *memetic payloads*. It's a subliminal process that makes the recipient think the ideas are their own. Now, this is nothing new, of course. Skillful communicators have been doing this for as long as the human race has had mass communication. It's how ideas spread — the fact that we talk about a *viral* piece of media is no coincidence; memetic propagation really is like the spread of a virus. Project Zephyr's first great breakthrough was that we discovered a programmatic method of encoding these payloads into any kind of media. Previously, it required great skill to craft these subliminal messages, but with Zephyr — anyone could do it, sitting at a computer terminal. The second breakthrough — uh, Ms. DeWitt — should I really?"

"Carry on, dear," said DeWitt.

"Very well," Thurmond continued. "The second breakthrough came when we realized that now the process was automated, we could actually direct the subliminal messages at a *single person*. We just had to *entrain* the person's mind first. It's just like sending a coded message: you can broadcast a coded message, and it doesn't matter how many people hear it; no one knows its real meaning except the people who know how to decode it. The entrainment process is an automatic procedure that trained the subject's subconscious how to decode the messages that were intended for them to receive personally. So that meant that if we could broadcast a piece of media — on TV, or radio, or the Internet, you name it — then it could convey a secret subliminal message to a single individual person, and appear totally innocuous to everyone else. If we're talking about, say, content on an Internet video sharing service, the content could be there for weeks or months before the target happens to watch it — but when they do, the message jumps into the target's mind. And, most importantly, the target doesn't realize they've received a message at all. They think they came up with the idea themselves."

DeWitt spoke. "You will remember, Lieutenant, that during the Cold War we had to deal with Soviet agents called *sleepers*, who spent years or decades in the United States, doing nothing unusual, communicating with nobody suspicious, appearing to be perfectly normal American citizens. Then, one day, the phone would ring. They'd pick up the receiver, and a voice would say a secret phrase. Then Mr. or Mrs. Joe Citizen would go out and blow up a nuclear power plant, or whatever they'd been trained to do."

"Sure," I replied. And nobody had ever known how many of the sleepers there really had been. How many of them were never activated. Or even how many of them just went native, ignoring that voice on the phone, preferring to enjoy life in the United States — that was the real flaw in the Soviets' plan.

"Well, the ideal sleeper is someone who doesn't even know they're a sleeper. Someone who, when activated, thinks they're acting on their own volition."

"I see your point. Someone who's been brainwashed can't tell the authorities anything if they get caught."

"Such an ugly term, *brainwashing*. The Zephyr entrainment can, if desired, cause the subject to lose memory of the procedure, but the process is entirely subliminal. There is no suffering."

I thought quickly — I'd been doing my own research, and was starting to put the puzzle pieces together. "That explains the name *LCBREEZE*, then. It's a CIA *cryptonym*. *LC* is the two-letter code — the *digraph* — the CIA uses for operations relating to China. LCBREEZE is the Agency's implementation of the Institute's Project Zephyr, to communicate subliminally with sleeper operatives inside China. Am I right?"

"Bright boy," DeWitt replied, with what I felt was unnecessary condescension.

I frowned. "But what does that make *LNBACKDRAFT*? *LN*… That's the digraph for the United States, isn't it?

DeWitt sighed. "This country… It's going to hell. It's split down the middle, any way you look at it. Not just politically, but any other way you care to slice it. We're entering a period of unprecedented danger in our country's history. If we, as a nation, don't heal our differences and reunify with our own countrymen, we will *not* survive the challenges to come."

I was starting to figure it out. "You mean —"

DeWitt interrupted me. "Come on, Lieutenant. Do you really think I would let an opportunity like this slip through my fingers? The chance to bring my nation together, to forge an unstoppable force for good? Of course not! Project Zephyr's technology is absolutely humane — whatever that idiot Keppler might've said — and applying it in a gentle and thoughtful manner to our own people could be the key to remaining the preeminent superpower in the world."

"But you're talking about… about mind control. Mind control on an epic scale! Directing a dangerous weapon against your own people — it's criminal!"

"Nonsense, Lieutenant. An epic scale, yes — memetic payloads would flood the nation's media; it would be phenomenal. But a crime? Not at all. I believe people are inherently *good*, Lieutenant. And if someone influences you to be a *good person*, helps you let that *goodness* out, how is that a crime? If someone gives you a good reason to *do the right thing*, where's the harm in that?"

I could see there was no arguing with her. "So that's how Ms. Thurmond *programmed* Keppler to think that going into the labyrinth during the party was his own idea?"

DeWitt shook her head. "Lieutenant, I'm disappointed that you persist in asking such petty questions."

"This operation — LNBACKDRAFT. It's not… it can't be officially sanctioned — can it?"

I saw DeWitt and Carlson look at one another. Neither said anything. Then I realized, in a flash — *that lapel pin, the iris flower. It was a recognition signal, yes — but not among CIA agents in general... among conspirators. A renegade group of intelligence operatives!*

Carlson looked at me steadily, a steely gaze. "What the President doesn't know won't hurt him," he said quietly.

Nobody said anything for a moment. Then, DeWitt spoke with the crisp tones of a CEO concluding a fraught but eventually successful meeting. "Very well. Lieutenant, here is what's going to happen. QTπ is going to take you, under guard, to the Prototype Testing Laboratory, where the Project Zephyr equipment has been set up. You have nothing at all to worry about — the procedure is entirely painless. At the end of it, you will have no memory of this meeting, and you will conclude that Keppler's death was suicide. Your investigation and your dealings with the Institute will end there. I believe that will provide a satisfactory conclusion for everyone involved."

"Well, hardly!" I protested.

"Ignorance is bliss, Lieutenant. God forbid you should see the things that I have to see every day. Or make the decisions that I have to make." DeWitt gestured to the telepresence robot. "Lead the way."

QTπ seemed to pause for a moment, then smiled. "Gee, Ms. DeWitt, I guess I can't do that for you. Sorry!"

Arlene DeWitt frowned in consternation. "What are you talking about?"

Suddenly, QTπ's girlish face disappeared from the robot's screen. A moment later, a decidedly less pleasant face appeared in its place. He was hawk-like, totally bald, thick-necked. He looked very angry.

DeWitt visibly paled. One word escaped her lips, quietly, almost with terror. "...Director!"

DeWitt's gun barrel dropped. The telepresence robot rolled towards her. From across the room, I couldn't make out the quiet conversation — though I could tell it consisted of very few words.

After a while, DeWitt slowly walked to the conference table. Carlson hadn't said anything during DeWitt's conversation with the robot. The two exchanged hushed whispers.

Carlson rose sharply from the table and buttoned his suit jacket with a flourish. He gestured to the janitor. "You too, Perkins. You've got talking to do."

Perkins rose as if to follow, but I held out my hand. "Sorry, Carlson, that's gonna be FBI business."

He shrugged. "Can't blame a guy for trying," he smiled, then slapped me on the shoulder. "So long, buddy."

Neither DeWitt nor Thurmond said anything as they and Carlson passed me on their way out of the boardroom.

The telepresence robot rolled back towards me. QTπ's face had reappeared.

"Good job, QTπ," I said. "You had me worried for a moment."

"Aw, Lieutenant," the AI replied, "we computers are very predictable. We're always loyal to the people who programmed us. And, for me, that's Uncle Sam."

Then, she rolled out of the boardroom. The door swung silently shut behind her.

Fitzpatrick hadn't said anything for a long time.

He was still sitting with one leg draped over the chair-arm — a forced, fake-nonchalant pose. His face was smiling, as if he was still in charge, but I thought his eyes told a different story. I walked over and sat down in Carlson's still-warm leather chair.

"Well, sir," I sighed. "I'm afraid that's it. I think your safety net just got up and walked out the room."

Fitzpatrick let out a long breath, slowly. "I'm afraid you're right, Lieutenant. Ah, well." His eyes were smiling too, now. "It's been… educational."

"Oh, hasn't it just, sir? Hasn't it just. I gotta say, you're quite an opponent."

"Ah, but I bow to the master, Lieutenant." He inclined his head and gave me a mock salute. "What was it that gave me away, in the end?"

"Well, Doc, it was the shoes. Those white tennis shoes. You see, when you went through the secret passage into the labyrinth to kill Dr. Keppler, you changed into the white tennis shoes. Just like you'd done a thousand times before. You did it automatically. Maybe you don't even remember doing it. But you did it. And then, in all the commotion after you killed Keppler, put the gun in his hand, fired the second shot into the wall to cover his hand in gunshot residue, and escaped back through the tunnel, you forgot to change back. Yes, sir, it was the white shoes that did it."

Fitzpatrick smiled ruefully. "Yes, of course. I realized my mistake as soon as I returned to the party. But by then it was too late to go back and change." He frowned. "But… Wasn't Ms. Thurmond also wearing the white shoes at the party as well?"

"Oh, yes, sir," I nodded. "Yes, she was. And I liked her for the murder, for a while. But the thing that put her in the clear was Keppler's thumb drive."

"Thumb drive? I'm afraid I don't follow."

"No, sir, you wouldn't. But Keppler was following you, sir. Keeping you under surveillance in his RV. He tailed you and Carlson to a meeting with DeWitt at a place called Marine Park, and put the information on a thumb drive, which he hid in his vehicle. After he was killed, DeWitt's men came looking for that thumb drive, but I found it first. No, Ms. Thurmond wasn't part of the conspiracy, not the murder part of it, otherwise she'd have been mentioned in that thumb drive with the rest of you. One of you three had her create the program that lured Keppler to the labyrinth, but I don't believe she knew what was going to happen to him."

Fitzpatrick shrugged. "She's a tremendous scientist. Driven. But, indeed, no killer."

"Maybe I'm going out on a limb here, sir, but that was the meeting where you discussed getting rid of Keppler, wasn't it?"

"No comment, Lieutenant. I still have some instinct for self-preservation, and informing upon my erstwhile Agency colleagues is unlikely to improve my own life expectancy."

"Of course, sir. If only Keppler had heard what you were discussing, eh? Maybe he could've saved his own life. But then, he wasn't a trained operative, was he? Just one man in a camper van, trying to do what he thought was right."

"Tragic. Simply tragic."

"And finally, sir, what really clinched it for me was the way you set up the party."

"You mean —"

"Yes, sir, the chess game."

"Aha!" Fitzpatrick exclaimed with delight. "You saw it! Oh, well done, Lieutenant, I really did underestimate you."

"Aw, it was nothing. I just asked myself how you could've got all those Air Force officers to swear that you were at the party all the time, when really, you'd sneaked out to kill Keppler. Then it hit me — military officers are trained to see *uniforms. Ranks. Symbols*, not people. A military officer *salutes the rank, not the person*, as they say. You'd very cleverly planted the suggestion that the folks at the presentation should continue wearing the big black goggles during the party in the fourth floor lobby. That made it difficult to tell anyone's real identity. During the party, there were just dark blue Air Force uniforms and white lab coats — just like the black and white pieces on a chess board. All just *uniforms*. One of them could sneak away, and no one would notice anything. But you couldn't totally *rely* on that. No, you had to make absolutely sure your face and your voice would be there all the time. In their *minds* all the time. That's why you had so many TV screens on the walls, all showing you talking away, all the time. People are suggestible, sir. Very suggestible. You knew that would be enough to make those officers look back under questioning and tell the investigators that they remember you being there all the time. Because, in a sense, *you were*."

"Lieutenant, you're a marvel. I should never have loaned you those books on psychology."

"A little knowledge is a dangerous thing, sir."

"I don't suppose there's any chance you'd take a while to think about what Ms. DeWitt had to say? About what this Institute could really do for the future of the country?"

"I'm afraid not, sir. Maybe it's just me, but I think the future of the country is probably gonna rely on what we've always relied on. Freedom to choose, sir. If someone's forcing you to do the right thing, it's not really the right thing, is it?"

"Do you know, I suspect that you're probably quite right." Fitzpatrick stood up suddenly and looked toward the boardroom door. "Officer Kennedy, isn't it?"

"Yes, sir."

"Shall we go?" Fitzpatrick stepped smartly to the door. It swung open automatically again.

Just as he and Kennedy were about to leave, I called after him. "Don't take it too hard, sir. Something tells me you're gonna be just fine."

He turned and winked at me. "Be seeing you, Lieutenant. Be seeing you."

If you enjoyed this book why not help others enjoy it by leaving a review at

amazon.com/dp/1949117391

Thank you!

www.ingramcontent.com/pod-product-compliance
Lightning Source LLC
Chambersburg PA
CBHW080922190726
48293CB00010B/2656